Dr Gribbles and the Beast of Blackthorn Lodge

By Simon Dillon

Copyright 2014 Simon Dillon

Published by Gajmo Publishing

Cover Design by Charles Bown

Dedication

For Thomas, whose highly imaginative
nightmares inspired this book.

Chapter 1: The Haunted House

September 1987.

Being trapped inside a haunted house was turning out to be every bit as terrifying as Tim had feared. He sat on the moth-eaten hallway carpet leaning against the crumbling plaster walls, putting his hands over his ears to shut out the horrible muffled roars.

Tim desperately tried to think of a way out, but his options were limited. The front door was blocked shut, as was the back door. That left the downstairs windows, but they were boarded up; as were most of the upstairs windows, except the small bathroom window on the top floor. But getting to it would mean climbing the dusty wooden staircase and it didn't look particularly stable...

The events that caused Tim Rawling to get trapped in the abandoned house on Cromwell Hill began when he was cycling back from the park. It was late on a Saturday afternoon, and he was returning home for dinner. His older brother Rob always prepared food for them at around 6 o'clock, as their parents ran a newspaper shop and often weren't home until later.

It had been a particularly warm September, with summer determined to linger into autumn. The large beech and chestnut trees on either side of the quiet lane that led up Cromwell Hill were still covered in thick leaves. Only the occasional sound of lawnmowers came from the gardens of the large detached houses that lined the road. But as Tim got further up the hill, he approached Blackthorn Lodge - an abandoned house that was beginning to fall into ruin. It lay at the very end of the lane.

A footpath continued further up which then wound round the hill for a while, before plunging back down towards the town of Plympton, just outside Plymouth. Normally Tim would have continued on his BMX bike back along the footpath, but today he glanced at Blackthorn Lodge. As he did, he thought he heard a muffled cry.

He pulled on the brakes and halted outside the house, staring at its boarded windows and overgrown garden. Long grass almost completely covered the broken paving slabs that led to the front entrance. The weatherworn brown paint on the door was peeling, and much of the red brickwork looked chipped. The walls were tangled in ivy and several tiles were missing from the roof. Twin chimneys loomed like sinister horns, casting dark shadows in the late afternoon light.

Tim stared at the house for a minute, listening carefully. But there were no more muffled cries. Perhaps he had imagined it. After all, there were many local stories about how the abandoned house on Cromwell Hill was cursed. The name Blackthorn Lodge itself sounded sinister. As to the specifics of why the house had this reputation, Tim didn't know for sure, but there were many theories. Some spoke of the place being haunted by the souls of children who were once imprisoned and murdered there by a deranged lunatic. Others said a spectre resembling a local woman, who had committed suicide after being jilted at the altar by her betrothed, was often seen drifting through the grounds. But the most popular theory was that of a savage demonic creature from the depths of hell lurking in the house. It was known as the Beast of Blackthorn Lodge.

Like most eleven year olds, Tim was morbidly curious as to the truth behind these stories. Since the house had only been abandoned for about twenty years, he doubted most if not all of the theories. The idea of it being genuinely haunted seemed ludicrous. Yet he could have sworn he heard *something* as he cycled past. That something had sent shivers down his spine, in spite of the fact that night was still a good two or three hours away.

Just as Tim decided he must have been imagining things, he noticed a gang of three other boys on bikes approaching from the footpath at the end of the lane. His heart sank as he recognised the leader of the gang: Jake Buxton. There was no way they would let him escape unscathed. Not after what happened earlier in the week at school.

Tim had just started at St John's Comprehensive, and in doing so made the unfortunate discovery that he and those in his year were frequently targeted by Jack Buxton and his gang. Most of the time they were just after lunch money, but sometimes they would throw a few punches to make clear who was in charge. Jake and his followers were three years above Tim and his classmates, so fighting back was often impossible, especially as Jake typically harrassed Tim or those in his year when they were alone.

Realising they had a problem, Tim set about solving it logically. But rather than go to his parents or tell the teachers, he came up with a far more profitable solution. He decided to start a protection racket.

Tim's secret weapon was his sixteen year-old brother, who had just started A-levels at the same school. Rob was tall, muscular and more than a match for Jake and his cronies. But because Rob was also very protective of Tim, or of anyone Tim told him about that needed protection, it was clear that there was a way to fight back. Of course Tim did not mention to his brother about the protection money he was set to make, as he knew his brother would not approve of such a scheme and would gladly have defended Tim simply because he saw it as the right thing to do.

But Tim's friends didn't know this, so Tim told them that they could buy protection - for a competitive price. They were initially sceptical that Tim could deliver, but eventually their classmate Ian Cole, who was being bullied worse than most, paid the 50 pence per week fee. Tim in turn informed Rob that he and Ian Cole were being badly bullied by Jake Buxton.

It was during morning break time on the previous Thursday when Rob had intervened, and Tim couldn't have planned it better if he had tried. Jake and two of his gang were accosting Ian Cole as usual, demanding his lunch money. Tim had already tipped off Rob to be by their lockers during their morning break, and sure enough he arrived just in time to witness Jake shoving Ian against the wall.

Rob had then charged up to Jake, pulled him away from Ian and dragged him by the scruff of his shirt into the boy's toilet. Once there he forced Jake's head into one of the toilets and flushed it several times. Eventually, Jake begged to be let go, spluttering a promise that he wouldn't bully Ian Cole any longer. Wet and humiliated, Jake then had to suffer the laughter of Tim and the rest of his classmates as he made his way back out of the toilets and along the corridors of the school.

It was a triumph for Tim, and as a result many others began to pay him their fifty pence's every week to pay for Rob's protection. But no doubt Jake had wind of the scheme by now, and wanted revenge. That is how Tim knew, from the look in Jake's eye, that he would not get out of this awkward situation easily. They weren't in school now, nor did Tim have his brother present to back him up.

'Well, well,' said Jake. 'Let's see if the Rawling runt is as tough without big brother to fight for him.'

Tim tried to think of a way out, but since he couldn't, he resorted to insults as he didn't want to let them see how frightened he was.

'I can always arrange another toilet water tasting for you if you like, Buxton. I hear you're something of a connoisseur.'

Jake was momentarily taken aback. 'A con…what?'

Tim smiled smugly. He loved using long words that the likes of Jake Buxton wouldn't understand. It made him feel superior, even if he did get punched for his trouble.

'Think you're so cool don't you, with your long stupid words and protection money,' said Jake. 'But I can see you're scared. And you should be.'

Jake glanced up at Blackthorn Lodge. 'You know what this place is, don't you?'

Tim shrugged. 'Just an old house.'

'Not just any house, dimwit. It's haunted.'

'Don't be stupid.'

'You're about to find out, Rawling runt, that there's much worse things than getting your head flushed. Like getting trapped inside there.'

Jake pointed to the house. Tim's stomach churned, especially after the cry he thought he had heard. He looked back at Jake and his two companions - Carl Ledger and Gary Price. Both were thick built and thuggish looking in their leather jackets and ripped jeans. Jake wore similar attire, but his jacket was open, revealing an Ironmaiden T-shirt underneath. In spite of his fear, Tim thought they all looked ridiculous - as if they couldn't make up their minds whether they wanted to look like rockers from the 1950s, or metallers from the 1980s. Tim on the other hand put a great deal of thought into the tracksuits and sports gear that he wore, making it clear that he was more a Run DMC/Beastie Boys kind of guy.

But despite their fashion sense (or lack of), it was clear there was no way Tim could get the upper hand in a fight with one of them, let alone all three. So he decided to attempt a negotiated settlement, vainly hoping to make Jake see that his actions would have consequences.

'Listen Jake, I know the three of you could easily beat me up now. And I know you're upset about what happened at school with my brother. But think about it logically. We could all make some real money here. You threaten to bully people. People pay me for protection. But you don't attack anyone because you pretend to be afraid of my brother. Then we split the profits. What do you think?'

Jake grabbed Tim by his tracksuit jacket.

'On the other hand, whatever you do to me now, my brother will hear about it in the end, and then he'll do something far worse than just flush your heads down toilets! Just be logical about this for one second…'

Clearly the logical acquisition of wealth wasn't foremost on Jake's mind. He, Carl and Gary dragged Tim up to the rusty gate by Blackthorn Lodge, opened it, and pulled him along the broken slabs of the overgrown path. The sinister house loomed over him, more threatening than ever. As he glanced up, Tim noticed that the bathroom window on the second floor was the only window not covered by chipboard.

Once they reached the front door, Gary and Carl held Tim in place, whilst Jake went back to fetch Tim's BMX. Jake then repeatedly kicked the back wheel until it buckled and the chain fell off.

'Wouldn't want you running off,' Jake said, as he gave the BMX one final kick.

Tim realised his situation was hopeless. Given the pointless damage Jake had just inflicted on his bike, it seemed clear that he was either about to sustain similar damage, or else something far worse was about to happen.

It turned out to be something far worse.

Jake pulled at the front door which swung open with an eerie creak. 'We broke into here months ago,' Jake said. 'But now we're going to make sure it stays shut.'

With that, Carl and Gary dragged Tim several feet inside the house before dropping him at the foot of a staircase in the dusty hall. They then rushed back out again, slamming the front door. Tim ran after them and pounded on the closed door, trying to force it open. But it was no use. Carl and Gary were putting their full weight against it whilst Jake placed objects against the door to wedge it shut.

'Let me out!' cried Tim.

'Not a chance!' Jake yelled.

Tim thumped and pounded on the door.

'Let me out! Please!'

The muffled sounds of Gary and Carl laughing enraged Tim, but try as he might he could not budge the door. He forced himself not to panic as he examined his surroundings – the ancient, moth-eaten maroon carpet, the crumbling plaster walls, the rotten wooden staircase, the cobwebs, the ominous closed doors, the dust-filled corridors…

The back door.

He ran past the staircase along a corridor that wound left then right until the ceiling got lower and eventually led to what must once have been a large kitchen with a great fireplace. But the surfaces and few remaining sticks of furniture had rotted and were covered in dust and cobwebs. A few mice scurried out of Tim's way as he rushed through, and after some fumbling around he discovered the back door. But as he attempted to turn the metal handle he found that it was locked. He tried to force it open, but after a great deal of pounding and shoving realised Jake and the others must have barricaded this door too.

Tim glanced around breathlessly, trying to think of another way out. Due to the boarded windows everything was dark and covered in shadows, but there were chinks of light here and there where the sun penetrated. Outside he could hear the muffled sounds of Jake and the others running back through the overgrown gardens, laughing and yelling at him.

'That's what happens to people who mess with Jake Buxton…'

'We might let you out in the morning, if the Beast hasn't got you first…'

Tim heard a few congratulatory exchanges as the sounds dwindled into the distance.

'Skill!'

'Wicked!'

Eventually silence fell. Shadows and passageways suddenly seemed a lot more threatening, as though they might genuinely contain spectres or demons. Although he was hot from trying to force his way out, Tim began to shiver at the thought that the house could be haunted. No, that was ridiculous. There were no such things as ghosts. The Beast was nothing more than a myth.

Tim refused to accept that he was trapped, and began to look for other ways out. He searched the ground floor thoroughly, opening all the doors that weren't locked and trying to break through the boards that were nailed onto the window frames. He found a couple of wooden poles and tried to smash through with those, but they simply broke in two, having succumbed to damp and decay. The rooms were mostly empty, with creaking exposed floorboards. Some had foul smelling carpets, and the odd piece of furniture. There were even a few old books scattered on the floor of one.

Despite all attempts to break out, Tim remained trapped. He tried the front and back door several times, but no amount of pounding and yelling did any good. He had yet to look upstairs, but didn't want to risk climbing the rotten looking staircase. The idea that he might really have to spend the night in this place horrified him. He thought about how worried Rob would be once he was late for dinner, and his parents' annoyance at the inconvenience he would end up putting them to. He imagined them irritably contacting the police and a search taking place.

That was when the roaring started.

It began as a low-pitched, muffled but loud growl. Tim realised in alarm that it was the same sound he thought he had heard when he cycled past the abandoned house earlier. What could it be? The house wasn't really haunted, surely? Perhaps some kind of animal had got trapped inside. But what kind of animal made a noise like that? It couldn't be the Beast. It couldn't be...

Tim listened again, and the growling became louder. He then heard a great muffled crash, as though something had been pushed over. The muffled growling then became muffled roaring, as though the animal was in pain. The sounds were vicious, savage and froze Tim's blood. For someone who didn't believe in ghosts, Tim was on the verge of becoming a believer, as he couldn't think of any rational explanation for what he was hearing. Were the stories of the Beast actually true?

Cautiously, he crept along the corridors towards the source of the noise. Eventually he reached a locked door and listened outside. The roaring was definitely louder here, but it seemed to be coming from underneath, perhaps a cellar.

Tim remembered the stories of children being murdered in this house. What if this Beast had been the true culprit? An icy thrill of terror shot through Tim, and he almost panicked. Then he forced himself to calm down. Whatever was in the cellar seemed to be trapped. Spectral monsters would be able to move through walls, so perhaps it was a creature of flesh and blood after all.

But what kind of a monster would make those agonised, painful noises? Although they sounded like an animal roaring in pain, the cries also sounded partially human. Yet whatever was in the cellar clearly wasn't human either. Confusion and curiosity temporarily overcame his fear, and Tim tried the cellar door once more.

The monster beneath must have heard or sensed Tim, because all at once it roared louder than ever. New terror swept over Tim as he realised he had now revealed himself to whatever lurked down there. He rushed to the front door and pounded on it with increased desperation.

'Help! Let me out!'

The roaring and snarling grew louder, and Tim began to fear what might happen if the monster were to somehow break out of the cellar with him trapped inside the house. His imagination went into overdrive, and he banged on the door more furiously than ever.

'Help! Help me! It's the Beast! The Beast!'

More sounds of smashing and raging anguished roars rose up from beneath the floor. Tim struck the door as hard as he could, pounding until his hands and fingernails were bruised and bleeding. Exhausted and terrified, he then slumped against the walls and put his hands over his ears, thinking over his options.

It was then that he remembered the bathroom window on the second floor, which was the only window not boarded up. He stood and looked again at the stairs. Although the wood was rotting there really was no choice. He would have to risk climbing up.

A particularly loud roar prompted Tim to begin his ascent. Instinctively he put his hand onto the banister but this was a mistake. It snapped off immediately, almost causing him to lose his balance and fall back down. Quickly correcting his footing, he continued up carefully, the floorboards groaning and creaking under his weight. Near the top of the stairs one of the wooden steps split beneath his feet, but he moved off it hurriedly, and a moment later stood on the dusty landing. Dark passages lay to the left and right, but Tim knew he had to continue up the next flight of stairs – all the way to the second floor.

Gingerly, Tim resumed the journey up the stairs, but the rotten steps were in worse shape further up. Several broke beneath his feet, and on one occasion his entire foot slipped through the staircase and smashed through the plasterboard, no doubt causing it to protrude from the slanted ceiling of the room below. Rusty nails and splinters of wood scraped against his skin. Tim hastily withdrew his foot and saw his leg was bleeding.

Alarmed at the prospect that he might fall through the staircase and smash all the way through the ground floor into the cellar, Tim moved faster, and eventually reached the second floor. Here the passages were less dark as they were illuminated somewhat by the light from the bathroom window. Tim headed towards the source of the sunlight, and turned right along the corridor, eventually reaching the bathroom.

There was no door on the bathroom. It was on its side in the corridor having been removed from its hinges. The bathroom itself had a dust and cobweb covered bath, basin and toilet, but no curtains. Tim stepped across to the window, and after wrestling somewhat with the handle, managed to wrench it open. The roaring continued downstairs, but it was more muffled, so seemingly the monster remained trapped in the cellar. That at least was a relief to Tim.

Tim looked out of the window and saw the street on the other side of the overgrown garden, well over a hundred yards away. It was unlikely anyone would see or hear him from there, and he couldn't see anyone in any case. He would have to climb through the window and get down somehow. He could jump, but it was high, and he would almost certainly hurt himself. Looking to the left he saw a drainpipe at an intersection of the house walls. If he could get out and manoeuvre onto the drainpipe he might just be able to escape without doing himself any serious injury.

Knowing there was little choice Tim climbed onto the basin and slowly eased himself through the narrow window frame, until he was outside hanging on to the window ledge. He found footholds in some of the crumbling brickwork and used the overgrown ivy branches as handholds. Bit by bit he made his way to the drainpipe, and by the time he got there he was sweaty and covered in dust and dirt.

But as Tim grabbed hold of the drainpipe, it creaked and began to pull out from the wall. Immediately realising he was going to fall, Tim slid as quickly as he could down the pipe before it gave way completely and fell to the ground with a crash.

Tim had a reasonably soft landing in a patch of grass and stinging nettles, but his back and legs ached where he fell on them. He was stung several times, but in spite of the pain was relieved to be out of the house, especially as he could still hear the snarls and roars from the cellar, although they were far less audible.

Grabbing his damaged bike, Tim limped as quickly as he could out along the overgrown path and back towards the gate. By the time he reached the road, he could no longer hear whatever ghost or monster lurked in the cellar, and part of his mind questioned whether he had ever heard it at all. Perhaps his imagination had simply got the better of him. Perhaps he'd had some kind of breakdown. He had read about such things in some of the magazines his parents sold in their newsagents.

Tim brushed himself down as best he could, realising he'd be late home as a result of his misadventures, and because his bike was broken. But such minor irritations were nothing compared to the relief he felt at escaping from that horrible roaring. He glanced back up at Blackthorn Lodge and shuddered. Whether he had imagined the Beast or not, it had been a most unpleasant experience, and one which he was determined would result in serious payback for Jake Buxton and his cronies. They were nowhere to be seen, but Tim decided it was best to make himself scarce, in case they should suddenly return and force him back inside.

Tim was mentally devising revenges that he and Rob could inflict on his tormentors when he suddenly noticed a figure running up to him from the opposite side of the street. To his surprise, he recognised his neighbour from a few doors down their street: Doctor Gribbles. Tim and others his age often referred to Gribbles as the neighbourhood mad scientist, even though he had retired and was a well-known and well-respected member of the local community. He was on friendly terms with Tim's parents and had even been invited to speak to pupils at St John's Comprehensive a few times. Today however - with his dark and worn trousers, scuffed shoes, white laboratory coat, untidy silver hair and intense steel eyed stare - Gribbles particularly looked the part of the mad scientist. He stormed up to Tim and grabbed him by the shoulder.

'I just saw you climb out of the top floor of Blackthorn Lodge!' Dr Gribbles exclaimed.

Although surprised by Dr Gribbles' manic demeanour, Tim wasn't really in the mood for explaining what had happened. He just wanted to get home.

'I was having a quick look inside,' said Tim. 'But got trapped so I had to get out somehow.'

'You went inside! Why?'

'Just curious, I suppose. Heard it was haunted and wanted to see for myself...'

'Curious!' Dr Gribbles looked left and right as though concerned he might have been followed then forced himself to calm down. He looked Tim straight in the eye, clearly making an effort to be calm.

'What did you find in there?'

'Nothing,' Tim lied. 'It's just a boring, empty, dusty old house.'

'Indeed,' said Dr Gribbles. 'However, it is also an *extremely* dangerous house as it is very old and rotten. Condemned properties are sealed off with good reason. You could do yourself a serious injury in there. I warn you: if I see you anywhere near this place again I will inform not only your parents but the police as well, for your own protection. Do not go in there again, ever, under *any* circumstances. Do I make myself clear?'

Tim nodded.

'Well, you'd better get off home.'

Dr Gribbles strode away looking somewhat flustered, back in the direction he had come. Tim noticed that his car, an old black Cortina, was parked a little way down the street. As Dr Gribbles got back into it, he did not start the engine. He seemed to be waiting for something, but what? For Tim to go away?

Tim was quietly intrigued as to why Dr Gribbles had turned up on Cromwell Hill at this precise moment, and why this former scientist was so concerned about him going into an abandoned house. It all seemed highly mysterious, and he wondered whether Dr Gribbles knew the stories about the Beast.

With such thoughts in his mind, Tim hurriedly made his way along the footpath, down the hill and back home.

Chapter 2: Dubblety, Dubbler and the Mad Scientist

Tim returned home via an entrance to his back garden from the pathway that led east to Cromwell Hill. Looking up at the brown brick, semi-detached house, he considered how long he had lived here, at number 4 Cumberland Close. It was almost his entire life.

For much of that life his parents had ran their nearby shop, and that kept them very busy. As Tim and his brother had got older, Rob was the one who cooked their dinner, helped him with homework and generally looked after him. Rob didn't seem to mind the extra responsibility, but whilst they had always been close, lately his brother had got more irritable, and the amount of time they spent together became less. Even worse, Rob was behaving more and more like an overly-fussy mother, and on this occasion he got particularly annoyed when Tim arrived home.

'You're over half an hour late!' Rob exclaimed, as Tim finally entered through the French windows. 'And you're filthy! What's happened?'

Tim rolled his eyes. 'Are you trying to sound like Mum? Or does it come naturally?'

'Hurry up! Dinners on the table, Dubblety.'

Dubblety or *Double T* was Robert's nickname for Tim. *TT* stood for *Tiny Tim*, which Robert used to call Tim when he was younger.

'Be there in a minute, Dubbler.'

Dubbler or *Double R* was Tim's nickname for Robert. *RR* stood for *Robert Rawling*.

Tim nipped upstairs to the bathroom to clean himself and change his dirty clothes. He wondered whether or not to tell Rob about everything that had happened. His brother would almost certainly laugh if he said there was some kind of monster trapped in the cellar of Blackthorn

Lodge, and Tim wasn't entirely convinced that he hadn't imagined the noises. Having recently read a great deal of Sherlock Holmes stories, Tim had decided he was an ardent rationalist. However ghostly or supernatural an event might appear, there would undoubtedly be a logical, scientific explanation - even if it was something highly unlikely. To that end, Tim had almost convinced himself that the moaning, snarling and roaring from the cellar had been the fear-fuelled product of a terrified mind. He decided not to tell his brother.

He also decided to leave out the encounter with Dr Gribbles. Although it had intrigued him, there was something unsettling and peculiar about their exchange, and he didn't want to say anything about it just yet. For one thing, it might make Rob think twice about the kind of revenge he was going to suggest against Jake, Gary and Carl.

After returning downstairs, Tim hurriedly told Rob the edited version of events in Blackthorn Lodge, in between mouthfuls of spaghetti bolognaise. Rob listened and frowned as he heard about what Jake and his gang had done. He ran both hands through his thick, dark hair, which he always did when he was annoyed. By the time Tim finished, Rob was on his feet pacing up and down the dining area. Tim wished Jake was there at this moment, facing up to his brother's intimidating near six foot height. In this state, Rob's retribution would be swift and furious.

'That odious, vindictive, jumped-up, cowardly little cretin,' Robert muttered as he paced. 'By the time I'm finished with him, he'll be longing for something as comforting as pain…'

Tim couldn't help smiling. There was something deeply satisfying about seeing his brother determined to exact vengeance on his behalf. But he had a better idea than simply unleashing his brother on Jake and having him pound his face to a pulp.

'I'd like to shut *him* in Blackthorn Lodge,' said Tim. 'Let's see how he likes being trapped in a haunted house.'

Rob laughed. 'You don't believe any of that nonsense, do you?'

'Of course not,' Tim replied quickly. 'It's just... Well, it's quite a scary place, and it would serve him right.'

'What should we do instead, Dubblety? Re-arranging their faces is too ordinary.'

'That's fine for Gary and Carl. They're like worker bees. They don't have minds of their own. They just exist to serve the hive ruler. Jake on the other hand... I need to come up with something really horrible, but I haven't thought of it yet.'

'Let me know when you do. You're the brains Dubblety.'

'And you're the brawn, Dubbler.'

They ate in silence for a while. Tim found himself thinking about when Rob used to take him into the woods to build dens, climb trees, light campfires and generally muck around. These days Rob went out with him less and less. He seemed much more focussed on spending time with his own friends, or even occasionally girlfriends.

'Of course, it never would have happened if you'd come with me to the park,' Tim muttered. 'Jake would have legged it the moment he saw you.'

Rob shrugged. 'Can't be everywhere. One of these days you'll have to fight back without me.'

'I don't do fighting. Too uncivilised.'

'The world's not a very civilised place, in case you hadn't noticed.'

'Yeah, but I still wish you did more stuff with me, like you used to.'

'Like what?'

'I dunno. Played football maybe?'

'Don't have time. I'm meeting up with friends.'

'You mean Louise Milner?'

'That's none of your business.'

'Does she know about Lucy Taylor? Or Jenny Smith?'

'For heaven's sake Dubblety, they're just friends. Grow up!'

'Perhaps I'll tell her about how you used to go out with them both. If she knew you still hung around with them she might not like it. I've heard she can't stand Lucy.'

Rob adopted a patronising tone. 'Really Tim, for someone your age, it's just not normal to pay such close attention to school gossip.'

'Information is an important commodity.'

'You're being a freak again. Shut up.'

'I wonder what Louise would say if she realised you hang around with Lucy because you like the fact that she still fancies you.'

'That is *not* why I hang out with her!'

Tim shrugged. 'It's not me you have to convince.'

'Tell Louise that and I'll break your face!'

'I'm not saying Louise *has* to know...'

Tim let his voice tail off and waited for the wheels to turn in Rob's head. On the one hand he had no intention of actually saying such things to Louise, but from the paranoid looks on his brother's face, he knew his observation based guesses were correct and that Rob wouldn't want to take the risk. Such subtle blackmail was an art, and Tim was quite proud of his finely honed skills.

Eventually Rob sighed irritably. 'Alright, fine! Tomorrow morning we'll have a kick around. But I meant what I said. You tell Louise anything about Lucy and I'll lock you back in Blackthorn Lodge myself!'

The following morning, Tim and Rob spent an enjoyable few minutes kicking a football around the road. Cumberland Close was a quiet cul-de-sac, so it was easy enough to get out of the way if a car drove into their street. The sun was high and clear in the almost cloudless sky, and it was still unusually warm for September.

Rob designated the goal area between a drain and a manhole cover. He practiced his goalkeeping whilst Tim attempted to get the ball past him. Rob had played on a number of football teams, and had been quite a good goalkeeper, but Tim couldn't help thinking his brother's skills were rusty. Perhaps it was the result of spending too much time with Louise Milner, who Tim disliked. He considered her brainless and shallow, not to mention patronising and unpleasant. She had even compared him to the Antichrist child from *The Omen*. Tim much preferred Lucy Taylor, who was intelligent and even played chess with him when she visited the house (much to Rob's irritation).

Unfortunately, Tim's enjoyment of once again playing with his older brother soon came to an end. After misjudging a kick, the football shot high in the air, far over Rob's head, across the street and smashed a downstairs window in number 17. Tim gulped. He knew all too well who lived at that address.

Dr Gribbles.

'Well done,' said Rob. 'Now go and tell the mad scientist you smashed his window.'

'It wouldn't have happened if you weren't such a rubbish keeper,' said Tim. 'You tell him!'

'You kicked it, you tell him,' Robert insisted.

Tim's stomach churned. The prospect of telling Dr Gribbles he had just smashed his window was not a happy one, especially after their last encounter. But Rob didn't know about that. He didn't want him to find out either.

'I'll buy another football,' said Tim, and he began to walk away.

But Rob grabbed Tim by the scruff of his T-shirt and hauled him across the road to number 17. A few seconds later, Rob had rung the doorbell.

'Dubbler, no!'

'You've got to own up to what you did.'

'But he's mad!'

'He will be once he sees what you've done to his window.'

'No, he really is. I'm sure of it.'

'Don't be ridiculous! They wouldn't let him speak at school if he was really nuts.'

The incident outside Blackthorn Lodge flashed through Tim's mind, but he didn't want to explain it to his brother. 'I've heard things,' he muttered feebly.

Rob rolled his eyes. 'As I keep telling you Dubblety, you shouldn't listen to gossip. Besides, even if he is mad, I'm sure we'll be perfectly safe telling him his window is broken. After all, what could he possibly do here, in full view of the entire road...'

Rob's voice tailed off as the front door opened. Tim gasped at the peculiar figure of Dr Gribbles in his white laboratory coat wearing a gas mask and holding up a canister that looked like a fire extinguisher. He then released a valve at the top, causing a strange green gas to be expelled directly into his and Robert's faces. Gasping and spluttering, the last thing Tim saw before he fell unconscious was Dr Gribbles' wide, excited eyes.

Tim awoke to find himself slouched on a black leather armchair in what appeared to be an underground laboratory. Beakers, test tubes and glass pipes filled with bubbling liquids had been set up across the wooden work benches. The cupboards were stacked with other glass bottles, many of which had dire warnings on their labels. There were also circuit boards and wires on other surfaces, books, scientific journals, papers, two computers and a cage filled with white mice. The place had a musty smell, mingled with a peculiar aroma...toast and tomato ketchup? Tim looked around and saw Rob nearby on another chair. Dr Gribbles stood over him, munching toast and scribbling frantic notes on a clipboard.

All at once Tim felt afraid. He remembered the green gas and wondered if Dr Gribbles had kidnapped them to use as human subjects in some kind of horrible experiment. In spite of his outward respectability, it appeared the jokes about Gribbles being mad might have some basis in fact.

Dr Gribbles noticed Tim stirring in his chair. He put down his clipboard, grabbed an iron bar from a nearby surface and rushed over to him. Fearing that he was about to be attacked, Tim instinctively covered his head.

'Quickly!' cried Dr Gribbles. 'Try and bend this bar!'

Puzzled, Tim looked up at Gribbles as he insistently handed him the bar. 'What did you say?'

'Bend it! Quick! Before the effects of the serum wear off!'

'Serum?'

Dr Gribbles pointed to two empty syringes on a work bench. 'I injected you both with my revised haemomuscular enhancing compound. Try it!'

Tim still felt confused. He took the bar in his hand, unable to take in what was happening.

'Bend the bar!' cried Dr Gribbles, almost hysterical.

Numbly, Tim tried to bend the iron. To his astonishment, he found it no more difficult than bending a thin stick. Dr Gribbles punched the air in triumph.

'Success! Let's just hope it worked on the older subject...'

'Older subject? You mean my brother!'

Dr Gribbles ignored Tim and stood next to Rob, watching closely.

'What have you done to us?' cried Tim.

'Oh, nothing permanent, or particularly dangerous,' Dr Gribbles replied. 'I've just temporarily increased your strength. The problems are twofold: making it last longer than a few minutes, and making it work on adults. If it works with the older subject, the chances are it will work with adult subjects.'

'We are *not* subjects!' Tim yelled, outraged. 'What was that green gas you sprayed in our faces?'

'Just something to knock you out, so I could get you into my laboratory without any unnecessary aggravation,' Dr Gribbles continued. 'I had just finished the revised compound and needed subjects to test it on.'

'Stop calling us subjects!'

'What do you expect me to call you? You haven't told me your names.'

'You know our names!'

'I cannot be expected to instantly recall every piece of information my mind has catalogued!'

Tim was so aghast that he didn't know what to say. In the end he settled for a straight answer.

'I'm Tim Rawling and this is my brother Robert.'

'Of course! The Rawling offspring. Well, I'm Archie Gribbles. You can just call me Gribbles. Or Archie if you like, but I prefer Gribbles. I'm friends with your parents.'

'I know!' said Tim. 'You've met us before, several times.'

'So I have,' said Gribbles, as though baffled at a great mystery. 'You've grown. So, why are you here?'

'We only knocked on your door because we accidentally kicked a football through one of your windows.' Tim looked around at the laboratory. 'Is this your cellar? Are we still in your house?'

'Of course! The gas only knocked you out for a couple of minutes...'

'What on earth just happened?' Rob interrupted, as he came round. He stared at his surroundings and Dr Gribbles in utter bemusement.

'I can bend steel bars!' cried Tim, picking up the bar and having another go. In spite of being drugged and experimented on, the sudden realisation that he had been dosed with something that gave him superhuman strength was undeniably exciting.

But this time it was much more difficult to bend the bar. Dr Gribbles nodded with interest and scribbled something on his clipboard. 'As expected, the effects of the serum are wearing off.' He turned to Rob. 'What am I thinking? Robert, try and bend this bar!'

Looking too confused to do anything but respond to Dr Gribbles' seemingly insane request, Rob attempted to bend the bar as Tim had done, but to no avail.

Dr Gribbles looked disappointed. 'Alas, once again it would appear post pubescent subjects are unaffected by the serum. Perhaps a higher dosage would yield better results?'

As Dr Gribbles continued to mutter indistinctly, Rob finally seemed to regain control of his senses. He stood and confronted this seemingly insane man, pointing an accusing finger.

'Who on earth do you think you are? You can't just drug and kidnap us? What have you pumped into our systems? For all you know there could be serious side effects!'

Dr Gribbles shook his head dismissively. 'Oh, I doubt that every much.'

'How can you be sure?'

'Well, you aren't dead for one thing.'

Tim and Rob both stared incredulously at Dr Gribbles, as he wandered back to his beakers and test tubes to examine a bubbling liquid.

'Thank you for your assistance,' said Gribbles. 'You can go.'

'I could report this matter to the police,' said Rob.

'You really can't just gas people and drag them in here to be experimented on,' Tim added.

Gribbles sighed. 'I suppose not. I should have asked your parents first.'

'They wouldn't have understood,' said Tim. 'Besides, they aren't there for you to ask.'

'It's Sunday. Isn't their shop closed today?'

'Yes, but they're visiting friends.'

Dr Gribbles' eyes darted from Tim to Rob and back again. He suddenly looked a little sad.

'Perhaps I do owe you an apology. Tim, would you like me to repair your bike?'

'How did you know his bike was broken?' Rob asked suspiciously.

'Oh, I saw him walking home the other day, and his bike was broken.'

'Jake Buxton's handiwork,' said Tim.

'In that case, repairing my brother's bike is the least you can do, considering you've performed dangerous experiments on us without our permission,' said Rob.

'They weren't that dangerous...'

'Even so, don't do it again or I really will tell the police. No shoving gas in our faces and injecting us with dodgy experimental drugs.'

'It was quite cool though,' said Tim, imagining himself squaring off against Jake Buxton and his gang. 'Think what we could do with some of that stuff. Think of the possibilities. Dr Gribbles, perhaps you should give us some of that serum so I can test it more thoroughly?'

'I need to revise the formula so it works with adults,' said Gribbles.

'I know, but in the meantime, that stuff you gave us works on me at least, so I could...'

'I can't believe you Dubblety,' Rob interrupted. 'We get drugged, kidnapped and experimented on, and all you can think of is getting even with Jake Buxton?'

Tim shrugged. 'Well, why not? I think this invention of Dr Gribbles is a very good one, even if he didn't ask before testing it on us.'

'It's not really designed for getting even with bullies,' said Gribbles. 'Still, I've got a batch I could give you in return for certain services.'

'What services?' asked Rob.

'You and your brother come back here and agree to let me test the revised versions of the haemomuscular enhancements on you.'

'And you still fix my bike as well?'

'It's a deal.'

Tim smiled, and shook hands cordially with Dr Gribbles.

'Wait a moment!' cried Rob. 'This is madness! I'm not agreeing to this!'

'Have some vision Dubbler,' said Tim. 'For scientific progress to be made, tests on human subjects are necessary. Besides, we can make a fortune with this stuff.'

'Oh no!' cried Dr Gribbles, suddenly alarmed. 'No, you mustn't sell it. It has to be our secret. You use it to get even with the bullies, nothing more. No bending steel bars or doing anything that attracts attention. It must simply appear that you were able to stand up for yourself. Otherwise, the deal is off.'

'Very well,' said Tim, a little disappointed that he wouldn't be able to make money from the deal. 'Do you have to take it with a syringe?'

'It can be taken orally as well. I'll put it in little vials so you can keep them in your pocket for emergences.'

'Very practical,' said Tim.

'Exactly what I thought. I can even flavour them if you like. Strawberry? Orange? Mint?'

'How about Loganberry?' Tim asked half-jokingly.

Gribbles smiled. 'I'll see what I can do.'

'I can't believe I'm going along with this,' Rob muttered as they strode home a few minutes later to get Tim's bike. 'This is insane. We really, really ought to call the police.'

'But they'll just spoil everything,' said Tim. 'Besides, we did a deal with him, and you're always going on about how important it is to stick to your word.'

'Giving my word to a mad scientist isn't something I would have done.'

'He isn't mad,' said Tim.

Rob laughed. 'Not compared to you. Have you forgotten what he did to us?'

'Well, you can't make an omelette without breaking a few eggs.' In truth, Tim wasn't too bothered about what had happened, since he had obtained superhuman strength as a result.

'What I want to know is why he's making this drug in the first place.'

'Perhaps he's got some new contract from the government.'

'He's supposed to be retired. Besides, if he was working for the government, developing a drug like that would be top secret. He wouldn't just test it on anyone who happened to kick a football through his window.'

'That reminds me. We forgot to get the football.'

In spite of Rob's misgivings, he and Tim spent the rest of the day at Dr Gribbles' house, and actually had a very interesting time. For one thing, Dr Gribbles fixed Tim's bike as he promised, before carrying cn with his work. Just as he had on the occasions when he had visited their home, Gribbles seemed very pleasant, although a little distracted and hyperactive at times. It was clear that Rob didn't trust him, but Tim found himself admiring this reclusive genius, and wondered what tcp secret government research he had worked on during his career. No doubt he would have signed the Official Secrets Act and be unable to talk about such things, but Tim was curious nonetheless.

In addition, Dr Gribbles had a surprising amount of toys in his home. Tim played for several hours with Mechano and Lego sets, whilst Rcb played computer games. Several of these had been written by Dr Gribbles himself and seemed far more advanced compared with the usual Spectrum or Commodore fare.

Throughout the day, Tim hoped that his encounter with Dr Gribbles outside Blackthorn Lodge would not be mentioned, but the scientist seemed to have forgotten the matter entirely. A curious part of Tim still wanted to know exactly what Gribbles had been doing there in the first place, but intrigue as to why the former government scientist was developing a drug to enhance strength was now his primary interest. Eventually, he asked Gribbles outright.

'Why are you making a drug that increases strength?'

Dr Gribbles put down the test tube rack he was holding, and fixed Tim with a wide-eyed, somewhat manic stare. 'Can you think of uses for such a drug?'

Tim thought of how he planned to take revenge on Jake Buxton, how he could lift heavy objects as and when necessary, how he could impress his friends and so on.

Gribbles seemed to read his mind. 'You see? If you can think of several, I can too.'

Dr Gribbles went back to work, and Tim realised that he hadn't really answered his question.

Just before tea time, the scientist produced a new, loganberry flavoured version of the drug that he tested on Tim and Rob, but the effects were no different. Tim was able to bend a steel bar and break a large chunk of wood with his bare hands. Rob remained unaffected.

'At least it tastes nice,' said Tim, impressed with the loganberry flavouring.

'Most frustrating,' Gribbles muttered. 'Trying to compensate for hormonal change is proving trickier than I thought.'

Tim was about to ask Gribbles to explain the problem more clearly when there was a knock on the door upstairs. Gribbles grabbed a gas mask and canister, but Rob blocked his path.

'I really wouldn't do that again if I were you.'

Gribbles looked confused. 'But we need more test subjects.'

'Not all subjects are likely to be as understanding as us.'

'Of course, quite right.' Gribbles put down the mask and canister and went upstairs to answer the door.

Rob rolled his eyes. 'I still think he's mad.'

'No, just single minded.'

'He's fun to be around, I'll give him that. Much more interesting than when he visits Mum and Dad for tea, or when he talks in school. Perhaps if he could just...'

'Shh!' Tim interrupted. 'Listen!'

From upstairs Tim and Rob could hear the sound of raised voices. Dr Gribbles was arguing with someone.

'...there are some lines that should never be crossed, and you are crossing them!' Gribbles yelled.

'Who are you that you should develop such moral scruples?' a man's voice replied. It was soft, yet somehow cold. Tim felt a shiver down his spine.

'I want you to leave now.'

'You were the one who initiated this project, so you only have yourself to blame. We will do this, with or without your help.'

'I want no further part in it. I am retired.'

'Men like you don't simply retire. I can only imagine what experiments you are undertaking in secret. If you come back to us, the possibilities are endless.'

'I will *never* come back. *Ever*. Not after what happened.'

The man with the cold voice sighed in exasperation. 'You really should let go of the past.'

'The past is the one thing keeping me human. If I ignore it, I become the monster. Heaven forbid that I should let go of the past! The price is too high. Tell London the answer is still no, and will remain no whilst I have breath in my body!'

There was a loud slam, followed by brief silence. Tim listened closely, and presently heard sniffing. He exchanged confused glances with Rob as they both realised in amazement that Dr Gribbles was crying.

Chapter 3: Into the Cellar

Tim and Rob stood at the foot of the stairs for a few minutes, waiting for Gribbles to return. It seemed best to leave him be rather than embarrass him by going upstairs, but at the same time Tim found himself wanting to find out what was wrong.

Eventually, Gribbles composed himself and by the time he returned to the laboratory he was smiling.

'That's got rid of him!' Gribbles declared.

'Who was it?' asked Tim.

'Double glazing salesman. Don't these people have better things to do on a Sunday?'

Tim could tell Gribbles knew they knew he was lying, but that it was his way of telling them to mind their own business.

'Anyone for scones?' asked Gribbles. 'I baked some yesterday, and they're rather good.'

They ate a surprisingly tasty afternoon tea of scones with jam and clotted cream, and chocolate cake; all of it home made. Discovering this supposedly mad scientist was also an excellent cook was a surprise to Tim, who was used to eating meals Rob had prepared. To be fair, Rob's cooking was getting better. He had once thought his brothers cooking should be outlawed by the Geneva Convention as a weapon of mass destruction, but now he thought casualties incurred as a result of eating his food were down to what the Pentagon might term "acceptable losses". Tim had learnt to cook a bit himself too, but unfortunately he only really had his brother to teach him, as his parents were too busy.

Just before they left, Gribbles asked Tim and Rob to return the following weekend, as there would be additional serums ready for testing. They agreed to this, although Tim could tell it was still against Rob's better judgement. But Tim didn't care. His mind buzzed with the possibilities of what he could do with the strength enhancing serum. He even thought of a name for it: Hec (HEC – Haemomuscular Enhancing Compound).

After going to bed that evening, Tim lay awake for some time. He wasn't just thinking about Hec but about the various mysteries around Dr Gribbles. For one thing, what was Gribbles hiding in Blackthorn Lodge? Then there was the mysterious caller who had been sent away so vehemently. It seemed apparent that he was a government agent of some kind trying to persuade Gribbles to return to a top secret project, but what project? And was this somehow connected to Hec? Above all, after the caller left, why had Gribbles been crying?

That night, Tim dreamt Dr Gribbles sprayed knock-out gas in his face then trapped him inside the cellar at Blackthorn Lodge. Here, shrouded in total darkness, he heard the piercing roars of the Beast, and although Tim desperately tried to take some Hec to fend off the monster, the extra strength proved useless. Amid the roaring Tim heard the sobs of Dr Gribbles, and the cold voice of his mystery caller.

You only have yourself to blame.

We will do this, with or without your help.

Tim awoke suddenly, his heart pounding. He felt afraid, and in the early morning gloom was confronted with a simple truth he had tried to suppress but couldn't.

He had not imagined the roaring in Blackthorn Lodge. There was something monstrous in that cellar, and what's more, it was highly likely that Dr Gribbles knew about it. Otherwise, why would he have warned Tim to keep away?

All thoughts of Dr Gribbles were banished from his mind throughout much of the following day, as school proved somewhat tricky. Rob had a cold, and was therefore off sick and unable to provide the necessary deterrent to Jake Buxton. Word of Rob's absence reached Jake, so those in Tim's year who normally paid protection money insisted on a discount until Rob returned to school. Irritated at what he saw as a slump in his business venture, Tim did his best to avoid Jake when he heard rumours that he and his gang were promising to get him back for escaping from Blackthorn Lodge. But he knew that if he did get cornered, he could always use Dr Gribbles' experimental loganberry flavoured Hec vials and try to defend himself.

By the time the school day ended, Tim was tired and fed up, but as he reached his front door he caught a glimpse of Dr Gribbles driving past in his black Cortina. His face was pale with blood all down one side. He appeared to have been attacked.

Intrigued, Tim went up to Rob's bedroom and explained what he had seen. His brother still felt ill, but was very interested in Tim's story.

'Perhaps he got injured during one of his crazy experiments,' Rob said thoughtfully.

An idea occurred to Tim. 'Perhaps he was driving to Blackthorn Lodge. I saw him over there the other day that time when Jake and the others locked me inside.'

'What did he say?'

Tim didn't speak immediately. He didn't really want to tell his brother the full truth about the roaring, but in light of the other strange events, it seemed a good idea.

'Look Dubbler, there's something you need to know. When I was inside the house, I heard muffled roars coming from the cellar.'

Rob raised a dubious eyebrow. 'You mean this mythical Beast?'

'I know it sounds ridiculous. I kept telling myself I was imagining things, but I can't ignore the evidence any longer. I definitely heard *something* trapped inside that cellar.'

'So you're saying the haunted house really is haunted?'

'No. There has to be a rational explanation. After I escaped, I saw Dr Gribbles. He seemed afraid, and was very angry with me for having been inside the house. He told me to stay away from it then went back and sat in his car. I wondered if he was just waiting for me to leave so that *he* could go inside the place.'

'Why would Dr Gribbles be interested in Blackthorn Lodge?'

'I don't know, but after all the other weird stuff that's happened, I want to find out.'

Rob sighed. 'Alright, so beside testing dangerous drugs on children, you're saying he's also pals with the spectral Beast of Blackthorn Lodge?'

'It can't be a spectre.'

'Perhaps it isn't, but it's something. I don't think you imagined those roars.'

Tim thought for a moment, before coming to a sudden decision. 'I'm going to take another look. Right now.'

'At Blackthorn Lodge?'

'Of course.'

Rob got out of bed and began to put on his clothes.

'What are you doing?' asked Tim.

'Coming with you.'

'But you aren't feeling well.'

'I can hardly let you go alone after what happened last time, and from the look on your face I can see you won't be happy until you've satisfied your curiosity. Besides, what if you run into Jake Buxton again?'

'I've got my Hec vials.'

'Yes, well it isn't just Jake that concerns me. It's what Gribbles has in that cellar. We know what he's capable of, and whatever is going on there, I doubt it's good.'

It was almost dark by the time Tim and Rob stood outside Blackthorn Lodge. Stars began to appear amid patches of cloud and lingering blue

34

light in the wake of the recently set sun. The cool, pleasant air still felt very much like summer.

However, as far as Tim was concerned, it might as well have been the height of winter with thunder, lightning and lashing rain. Such typical gothic horror weather would have suited how anxious he felt. He recalled in vivid detail the terror of being trapped inside, and although he knew it was unlikely that the entrances would end up barricaded again, he was nevertheless very tense.

'Are you sure you want to do this?' Rob asked.

'Of course.' However afraid he felt, Tim's determination to get answers to the peculiar occurrences surrounding Dr Gribbles overrode all other considerations.

Rob nodded. 'Right. After you?'

Tim led the way to the front door through the overgrown garden. The broken draining pipe he had climbed down to escape remained visible on the ground, exactly where he had left it, but the barricades Jake and his cronies had used to trap him inside where gone. Tim wondered how much time had elapsed before Jake and the others returned. He had no reason to believe that Jake wouldn't have done exactly as he said he would do, and leave him there all night.

His heart racing, Tim stared up at the looming, boarded-up house. The ivy and creeping plants rustled in the gentle breeze. A blackbird crowed nearby. Tim was glad of Rob's presence, as he didn't know whether he would have had the nerve to try the front door and re-enter the sinister house without him.

Inside, all was quiet. Tim crept ahead with Rob following, examining their dusty, decaying surroundings. A little way into the hall, Tim found the fallen rotten plasterboard from where he had stepped through the upper staircase in his desperation to reach the upstairs bathroom.

Rob took a torch from his pocket and switched it on in the gloom. Tim did likewise, and shone his light into the various corridors leading off the hallway. The silence was ominous, and Tim began to wonder if he really had imagined the noises from below.

'So where's this cellar?' asked Rob.

Tim put his finger to his lips, and indicated the corridor on their left. They crept gingerly along, feet stepping on creaking floorboards. Cobwebs occasionally brushed through their hair, causing them to jump in alarm. Dust came up from the floor, provoking a violent sneeze from Rob.

'Shhh!' Tim hissed.

'Oh for heaven's sake Dubblety, this house isn't haunted! It is creepy, I'll give you that, but ghosts?'

'I didn't say it *was* haunted,' said Tim, irritation overcoming fear. 'I always said there was a plausible explanation for what I heard. Either I imagined it, or...'

His voice tailed off as they reached the door to the cellar. They stood there for a moment, examining the metal handle.

'Well, are we going to open it or not?' Rob asked.

'Last time it was locked,' said Tim. 'We'll probably have to break the lock.'

But to his surprise, the door swung open with an unsettling creak, revealing a set of stone steps leading steeply down into darkness. A cool gust of air rushed upward, and as Tim and Rob shone their torches into the cellar, they could not see the foot of the stairs.

Tim shivered, realising what the unlocked cellar door meant. Someone had been to the house since he had been trapped inside, and had unlocked the door. He doubted very much that Jake Buxton was responsible, so that left one other suspect.

Rob voiced what Tim was thinking. 'What *is* Dr Gribbles up to down there?'

Tim shrugged. 'I don't suppose we'll find out by waiting here.'

They began to creep slowly down the stone steps. Their feet echoed louder than Tim would have liked, and it seemed far cooler than it had on the ground floor. The hairs on the back of his neck began to stand up, and he tried to put all thoughts of ghosts and spectres out of his mind. There *had* to be a rational explanation for what was happening.

They stole downward, to the foot of the steps. With their torches they could make out a second door, just ahead of where the stairs ended. The door was covered in pale blue, peeling paint. It had a latch but no key.

Tim and Rob exchanged nervous glances before slowly opening the latch. The squeak of the door as it swung inward seemed very loud in the silence, and Tim held his breath as he shone his torch into the gloom. A large room lay on the other side, with empty wooden wine racks lining one wall. There were also a few empty cases on the floor, as well as some old rusty tools – including a spade and a crowbar. The air was musty, damp and cold. Tim almost felt disappointed.

'Just as I expected,' he said. 'I imagined it all.'

'Let's take a closer look,' said Rob. 'Whatever you heard might have gone, but we might find some clues that will tell us what it was.'

Tim and Rob moved slowly inside the room, scanning their torches around in the dark. The floor was set with large flagstones, and the walls were damp. Tim bent down to examine the tools, but as he did he noticed something else amid the dust and cobwebs.

'Footprints!'

Rob joined his brother and glanced at the muddy prints that had dried onto the stone floor. 'These look recent,' he said. 'There isn't as much dust around them.'

'What about this?' Tim said, pointing his torch to another dried mud patch.

'Too big to be a footprint,' said Rob.

At first Tim thought his brother was correct, yet as he stared at the dark mud he began to see this might not be the case.

'It's not a human footprint.'

'What are you suggesting?'

'It looks like some kind of gigantic paw print.'

'Made by what?'

'I've no idea, but I hope whatever made it isn't here anymore...' Tim's voice tailed off as he examined the far end of the cellar. There were additional paw prints, more scattered, and older than the more recent human footprints. Something on the wall caught Tim's eye, and he shone his torch on an area of brickwork that had several lines scored diagonally across the stone.

'What is this?' Tim murmured.

Rob examined the wall. 'It's like someone, or something, has been clawing at the wall, gouging at it...'

His torch stopped on a part of the wall that was dark red. Tim prodded the red area and it flaked off onto his fingers.

'Dubbler, please tell me that's not what I think it is.'

Rob examined the red flakes, sniffed at them and nodded slowly. 'Dried blood. Quite a bit of it too. There's a trail...' Rob followed the dried blood to an area in the centre of the room where a couple of old wooden crates had been carelessly stacked. Rob moved them aside, revealing a wooden trapdoor with an iron ring attached to it. It was bolted shut.

For a moment Tim and Rob stood next to the trapdoor, shining their torches on it in trepidation.

'Do we open it?' Rob wondered aloud.

'Of course,' said Tim, in spite of his anxiety. 'We've come this far.'

'But is it wise? I can't help wondering; if we were to just turn around now, leave this place, and forget all about what Dr Gribbles might be up to, perhaps we might thank ourselves in the long run.'

'In the long run, we'd always wonder what he was up to,' said Tim.

Rob sighed. 'You're probably right. Still, there's a particular pop group springing to mind whose name is appropriate to this situation.'

Tim stared in bemusement at his brother.

'Curiosity Killed the Cat,' said Rob.

'Didn't know you were into them,' said Tim.

'I'm not.'

'Didn't think so. All I ever hear from your room is New Order and The Smiths.'

Tim unbolted the lock and began to pull at the iron ring. Slowly the trapdoor swung up and over on it's rusty, creaking hinges, until it was lying flat on the floor of the cellar. A metal ladder led down into the darkness, but it wasn't completely black. Faint light illuminated what seemed to be another stone passageway below, though the source of the light wasn't clear. A machine-like humming could also be heard.

'Strange,' said Rob. 'Another tunnel beneath the cellar that's been deliberately hidden. Odd marks and footprints. And what's that noise?'

Tim and Rob listened for a moment to the low hum from the tunnel. It sounded like the muffled whirr of a washing machine or tumble drier.

'What *is* going on down there?' Rob muttered.

'Let's find out.'

'I wonder. Perhaps we really should just leave this.'

'Why do you keep saying that? Of course we can't leave it! It's a mystery, and we've got to get to the bottom of it.'

Tim began to climb down the ladder into the tunnel beneath the cellar. Rob followed reluctantly. 'I still think this is a bad idea,' he muttered.

The ladder had about twenty rungs, and eventually they found themselves in a dark, damp stone tunnel, unquestionably man made. To their left, the tunnel came to a dead end. On the right, the tunnel continued for about seventy yards, but there was a dim light coming from beneath a closed steel door at the far end.

'That humming must be from an electrical generator,' Rob whispered.

'Why are you whispering?' Tim asked.

'In case someone overhears us.'

'Who?'

'Whoever is in that room!'

'How do you know there's someone in it?'

'Because the light's on, you nitwit!'

Tim thought about this for a moment. 'That doesn't mean there's someone present. It could be that he just left the light on after he left.'

'After *who* left?'

'Dr Gribbles of course! I reckon on the other side of that door is some kind of secret lab. Perhaps those roars I heard were just noises he plays to scare people away, and make them think the place is haunted.'

'You really are determined to find that rational explanation, aren't you?'

'Well, he can't be keeping an actual ghost here, but I still want to know what he's up to.'

They began to creep along the tunnel towards the door. The light that shone from beneath it grew brighter as they approached, and the humming grew louder. After about twenty yards, Tim noticed a passageway leading off to the right, next to the door, and as he got closer still, he saw it led to a second steel door. There was no light coming from this second room, but the humming seemed to originate there.

'Let's check out the room with the light first,' said Tim.

'Shh! Keep your voice down!' Rob hissed.

But amid all their discoveries, Tim was feeling excited rather than scared. 'Look, there isn't a ghost down here. It's perfectly safe to talk as loudly as…'

40

At that moment, Tim was interrupted by a growling that escalated into a hideous roar.

His blood ran cold. It was the same sound he had heard before – the snarling cries of a savage predatory animal.

'That's no ghost,' Rob whispered.

'It came from the room,' Tim whispered back. 'The room with the light.'

'We should get out of here now.'

'No!'

Tim was determined, even though he was terrified, to find out what lay beyond in the room with the light.

'Are you mad?' Rob hissed. 'Gribbles could have something really dangerous in there!'

'It's got to be in a cage or something,' said Tim. 'Otherwise, he wouldn't be able to experiment on it.'

'But what's he got that he's experimenting on?'

Another vicious roar echoed from the other side of the door. It rang along the cold passage, causing Tim to shiver with fright.

'It sounds like a lion or tiger,' said Rob. 'But it's also different, like a person that can't talk.'

The roaring continued. Tim and Rob remained rooted to the spot. The cries were horrifying, and with them now came sounds of clanking chains.

'Whatever it is, it's trying to escape!' cried Rob. 'Obviously, it heard us.'

'Gribbles will have it well chained up,' said Tim.

'That's what they thought in *King Kong*, before Kong went on a rampage!'

'Whatever is in there is not a giant gorilla,' said Tim.

'I don't care what's in there. We need to get out of here.'

'Not before I see what it is,' said Tim.

'Forget it! You are not opening that door!'

But Tim ignored Rob and rushed forward. The snarling and roaring became louder and more frightening than ever. Clinking chains being strained could also be heard, amid the thudding footsteps of a creature desperately trying to escape.

'Tim, you're insane! Come back!'

Rob ran after his brother, but by the time he caught up, Tim had already examined the door and discovered a shutter like those on prison cell doors. Tim opened the shutter and glanced through.

The large room beyond was lit by a single light bulb that dangled overhead. It contained a desk on the right hand side covered with test tubes, Bunsen burners and other scientific apparatus. At the back of the room was a large metal rectangular structure with a glass pane that looked like an airlock from a science fiction film. It was big enough for a human to fit inside. Cables ran from the device to a hole in the wall that presumably led into the other room that housed the generator.

The sounds of snarling and clanking chains emanated from the left hand side of the room, from an area that could not be seen. However, Tim could make out bones and water in a large plastic container. There was an extremely unpleasant stench from inside the room, like an animal cage in a zoo that hadn't been cleaned for a long time.

'What is it?' Rob asked, curious in spite of everything. He shoved Tim aside and glanced through the shutter. He stared at what he saw for some time, before withdrawing and blinking incredulously at Tim.

'Whatever that is is no ghost,' said Rob.

The terrible snarling continued. In spite of feeling utterly terrified, Tim was surprised to find a small amount of sympathy buried beneath his fear. Although it sounded dangerous and very frightening, the monster was obviously miserable too, bitterly resenting its captivity.

Still the monster roared and tugged at the chains, but to no effect. It seemed the Beast could not get free. Tim listened in fascination and fear for a few seconds then took another look, trying to catch a glimpse of the Creature. But the monster remained frustratingly out of view.

'No doubt the Beast made those marks and footprints in the cellar,' said Rob.

'Perhaps Gribbles had to force it down here,' said Tim. 'He'd have had to drug it. Or else he would need to be incredibly strong...'

Tim's voice tailed off as he felt the Hec vials in his pocket.

'It knows we're outside the door,' said Rob. 'We ought to leave. We're just upsetting it.'

'But what *is* it?' Tim exclaimed. 'This Beast, where did it come from?'

'I don't know, and to be honest I don't care. I just want to get out of here.'

Tim thought for a moment. 'We have to ask Dr Gribbles. If we tell him we've seen it, he'll have no choice but to tell us the truth.'

'Or he might kill us,' said Rob. 'He used to work for top secret government projects, remember? What if this is one of those? An experiment that went wrong?'

'Well, whatever it is, that creature is hungry or upset about something,' said Tim. 'We can't just leave it like this. We have to get some food.'

Rob stared at Tim in disbelief. 'Have you completely lost your mind? You have no idea what this thing is, and how dangerous it is. For all you know, feeding it could turn it into something even worse! Like in *Gremlins*.'

'Don't be ridiculous,' said Tim. 'This animal has probably been cruelly neglected.'

'It's probably chained up with good reason!' cried Rob. 'You know what, forget Dr Gribbles. We should go to the police right now.'

'No,' said Tim. 'We should find out more first.'

'What else is there to know? There's a vicious creature chained up underneath the haunted house on Cromwell Hill. We don't know who put it there, but it might have been Dr Gribbles.'

'I want a closer look.'

'Dubblety, no! Absolutely no way! This thing could kill you!'

'But it's chained up! It can't escape.'

'You are not going in there.'

'Who put you in charge?'

'I did. When Mum and Dad aren't around to look after you, which let's face it is most of the time, I am in charge.'

'Sorry Dubbler, but in the interests of discovering the truth, we've got to go in.'

Tim took another look inside the room. A series of savage snarls and chain pulling sounds slowly degenerated into the noise of something slumping against the wall. There then followed a loud, piercing snorting.

'I think its crying,' said Tim. 'Dubbler, we can't just leave it.'

Rob was not convinced. 'I'm sure the poor helpless savage beastie can take care of itself for a few more minutes whilst we call the police. Now come on!'

Tim knew there was no way he could convince his brother to open the door, but he wanted to prove the Creature wasn't dangerous. Clearly if Dr Gribbles had a work station inside the room then the monster must at least be safe chained up. He was determined to see the Beast and so recklessly came up with a plan.

For a long time afterwards Tim wondered what possessed him to act so arrogantly and foolishly; to knowingly step into a room with an unknown and in all likelihood hugely dangerous monster. The only reason he could give was simple curiosity, but such a motive seemed strangely inadequate considering the catastrophic nature of what happened next.

Tim pretended to move away from the door, but when Rob followed, he darted back and hurriedly opened the bolts that were keeping it shut. Rob tried to grab him, but it was too late. The door was open.

At this, a deafening roar pierced the air, followed by the clanking of a chain being tugged. But this time the noise was accompanied by sounds of crumbling masonry. In that split second, Tim knew the Beast had torn itself free. Immediately Tim and Rob tried to shut and bolt the door again, but they were too slow. Something huge smashed into it, slamming the door against Tim so violently that he was unconscious before he hit the ground.

Chapter 4: Project Centaur

Tim awoke with the taste of blood in his mouth. He gradually became aware of a furious row taking place between his brother and Dr Gribbles as they stood in the corridor beside the now buckled door. Tim noticed Gribbles had a dried cut on his head, and remembered how he had seen him with blood on his face earlier that day.

'You have no idea what you've done!' cried Gribbles. 'Why didn't he listen to me? I told him to keep away from this place!'

'You can't blame him for being curious!' Rob yelled.

'Oh yes I can! And as for you, someone your age ought to know better!'

'You still haven't told me why we can't just go to the police and tell them what happened.'

'Police? Is that the limit of your vision? The police can't handle something like this! They have no idea what's at stake, and neither do you.'

As he pulled himself up, Tim rubbed a large bump on his head. He felt sick and dizzy as Dr Gribbles turned on him.

'You've been a very foolish young man. I cannot begin to say how disappointed I am. You are now responsible for every death that takes place as a result of your actions. Their blood is on your hands!'

'Enough!' cried Rob. 'Stop talking to my brother like that! Let's not forget who decided it would be a good idea to experiment on a monster in a place like this! It's your fault Dr Gribbles!'

'You let out the Creature,' said Gribbles.

'You didn't chain it up properly,' said Tim. But deep down, he knew Gribbles was right. It was entirely his fault that the monster had escaped. If he had only left that door alone…

'Well, it's no use blaming each other now,' said Gribbles. 'The pair of you will have to help me put this right. We've got to hunt him down.'

'You mean the monster?'

'It is not a monster.'

'Then what is it?'

'A hybrid. Look, I haven't time to explain, but if this Creature is seen, all hell will break loose. It is the fastest, strongest, deadliest killing machine you can possibly imagine. It is also hungry, and will maul whatever it can get its hands on first, whether human or animal.'

'Dr Gribbles had just arrived to feed it when the monster escaped,' Rob explained.

'How long was I unconscious?' asked Tim.

'Only a couple of minutes,' said Rob. 'I was knocked unconscious too so I didn't see the Beast, but it must have climbed out of the cellar and out of the house. It passed Dr Gribbles on his way in, but he couldn't stop it.'

'Nothing can stop it,' said Gribbles. 'The only thing we can do now is hunt it and hopefully tranquilise it before it kills anyone.'

'Why not tell the police?' asked Tim.

Dr Gribbles shook his head. 'You really haven't a clue what you've got yourselves into. You are in very, very serious trouble, especially after what you've seen and done. If *only* you hadn't opened that door.'

'But what is that Creature, and why was it here?' asked Rob.

'That doesn't matter right now. What matters is we have to get out there and find it.'

'We're not going anywhere but home,' said Rob.

Dr Gribbles pulled a handgun from his pocket. Tim gasped in horror.

'I'm sorry, but there is no alternative,' said Gribbles. 'Given the highly sensitive nature of what you have seen, I ought to kill you both where you stand. But I need your help. Neither of you are going home until you have put right what you have done. Of course, we might be killed in the attempt, but that is our path whether we like it or not.'

'Dr Gribbles, please calm down,' said Rob, clearly rattled at having a gun pointed in his face. 'There is no need to threaten us. We'll come with you, but please put that away.'

Gribbles lowered the weapon slowly. 'Alright, but no tricks! Whatever happens now, you need to do exactly as I say, at all times. If we don't track down the Creature, the consequences will be disastrous in more ways than you could possibly imagine. Now follow me! We're going back to my laboratory.'

'Why?' asked Tim.

'No questions! Do as you're told!'

Tim and Rob were marched out of the tunnel, up the ladder, out of the cellar and out of Blackthorn Lodge. Outside the sky was dark. An owl hooted in the gloom, and although it was still relatively warm, Tim found himself shivering.

Dr Gribbles led them to his car, and once inside, they drove away from Cromwell Hill and back to Cumberland Close. To describe Gribbles' driving as erratic would have been kind. *Reckless* or *life-threatening* would have been more accurate descriptions, and by the time they screeched to a halt outside Dr Gribbles' garage, Tim felt as though all his insides had been churned up. Part of it was guilt at what he had done, but a part of it was the result of being hurled around corners at such alarming speeds.

Gribbles got out of the car and hurriedly escorted Tim and Rob inside the hallway of his house. After locking the front door, he opened his garage and parked the car inside. He then closed the garage and entered his house from a side door, returning to where Tim and Rob stood in bemusement.

Tim moved his hand towards the light switch, but Gribbles stopped him.

'Don't!'

Gribbles peered through a small window, scanning the street anxiously.

'What's the matter?' asked Rob.

'Checking we haven't been followed.'

'The way you were driving, I doubt anyone could have chased us,' said Tim.

'There are other ways of tracking people,' Gribbles said ominously.

'Look Dr Gribbles,' said Rob. 'At the very least, we need to let our parents know where we are, or they will start to worry.'

'I doubt that,' said Gribbles. 'Aren't they used to you going off by yourselves?'

'Well, yes. But if we aren't there by morning, then they'll call the police.'

Gribbles nodded thoughtfully. 'In that case, we have a bit of time to make sure they aren't watching your house. If they aren't, you can go back in a bit. But once you have made up some kind of convincing excuse to placate your parents, I will need your help hunting the Creature.'

'Who's *they*?' asked Rob.

'Enemies,' Gribbles replied simply. He did not elaborate.

Rob sighed in exasperation. 'I really think you ought to tell us exactly what's happening here, Dr Gribbles. Why were you keeping that monster underneath Blackthorn Lodge?'

'I've already told you, it's not a monster. It's a human animal hybrid, genetically bred mingling human and cheetah DNA.'

'Who bred it?'

'I did.'

Tim stared at Gribbles in amazement.

'You really are a mad scientist!' cried Rob. '*Frankenstein* is supposed to be a cautionary tale, not a scientific text book!'

'Why did you breed it?' asked Tim, who still couldn't quite believe what he was hearing.

'It was a top secret government research operation, codenamed Project Centaur. The objective was to concoct a serum we could use to increase strength and thus create a supersoldier.'

'Like Captain America?'

'Sort of. Originally, we had only been experimenting with strength drugs – the haemomuscular enhancing compounds that I've subsequently been trying to recreate. But then we began to investigate animal genetic components to try and increase speed and stamina. At first we simply mingled the DNA and experimented on mice, but then it got out of control. There were chickens that could fly, goats that could produce milk containing spider web. All kinds of strange combinations.'

Tim was baffled. 'Milk containing spider webs?'

'The point is we eventually mingled human and animal DNA – specifically cheetah DNA. The Creature you allowed to escape was the result.'

'You've got to be joking,' said Rob.

'I wish I was. Unfortunately, the Creature was extremely unstable and dangerous. The government shut down the project and ordered that all the evidence be destroyed. But I refused to kill the Creature. It's a sentient being with feelings, emotions and intelligence.'

Tim remembered how he had felt sorry for the monster as it tried to break free from its chains.

'So you hid the Creature?' said Tim.

Gribbles nodded. 'The secret tunnels beneath Blackthorn Lodge were an ideal hiding place. Getting the Creature there was something of a struggle. I had to use what was left of the haemomuscular enhancing compounds we had put together in the London laboratories in order to have the strength to wrestle the Creature down into the cellar, but even that wasn't enough. In the end, I had to use tranquilisers.'

'So now you want our help to track it down and tranquilise it again?' asked Rob.

'Precisely.'

'Was that why you've been trying to make Hec that works on adults?' asked Tim.

'Hec? Oh I see! Haemomuscular Enhancing Compound. Very clever. Yes, that's why. Unfortunately I've been unable to duplicate what I achieved in London. My equipment isn't sufficiently sophisticated.'

'How did you manage to trick the government into thinking you'd killed the Creature?' asked Rob.

'It wasn't easy. Part of my cover was leaving the job in protest after Project Centaur was terminated. Unfortunately, despite all precautions, it didn't quite work.'

'What do you mean?'

'Some who were involved in Project Centaur suspect that I pulled the wool over their eyes. These people are very dangerous, and will do anything to get the Creature back.'

'Why?'

'Because they want to experiment on him themselves, and when they're finished, they want to cut him up in an autopsy. I can't let them do that.'

'But I thought the project was terminated,' said Rob.

Gribbles laughed grimly. 'Government research projects like that are never terminated. They are simply started again under a different name to dispel rumours of their existence. The only reason Project Centaur was shut down was to put off a few nosey journalists. I can guarantee you the research is continuing, just under a different name.'

'How do you know?' asked Tim.

'Because ever since I resigned they've kept offering me jobs on different projects which I know are continuations of Project Centaur. But I will never go back. Not after what happened with...the Creature.

Besides, the man running the latest version of the project is the same man who ran Project Centaur, and I don't trust him.'

'Why not?'

Gribbles face darkened. 'That hardly matters. We need to focus on recapturing the Creature. But we also need to know if you are being watched.'

'Of course we aren't being watched,' said Rob.

'Then what is that blue van that just pulled up near your house?' asked Gribbles. 'It wasn't there a moment ago.'

Tim looked out. Sure enough a blue VW van with three occupants had parked a little way up the street from his home.

'It's the same van the Libyan terrorists used in *Back to the Future*,' Rob muttered.

'Have you seen it round here before?' asked Gribbles.

'No, but that doesn't mean it's full of government agents,' said Tim.

Rob began to laugh. 'I'll go and check the van for you.'

'Don't be a fool!' Gribbles hissed. 'Think! An unfamiliar van in your road, possibly watching your house. They are waiting for you to come back. Why are they waiting? Because they have already seen you with me. That means, they think you might know something and want to question you. Since you now know quite a bit, as a result of your own inquisitiveness, you are in serious danger.'

'If you're right, should we just wait here until the van leaves?' asked Tim.

'That van won't leave. They won't just be watching you. They'll be watching your parents as well.'

'There are no lights on in the house, so they can't be back from the shop yet,' said Tim.

'Obviously they are waiting for *all* of you to return.'

'But our parents have nothing to do with this!'

52

'Our enemies don't know that. But by now they are probably aware the Creature is still alive.'

Rob didn't look convinced. 'Enemies, enemies...How do we know you're not the enemy? What are you going to do with that Creature when you've recaptured it?'

'That isn't your concern.'

'Look, why don't we just telephone our parents from here, once they get back?' asked Tim.

'The line will be tapped,' said Gribbles.

'Why aren't they pounding on your door?' asked Rob, indicating the people in the van.

'Who says they won't be soon enough? I'm keeping the lights off to deter them, but eventually they'll think I'm out, so they'll come and search the house.'

Rob shook his head. 'You're being completely paranoid. Open this door right now or I'll...'

'Shh!' Tim interrupted. 'Look!'

He had noticed his parents returning from the shop. As it was just a five minute walk away they were on foot. They strode past the VW van and walked up the drive to their front door. As Tim watched his mother putting her key in the lock, three men in dark suits got out of the VW van. They strode up to his father and began to converse with him. Tim couldn't tell for sure, but from their body language his parents didn't seem particularly alarmed. A moment later his mother smiled and gestured for the three men to enter their home.

Gribbles turned to Tim and Rob as the front door closed. 'Now do you believe me?'

Rob looked at the scientist suspiciously. 'That all appeared perfectly civilised to me.'

'It always does,' said Gribbles. 'They won't alarm your parents unnecessarily, but they will say they need to find you for questioning.'

Rob shrugged. 'Then let's go and be questioned.'

'Don't be a fool!' said Gribbles. 'Your absence could well be the only thing keeping your parents alive. If you go back there they might kill you all!'

'But we've got to help them!' cried Tim.

'They'll be safe enough once our enemies leave. It's you they're after. But if you go back now, your parents could be killed too. These people don't like witnesses.'

Tim didn't know what to think. Rob continued to fix Gribbles with a dubious stare, but the scientist was insistent.

'You really have no idea what you've got yourselves into. I've explained what I can, and what must be done, but there are other matters here that you do not need to know about; suffice to say, our enemies take this very, very seriously. The three of us are all that stands between them and disaster, and to prevent that we *must* recapture the Creature.'

Gribbles began to walk away.

'This place isn't safe for us anymore. Whilst they are inside with your parents they won't be watching this house. We must take that opportunity to leave as they'll soon be back. When they come they will search this place. We must be long gone.'

Chapter 5: The Hole in the Ceiling

Tim felt somewhat in a daze as Gribbles barked instructions to him and his brother; urging them to pack various rucksacks with food, medical supplies, tents, ropes, torches and other camping equipment. He was also alarmed to see Gribbles pack two handguns and ammunition, as well as tranquiliser darts.

By now Rob seemed to have reluctantly accepted that sticking with Gribbles was their best chance of keeping their parents safe, so he and Tim both began to obey his instructions without question. After packing what was needed, they got into Gribbles' car and he drove them away. Tim glanced back at the empty VW van as they passed. It appeared the three men in black suits were still inside his house.

'Where are we going?' Tim asked.

'Back to Blackthorn Lodge,' Gribbles replied. 'We'll sleep there for the night then in the morning we need to start tracking the Creature.'

Tim was appalled at this idea. 'We can't sleep in Blackthorn Lodge!'

Gribbles shrugged indifferently. 'Well, you can't sleep at home, and they will be watching hotels. At this point they probably won't use the media, but I wouldn't be surprised if that didn't follow eventually.'

'But Blackthorn Lodge is...'

'Haunted? The paranormal is outside my field of expertise – suffice to say, I think we shall have to risk it.'

'What if the Creature comes back?' asked Rob.

'We'll set a watch,' said Gribbles. 'If he comes back, whoever is on watch will have to shoot the Creature with a tranquiliser dart.'

'I can't do that!' cried Tim.

'Yes you can. I'll show you how it's done before we go to sleep.'

Tim began to think he was trapped in some kind of bad dream. How could any of this possibly be real? How could he actually be about to spend the night in a haunted house with a tranquiliser gun, taking turns to stay awake and shoot a monster? The idea of it made his stomach churn. He glanced uneasily at Rob, but his brother was lying back in his seat with his eyes closed. Tim had forgotten Rob was feeling ill when they had come out to investigate Blackthorn Lodge.

'How do you know Blackthorn Lodge isn't being watched?' asked Rob.

'They won't be on to this place until the morning at least,' said Gribbles. 'But they almost certainly know about the Creature.'

'How?'

'Surveillance. No doubt I got careless. For example, buying large amounts of meat to feed the Creature would have been suspicious, and if they have been watching me, they will have picked up on such things.'

A moment later, they pulled up outside Blackthorn Lodge. Tim got out of the car and stared up at the sinister house. In the darkness it loomed more menacingly than ever. The idea that he was going to spend the night in this place filled him with dread. If he had to confront the Creature, he would rather it wasn't in a haunted house at the dead of night.

Tim and Rob took some of the rucksacks then followed Gribbles up to the front door. It opened with an eerie creak and they stepped inside cautiously. An alarming thought occurred to Tim, which he then whispered to Gribbles.

'What if the Creature is already back?'

'We'll make a complete search of the house,' Gribbles replied. 'I'll take the cellars and the tunnel, you can search this floor, and Rob can search the upper floors.'

Dr Gribbles took off his rucksack and rummaged around in it for a few seconds. He then handed them each a torch and a tranquiliser handgun resembling a miniature harpoon, with a dart placed inside. The gun felt heavy in Tim's hand.

56

'Be very careful with these,' Gribbles whispered. 'Those darts are probably deadly to humans, but they'll put the Creature to sleep without harming it. The effects last between five and six hours.'

'Do you have any spare darts?' asked Rob. 'In case we miss.'

'If you miss, you won't get the chance to reload,' said Gribbles. 'The Creature will almost certainly kill you. It's a miracle he didn't when you let him out.'

'Perhaps it was *because* we let him out,' said Tim. 'Perhaps he thought we were being kind.'

Gribbles shook his head. 'He is a Creature of pure instinct engineered to be a killing machine, nothing more.'

'All the same, I felt sorry for it.'

Gribbles stared curiously at Tim. 'It's a *him*, not an *it*,' he said presently. 'We'd better get on with searching the house.'

Gribbles and the others crept silently into the hall. Near the staircase, Gribbles indicated silently for Rob to go upstairs and for Tim to check the corridors and rooms downstairs. He then stole quietly along the corridor to the cellar door, unlocked it, and descended the dark staircase.

Rob and Tim had not moved from the foot of the staircase. Tim felt literally frozen with terror at the prospect of searching the house at night, knowing that the Beast could be lurking in any dark corner. There was certainly no way he was going to do it alone. Luckily his brother seemed to read his mind.

'There's no way I'm letting you search on your own, no matter what that lunatic says. Shall we begin with upstairs?'

Tim nodded. 'You go first.'

Rob led the way as they slowly climbed the stairs. The floorboards creaked louder than ever amid the gloom, and although their torches illuminated the darkness somewhat, they also created dancing shadows that fluttered in and out of ominous corners. On more than one occasion Tim jumped out of his skin as he thought he saw the Creature hiding in the blackness.

'I can't believe we're actually doing this,' Rob muttered, as they reached the landing.

'It's my fault,' Tim whispered back. 'If only I hadn't opened that stupid door.'

Rob shrugged. 'Can't be helped now.'

Tim didn't feel reassured. If anything, he felt guiltier than ever at what he had unleashed. His heart began to beat faster as they checked each of the bedrooms in turn. They were empty, but at one point they heard a mouse scuttling along the floorboards which made them almost fall over with fright. The dusty rooms made Tim want to sneeze, but he kept suppressing the urge, in case he disrupted the Beast.

'We'd best check the top floor,' said Rob.

But when they reached the staircase that led to the top, Tim suddenly remembered how part of the stairs had collapsed when he had been trapped inside previously. There was no way they could easily get to the top floor now. A great gap and a hole in the ceiling were visible where Tim had almost fallen through.

'If the Creature does come back, I doubt it will be able to get past that hole,' said Rob.

'I don't think it would hide up here, even if it did return,' said Tim. 'Let's go back downstairs.'

They crept back down, and made a thorough search of the ground floor. Apart from a couple of mice they overheard in the kitchen, they found nothing. But each room appeared dark, dusty and more sinister than ever. Tim could no longer suppress the sneezes, and there were several, one after the other.

'Just as well there's nothing here, given the racket you're making,' said Dr Gribbles, as he rejoined them at the foot of the stairs. 'Did you check upstairs?'

'Yes,' said Tim. 'No sign.'

'What about the top floor?'

'We can't get up to it. Look!' Tim shone his torch at the underside of the staircase that led to the second floor. A yawning hole gaped in the ceiling, and a load of plaster and rubble lay on the ground nearby.

'That happened when I got trapped inside,' Tim explained. 'I managed to get out through a bathroom window at the top.'

'I see,' said Gribbles. 'Well, there's nothing else we can do now. We should get some sleep. I suggest we stay here at the foot of the stairs. It's as good a place as any. I'll take the first watch. Rob, you can take the second. Tim, you can take the third.'

'How long *is* a watch?' Tim asked.

'It's now eleven o'clock,' said Gribbles. 'I'll stay awake until two o'clock then Rob will watch until four. Tim, you can take the final watch, until whenever we all wake up.'

'But what do we do?' asked Tim.

'Just that: watch. Stay awake and alert, ready to fire a tranquiliser dart should the Creature come back. Frankly, I don't think he will, but better safe than sorry.'

Gribbles gave Tim and Rob some hot chocolate from a thermos flask. It was warm and invigorating, and Tim briefly forgot his ominous surroundings. They then got out some sleeping bags and settled down for the night.

For a while, Gribbles sat with the gun in his hand, waiting in the night in case his monstrous creation should return. But after a while he took a couple of small circuit boards and a few wires from a rucksack, along with a screwdriver and other tools.

'What are you making?' Tim asked presently.

'Never mind that now. Just try and get some rest,' Gribbles whispered back.

Tim indicated the cut on Gribbles' head. 'Did the Creature do that to you?'

Gribbles nodded.

At first, Tim found it very difficult to get any sleep. His mind kept replaying all that had happened that evening, and it seemed too much to take in. The sight of Gribbles' bloodied face had prompted their investigation of the Blackthorn Lodge cellars, but the release of the Creature and their present predicament meant that Tim simply could not calm down.

He was worried about what the Creature might do, and had visions of it breaking into homes and mauling the occupants. He imagined it charging through populated areas causing widespread panic. He then imagined himself on trial for mass murder because he had released the Beast. He imagined the harsh words of a judge sending him to prison for the rest of his life.

Gribbles was right. They had to find it. That was the only way to make amends for his curiosity. But Tim was very scared – not just of the Beast, but of Gribbles' mysterious enemies. It occurred to Tim that he had never been more afraid in his life. In the past, when difficulties had arose (such as his problems with Jake Buxton), he had always managed to scheme his way out of trouble one way or another. But try as he might he could not think of a cunning way to manipulate his way out of this mess. They were entirely dependant on the plans of a probably deranged ex-government scientist.

Looking miserably up at the ceiling, Tim stared at the gaping hole in the staircase, which was lit in shadow from the light of Gribbles' torch. From where he lay it appeared very sinister – like a portal to some hellish alternative dimension. The opening was even darker than the blackness of the ceiling around it, and the more he looked at the hole, the more Tim had the uneasy feeling that it was staring right back at him.

Tim told himself it was just his imagination, but now the thought had taken root in his mind, he couldn't ignore it. The notion that this black hole was observing him caused his mind to run riot. What if the place really was haunted? What if spectres flew out from the portal in the dead of night to claim his soul?

Shivering at the thought, Tim looked away to where Rob slept peacefully. How his brother had nodded off in such an unwelcoming place was beyond him, but then Rob had always been a heavy sleeper. Besides, he still wasn't feeling well and was no doubt exhausted.

Dr Gribbles sat up on watch, silently staring into the gloom. His black silhouette was not particularly reassuring, and Tim still found it difficult to fully trust him. What if this entire course of events had somehow been engineered to get them into Blackthorn Lodge at the dead of night? What if Gribbles was really a deranged serial killer? What if he murdered him and Rob in their sleep?

Be calm, he told himself. *Be rational. He is a friend of Mum and Dad. Besides, if he is a serial killer, where does the Beast fit into Gribbles' plans?*

Tim turned on his back and stared up at the ceiling once more, but that just got his mind onto the black hole again. He tried closing his eyes, but he could still see it in his mind; staring relentlessly down at him, glaring at him in the unfriendly night. He couldn't understand it, but he definitely sensed a lurking presence; a watchfulness, a feeling of being observed by something angry.

Keeping his eyes squeezed shut Tim tried and tried to think of something else. He thought about how much he had laughed when his brother – a big Pet Shop Boys fan – had been irritated to the point of vigorously defacing *Smash Hits* posters of Rick Astley, since he had beaten their latest single to number one in the charts.

But all the time, Tim's mind kept returning to the hole in the ceiling.

He thought about Sylvester McCoy, who had just taken over as the new *Doctor Who*. Tim thought he was a good choice for the part, but the stories were weak. His brother, a big Tom Baker fan, had said no-one would ever be as good and that the series was in decline.

The hole in the ceiling looked at him.

Tim desperately thought of holidays he had enjoyed, pranks he had played, teachers he had annoyed, and of how much he disliked his brother's present girlfriend. He even thought about Jake Buxton and how much he would like to punch him after taking a dose of Hec. But that just made him think of Dr Gribbles and his crazy experiments, which in turn made him think of how they had let the Beast out and consequently...

The hole.

Unable to bear it any longer, Tim opened his eyes and stared back at the hole, as though daring it to do its worst. More than ever he sensed something staring down at him, and wondered whether or not he should tell Gribbles. It didn't seem possible as they had checked the house thoroughly, but what if the Creature had somehow been hiding on the second floor? Or even in the attic?

No, he told himself. He was jumping at shadows. There was nothing. Gribbles would insist it was his overactive imagination. Determining that this was indeed the case, Tim resolved once more to close his eyes and go to sleep, and to deliberately ignore whatever he sensed looking at him. He was about to do this when he suddenly saw – or thought he saw – a dim glimmer like the reflection of light in a set of blinking eyes.

Tim stared up in alarm. Perhaps it was just a mouse in the rafters that had stopped to look down. He squinted, peering into the gloom, but the eyes, if eyes they were, had gone.

Tim rubbed his eyes. He really was tired, and exhaustion finally began to get the better of him. Telling himself that his mind was playing tricks, he turned on his side and settled down. But a small voice in the back of his head reminded him what had happened the last time he insisted that his mind was playing tricks. He told himself he had imagined the roars and snarls from the cellar, and look how that had turned out. In his dreams, Tim saw the blinking eyes in the black hole again and again. He kept not quite waking up, and felt cold and afraid.

Eventually he was shaken awake by Rob, as it was his turn to watch. In the small hours of the morning it was colder than ever, and he shivered in the darkness.

'I'll stay up with you,' Rob whispered. 'I can't sleep anyway. I don't feel well.'

Once again Tim felt guilty, knowing his brother ought to be resting and getting well.

Rob seemed to read Tim's mind. 'It isn't all your fault Dubblety. I should never have agreed to come with you to this place. If I'd stayed put I doubt you would have come here on your own.'

That was true enough. Tim felt a little better at his brother's kind words.

'Seen anything at all?' Tim asked.

Rob shook his head. 'Heard a few mice, but that was it.'

They sat in silence for a while, amid the loud snores that were coming from Dr Gribbles. Presently they both began to laugh quietly.

'I'm not sure I could have slept with that racket anyway,' said Rob.

'Do you think Mum and Dad are OK?' Tim asked.

'I'm sure they're fine.'

'Do you really think we should trust Dr Gribbles?'

'I don't see what choice we have. He's the one with all the answers. I bet there's a lot he isn't telling us.'

'About the Beast?'

'About everything.'

The minutes dragged on, and Tim wrapped a blanket around himself to keep warm. He glanced at the tranquiliser gun in his hand and wondered whether he would be able to fire it if he was suddenly confronted with the Creature. After shining a torch at his watch, he saw it was 4:43am. Dawn was still over an hour away.

At that moment, Tim heard a scuttling above his head. It sounded like it came from the top floor.

'What was that?' Tim whispered.

'Probably just another mouse,' said Rob. 'I've heard them moving around upstairs quite a bit.'

Tim looked up at the hole once again, and the horrible blackness seemed to stare back. He strained his eyes in the darkness, and for a second thought he saw a shadow moving around. The movement was accompanied by the sound of creaking floorboards.

Rob looked up in alarm, and indicated for Tim to pass him the tranquiliser gun. Tim handed the weapon to his brother with shaking hands.

'Did you see it?' Tim whispered, hardly daring to breathe.

Rob put a finger to his lips and indicated that Tim should shine his torch at the ceiling. Slowly and deliberately he shone it up into the hole. The darkness around it slowly dispersed. Further creaking sounds and noises of shuffling and grunting followed. Whatever was up there was no mouse.

Tim's heart was beating so fast he thought it would burst from his ribcage. His hands trembled as he moved the torch beam to the centre of the black hole. What it revealed caused him to cry out in terror at what his eyes stubbornly insisted was before them: the gigantic head of a monster.

The horrifying face resembled a cross between a human and a panther. Great salivating fangs were visible as the Creature snarled, and its emerald eyes burned with rage.

64

Tim's cries roused Gribbles from his slumber. At the same time, Rob leapt to his feet, aimed the tranquiliser gun and fired. But he was too late. The shot went wide.

Roaring in fury, the Beast smashed at the plaster and came crashing through the floorboards. Tim and Rob dodged as the Creature fell, and Gribbles rolled aside just in time.

Tim half expected the Beast to be dead or at least injured as a result of his fall, but he got up immediately, looming menacingly at his nine foot height. The Creature had huge muscles around three times the size of the most muscular athlete or boxer, and although humanoid in appearance, the hands and feet were like those of a big cat; disproportionately sized with savage, razor sharp claws.

'Your gun!' cried Gribbles. 'Quick!'

'I missed!' said Rob.

Gribbles tried to grab his gun from the floor, but the Beast leapt across and kicked it out of reach. With astonishing and terrifying agility, the Creature then grabbed Gribbles by the throat and began to throttle him.

Tim watched helplessly, completely frozen to the spot. He had no idea what to do. Nothing his brain came up with offered any help.

But Rob acted desperately, lunging at the Beast and launching himself onto its back. The Creature let go of Gribbles, grabbed Rob, and slung him onto the floor. Rob yelled in pain and crawled as quickly as he could away from the staircase along one of the corridors.

'Reload whilst I've got it distracted!' cried Rob.

But the Creature was enraged, and from the look in his eyes, about to kill. Gribbles had no time to reload. Instead he grabbed a piece of wood that had fallen from the ceiling and began to batter the Beast. Turning to Gribbles, the monstrous being roared louder than ever and swiped at the scientist; swatting him aside as though he were nothing more than a fly. The Creature then returned his attention to Rob, and to his horror

Tim watched as the Beast slashed at Rob's arm, cutting a deep gash with his claws. Blood began flowing from the wounds and Rob yelled in agony.

In sheer desperation, Tim ran in front of the Creature and shouted at him.

'No! Leave him alone! Please!'

Surprised, the Creature stared at Tim in confusion. He then roared in his face. Tim thought his eardrums might burst, and in that moment squeezed his eyes shut. He was probably going to die, but he couldn't stand by and do nothing whilst the Beast devoured his brother.

Yet to his surprise the Creature did no such thing. Instead its roar became a low growl, and after eyeing Tim dubiously it bounded along the hallway, smashing its way out through the front door.

Gribbles pulled himself to his feet.

'Are you alright?' Tim asked.

'I'll live,' said Gribbles. 'It's your brother I'm concerned about.'

Tim and Gribbles knelt at Rob's side. He spluttered blood and bled profusely where the Creature had slashed at him.

'It looks just as bad as it feels,' Rob groaned. His face turned pale.

'He's losing blood fast,' said Gribbles. 'We have to get him to a hospital. Help me get him out of here.'

'But the Beast is out there!' cried Tim.

'We'll have to risk it,' said Gribbles.

Tim and Gribbles helped Rob to his feet and the three of them staggered along the corridor back to the staircase and out of the front door. Outside the night was old but the darkness remained thick. They crossed the overgrown garden and out through the gate into the street, where they lay Rob on the pavement and made him as comfortable as they could. Gribbles then rushed to a red telephone box about fifty yards away to call for an ambulance.

'What will he say to them?' Rob muttered.

'Probably that you've been attacked by a genetically engineered mutant creature,' Tim replied with a shrug, trying to keep cheerful for his brother's sake. Rob didn't look in good shape at all. Tim's stomach gave a horrible lurch at the prospect of losing him.

'Don't worry Dubblety,' said Rob. 'At least this way I'll be out of danger.'

'But what if those government agents find you?'

'It's either risk that or bleed to death here,' said Rob. He sighed, and spluttered more blood. 'I really, really wanted to be the one to bring down that monster. If only I hadn't missed. Films make it look so much easier.'

'You'll have to do some target practise,' said Tim. He leaned forward and whispered to his brother.

'Dubbler?'

'Yes?'

'I'm really, really scared.'

Tim didn't often make completely honest statements like that. Now that he had, he found he had tears in his eyes.

'Gribbles will look after you,' said Rob. 'I mean, okay, he's a lunatic and should be locked up. But we need him. I think he's just crazy enough to keep you alive, but not too crazy so that you get killed.'

Rob sighed. 'Still wish I'd bagged the Creature.'

'I still wish I'd not let it out in the first place.'

'Well, I shouldn't have brought you here to look for it, and Gribbles should never have brought it here either. Looks like we all share the blame.'

A moment later Gribbles came running from the phone box. 'Right! Let's go!'

'We're just going to leave him here?' asked Tim.

Gribbles nodded. 'The ambulance will take care of him. I've also called your parents to let them know.'

'I thought you said the phone was tapped?'

'It probably is, but we had to risk it with your brother's life in danger.'

'What about Rob? Won't they kill him?'

'Doubtful. Not if we're still at large. We have to start hunting the Creature at first light. Look!'

Gribbles pointed to the eastern horizon. Dawn was breaking.

'He's right,' said Rob, looking paler than ever. 'If you don't start looking for the Beast, more people could be hurt or killed.'

'We need to hide until the ambulance has been and gone,' said Gribbles. 'After that, we're going after the Beast.'

'Well, this is goodbye then,' said Tim, feeling utterly miserable.

'I'll be fine,' said Rob. 'Besides, I'll tell them nothing.'

'Don't be a fool,' said Gribbles. 'You need medical help so there's no point in secrecy now. Just tell them you were attacked by some kind of monster and leave it at that. You don't have to say anything about me or Tim.'

'Alright,' said Rob. 'Look after Tim. Don't inject him with anything that has dangerous side effects.'

'I'll take care of him,' said Gribbles.

With that, Tim and Gribbles made their way back to Blackthorn Lodge and concealed themselves behind some large, overgrown hydrangea bushes in the dim morning light. The sounds of an ambulance siren could be heard approaching in the distance.

Chapter 6: The Hunt Begins

Tim watched as the ambulance crew carefully placed Rob onto a stretcher. He appeared to be unconscious, but Tim wondered if his brother was faking, in order to avoid difficult questions. Certainly the ambulance crew seemed baffled as to the cause of his injuries.

'Looks like an animal did this to him...'

'Some kind of mad dog?'

One of the paramedics glanced around nervously.

'Don't think so. What dog could do that?'

'No sign of the caller. Better let the boys in blue know about this one.'

Tim listened closely, but couldn't overhear the muttered voices as one of the paramedics spoke into his radio, evidently notifying the police.

'Righto! Let's move him...'

The paramedics lifted Rob inside the ambulance. They shut the doors, and Tim watched as they drove away. Seeing his brother carted off to hospital in this fashion was somewhat upsetting, but he knew there was no alternative. At least his parents had been told and could look after him.

'We'd better get going too,' said Gribbles.

They went back inside Blackthorn Lodge, which looked as eerie as ever even in the morning light. Gribbles told Tim to wait as he briefly visited the cellar. He returned a moment later hauling large, heavy-duty bags. Tim glanced inside one and saw what looked suspiciously like sticks of dynamite.

'What are you doing?' asked Tim.

'Being prepared,' said Gribbles. 'Just in case.'

Gribbles set about placing explosives and detonators in various places around the ground floor, often cutting holes in walls and running fuse wires between each set of dynamite sticks.

Tim was somewhat puzzled at Gribbles actions. 'Are you going to blow up the house?'

'Not if I can help it.'

The scientist did not elaborate so Tim thought it best to leave him to it. After a few more minutes, Gribbles had finished. They collected their backpacks, weapons and other equipment and returned outside to the grounds. Gribbles took a small electronic device from his pocket and switched it on. A red light blinked slowly amid barely audible sounds of radio static.

'Is that what you were building last night?' Tim asked.

Gribbles nodded. 'Homing beacon. I injected a small electronic tracking chip into the Creature, in case he should ever escape, but hadn't got round to making the tracking mechanism. I just hope it works. It doesn't let me know the location. Only if the Creature is close.'

'And is it?'

Gribbles scrutinised the device. 'No. I'd say it's a good three or four miles away already.'

'So how will we track it?'

'The red light will flash more quickly the closer we get. Also we can use old-fashioned hunting techniques. For example, we can follow his footprints.'

Tim stared at the grass in the early morning light, but couldn't make out any discernible trail, especially as they had been back and forth through the grounds many times themselves. Gribbles also examined the overgrown gardens for a moment then produced a pair of what appeared to be red tinted goggles from his rucksack. A wire ran from them, which was attached to another small electronic device. Gribbles turned a switch and put the goggles on.

'Take a look through these,' said Gribbles.

Tim put them on and gasped. Amid the grass he could see several sets of footprints going to and from the house, some of which obviously belonged to them. But there were also a set of large paw prints leading out into the road.

'The goggles are infra-red sensitive and detect recent body heat,' Gribbles explained. 'What do you notice about the footprints?'

'Some are fainter than others,' said Tim. 'But the paw prints are very clear.'

'That's because they were made recently. All the prints will fade in the end, but at the moment the most recent tracks are the most visible.'

'So we just follow the paw prints?'

'Exactly. But after some breakfast.'

Tim and Gribbles sat behind the hydrangea bushes so they would be out of sight of the road, and ate a hurried breakfast. Tim would have preferred some toast, but the bread and jam felt like a feast after the horrible events of the night, especially washed down with warm tea from Gribbles' thermos flask.

'Can you manage on that for now?' Gribbles asked as they finished.

Tim nodded.

'We'll try and have another breakfast later, if we can. But we're going to have to move quickly to find the Creature, before the others.'

'Can they track him?'

'It's possible. They don't know I've injected a tracking chip, but they are likely to make that assumption and try to discover the frequency it transmits on. If they do, they could well find the Creature before us, which is why we have to get there first.'

Tim and Gribbles got up and walked out from the grounds of Blackthorn Lodge. The sun rose slowly, casting a bright orange glare on the surrounding houses and trees. The road was quiet and empty. Gribbles looked through the infra-red goggles and indicated the direction the paw prints were headed – back down the hill, along the lane towards the countryside.

They followed the paw prints for about half a mile. Running parallel with the road on the left side was a thick hedge and a footpath beyond it. Eventually they came to a large gap in the hedge where branches had been thrust aside violently. It was clear the Creature had forced his way through, perhaps to avoid an oncoming vehicle.

The prints ran along the footpath a short distance, before turning left again across a wooden fence into a field. The fence was broken in several places, and there were tracks across the grass that could be clearly seen without infra-red goggles.

'The Beast should be easy to find, if he keeps leaving marks like these,' said Tim.

'Once he gains some distance from where he was imprisoned, he will be more careful,' said Gribbles. 'The Creature has also been genetically programmed for stealth, and will do anything he can to avoid detection. He will try to mislead us. That is part of the reason I am so keen to recover him as quickly as possible. The longer we leave this, the greater the chance he will elude us for good.'

'But you have the tracking chip.'

'I can only track him within a forty mile radius. After that, we've lost him.'

Tim and Gribbles plunged into the field and followed the tracks. The ground was mostly hard, but the lowest parts of the field were sufficiently muddy to leave deep impressions in the earth. Gribbles paused and examined the footprints for a moment. He then looked up towards the horizon.

'He's heading for the moors.'

Once again Tim was overwhelmed with the madness of their situation. They were attempting to hunt down a genetically engineered killing machine that *he* had foolishly released - a monster that was now seeking shelter on Dartmoor. He realised he ought to be grateful that the Creature was heading away from densely populated areas, but traipsing across the moors in search of this terrifying being was not a pleasant prospect.

They continued through the field and eventually came to a stream, but from the marks on the embankment on the far side it was still clear the Creature had come this way. The tracks led north, through the field beyond. After crossing the stream Gribbles put on the infra-red goggles again to be sure of their path. The trail led them through, to a hedge and a road on the other side. The hedge had a gap where the Creature had lunged through, and beyond the road there were more tracks.

The field on the other side of the road had been recently ploughed, and the tracks in the mud were easy to follow. Upon reaching a stone wall at the far side of the field the trail went cold. Gribbles spent some time looking to and fro with his goggles, trying to find more tracks. The sun continued to climb, and Tim felt a little warmer. But he was tired and still hungry in spite of their brief breakfast. He wondered how Rob was getting on, and whether he was safely out of danger. Or would Gribbles' enemies go looking for him?

'A-ha!' Gribbles cried suddenly. 'Here we are! The Creature scaled the wall and walked along it some way west, before leaping off and continuing north. You can see his tracks in the next field. We'd better keep going.'

They climbed the wall at the point where the Creature had leapt off into the next field. Here they found more tracks. The trail eventually led to a farm path at the other side. The path headed north along an upward slope and ended at the entrance to a sheep field. Tim was alarmed to see a metal gate had been torn from its hinges, and now lay in a twisted pile at the side of the path.

'It's getting stronger,' Gribbles muttered, staring at the wrecked gate in alarm.

Tim didn't like the sound of that. 'Stronger?'

'The Creature was genetically bred to gain strength over time, but he ought to have stabilised by now. However, it hasn't stopped. He's getting stronger and stronger. That's how he was able to break free from the chains in the cellar...'

'So it wasn't entirely my fault?'

'Oh, your presence would have encouraged him. But in the end, yes, I fear he would have broken free, which is why I was about to make him more secure.'

'But we spoilt that.'

'What you did can't be undone, but there is still a small chance that we might...'

Gribbles' voice tailed off. He had caught sight of something that alarmed him and began walking into the sheep field. Tim followed, and it didn't take him long to see where Gribbles was headed. A few yards into the field, lying next to a clump of thistles, lay the remains of a mutilated sheep. The bones had been torn from its body, and the fleece was soaked in blood and entrails. Much of the meat had been gnawed and consumed, and flies buzzed around the carcass. Tim found himself retching in disgust. Staring at the bloody mess, he tried desperately to think of some way around their problem, but couldn't come up with anything.

'Let's hope he doesn't start picking off walkers,' Gribbles muttered.

Tim swallowed hard, resolving that they would catch the Beast. A moment later they continued on their way, following the Creature's trail across the sheep field and slowly up. A small woodland lay to their right, and to the left the farmland stretched far and wide. Behind they could see the hamlets of Hemerdon and Sparkwell, as well as Plympton getting smaller in the distance. As they stepped over a style at the other side of the field they began to follow a track that took them higher still, up towards the China Clay pits and stone quarries near the villages of Wotter and Cadover.

The sun gradually came up and by the time they were on the ridges near the quarries, the weather had turned quite warm. They saw no further dead animals, but the Beast's trail was still easy to find. Tim began to feel thirsty as well as hungry, but didn't complain. His greatest hope was that they would find the Creature taking a nap somewhere and that it would be easy to tranquilise.

The countryside became more rugged as the trail led north onto Dartmoor. The tracks of the Creature traipsing through the heather climbed up an even steeper slope past jagged granite rocks, and eventually led to a triangulation point. In a sheltered dell near this summit Tim and Gribbles ate a second breakfast of sorts, and drank more tea.

All that morning they followed the Beast, passing Cadover and the road far below on the right, across the moors and over the Plym river by Giant's Hill, before turning north-east into wilder country. Around lunchtime, around a large tor, they stopped again, and Tim could see Burrator reservoir in the distance to the west. There was still no sign of the Creature.

Their search continued into the afternoon, and as the miles wore on Tim became weary. The trail turned north again, over many hills and tors. The Creature's tracks took them over rough and uneven places; often boggy or mired in marshes and reeds on the lower ground. The going was tough, and Tim began to wonder if they would ever catch up with their target.

Tim had been on several walks on Dartmoor over the years, but they had typically taken him on well trod paths. It seemed the Creature had no intention of sticking to established routes, and was instead determined to lead them north the most awkward and tiring way imaginable. Tim wondered what they would do if they still hadn't found the Beast by the end of the day. Would they continue the hunt by night?

Eventually Gribbles came to a halt near the top of a tall hill after climbing a bolder strewn upward slope. He glanced down at the ground with his infra-red goggles again and again, walking in circles and thoroughly searching the grass, heather and rocks. Tim watched anxiously, fearing that they might have lost the trail, but a moment later Gribbles eyes widened and he smiled.

'I've found the trail again,' said Gribbles. 'He's trying to lose us. I was afraid this might happen. But I think we've got him now.'

'Is he close?' asked Tim.

Gribbles took the homing device from his pocket and switched it on. The red light flashed rapidly, indicating that the Creature was close by. Tim's heart beat faster, and he glanced around frantically, worried that the Creature might suddenly leap out from behind one of the boulders.

'He's close,' said Gribbles. 'But he's doubled back towards the south-west.'

Gribbles and Tim climbed down the hill and back the way they came. Tim glanced around nervously for a glimpse of the Creature. Gribbles kept checking the homing device whilst following the tracks. But they did not see any sign of the Beast or any other clue as to its whereabouts.

'I wish this device could actually locate the Creature,' Gribbles said presently. 'He is genetically engineered to conceal himself, so for all we know he could have us walking round in circles.'

Tim didn't like the sound of that. It was one thing tracking a savage, hungry genetically engineered monster with superhuman strength, but it was quite another hunting one that could outwit them with such deviousness.

The skies began to cloud over as the afternoon wore on. Tim felt extremely tense as they trudged back over the uneven ground they had slogged through earlier that day. But as yards turned to miles, this tension gave way to exhaustion. His legs ached, and he felt less afraid and more utterly weary at their seemingly unending hunt.

Eventually they reached Fox Tor, and once again Gribbles was uncertain of their direction. The tracks seemed to disappear completely, and even with his infra-red goggles, locating a trail proved difficult. Eventually he did find another set of tracks, but they were confused, and it seemed the Creature had taken a great leap from the granite rocks around Fox Tor to try and shake off pursuit.

'He's toying with us,' Gribbles muttered under his breath.

'Is there still a trail to follow?' Tim asked.

'Yes, but now it's heading north-east again, back the way we came.'

'What about your homing device?'

Gribbles looked at the flashing red light. 'Inconclusive. It hasn't really changed, which would indicate that we haven't got much nearer or further away from the Creature.'

'But that means…'

'He's watching us, yes. Probably following at a distance.'

Tim's blood ran cold. He glanced in every direction looking for signs of the Creature but found none. The thought that he could jump out at them at any second, or was wearing them down, chilled him to the bone.

'If the Creature is watching us, where is it?' Tim asked, barely daring to whisper.

'He won't be easy to spot. The only choice we have is to continue following the trail.'

Gribbles squinted through his infra-red goggles. 'Judging by the heat patterns, this trail is the newest, so if he is attempting to get us running in circles, we should catch up to him eventually.'

'But you can't be sure.'

Gribbles shook his head. 'No, I can't.'

Tim continued to look around, and the light began to play tricks on him. Every tiny movement in the heather or shadow on the rocks seemed to indicate the presence of the Beast. But at no point did the monster actually appear.

They turned back towards the north-east and picked up the trail again. But it became sporadic, and many times it appeared the Creature had leapt from rock to rock; often great distances. There were many frustrating intervals spent trying to ascertain which direction the Creature had followed, and which tracks were more recent. All the time Tim kept a sharp eye on their surroundings, checking for the monster that Gribbles was convinced was stalking them. The idea that the hunters had become the hunted filled Tim with rapidly escalating panic.

Eventually the reached Cater's Beam; a largely featureless, fen covered hill that Tim was familiar with from previous walks. It always seemed perpetually wet, even after a long spell of warm weather. Amid the terrain lay an upended railway sleeper that had become a famous landmark on the moors. From here they could see a long way in all directions, but there were still plenty of places the Beast could hide. Gribbles searched the ground looking for clues but to Tim's dismay found that the Creature had seemingly turned south-west again, back towards Fox Tor.

'He *has* got us running in circles,' said Gribbles.

'But why?' asked Tim. 'To make us give up?'

'No. To wear us down, so he can move in for the kill.'

'Tell me the truth Dr Gribbles, don't sugar-coat it.'

'Very well,' said Gribbles, taking Tim's sarcasm at face value. 'He will probably keep us following his trail until darkness falls, by which time it will be much harder to find our way. After that, when we make camp, he'll sneak up to us and tear us apart. Then he'll probably eat us piece by piece.'

Tim grimaced. 'On second thoughts, stick to the sugar-coating.'

'Or he might not be hungry. He might just kill us as we're a threat. He is engineered as a soldier after all.'

'Alright, so a summary of my life as it presently stands: A powerful government agency is trying to track down a monster that *you* created. For some crazy reason you want to recapture it before they do. My brother is in hospital having been attacked by this genetically engineered Beast. His life and the lives of my parents are probably in danger. In the meantime, we're on the moors trying to hunt down the monster. Only it's now hunting us instead, and will end up either killing and eating us, or just killing us. Either way, by the end of today we'll probably be dead.'

'A fairly good summary, although don't forget you bear some of the responsibility for what happened.'

'My point is this: instead of getting dead, which I think is a really, really bad plan, why don't we get out of here and start the hunt again tomorrow?'

'And go where exactly?'

'Somewhere we won't be killed!'

'There is a chance we'll survive if we remain sharp and alert whilst we camp. We can take it in turns to watch, and if the Creature approaches we can tranquilise him.'

'That was our plan last night and look what happened!'

'Your brother missed. You mustn't.'

Gribbles paused for a moment and stared at Tim, as though assessing him.

'We should give you some target practice tonight.'

Tim felt scared, but deep down he knew Gribbles was right. They had no choice. It was their fault the Creature was free.

'I still don't see why we can't just tell the police or the army or something,' said Tim.

'I'm sorry Tim, but we really can't. I may tell you why at some point, but for now you're going to have to trust me.'

They decided to make as much use of the light as they could before night fell, so Tim and Gribbles set off once again, following the trail back towards Fox Tor. The trail crossed back on itself several times, often ascending to higher ground or behind rocks and thick briers or patches of heather. It seemed they had reached the point in the trail where the Creature had begun to observe them. Gribbles kept checking the homing beacon, which did not flicker any more or less than it had previously, indicating that the Creature was consistently maintaining a similar distance from them. In the evening light, Tim noticed it had clouded over considerably. Mist crept into the valleys and the temperature dropped rapidly. The wind began to pick up.

By the time they reached Fox Tor, the trail disappeared again. Gribbles cried in weary exasperation as he darted from rock to rock, searching for fresh signs of the Creature. It was a full twenty minutes before he found anything, by which time the sun was low in the sky. Tim was exhausted and footsore, but knew they had no choice but to continue the pursuit.

'The trail has turned towards the north-east, *again*,' Gribbles announced presently. 'I'm afraid there can be no doubt that the Creature has us exactly where he wants us. The question is will he leave us alone by nightfall?'

'I thought you said he would kill us or kill us and eat us,' said Tim.

'I'll admit there is a slight chance of a third possibility: he may simply want to get away from us.'

'How will he do that?'

'By waiting until night, so we cannot track him. If he makes good his escape before morning he will be much harder to track.'

Tim thought back to the time he had been face to face with the Beast in Blackthorn Lodge, and remembered how instead of killing him the monster had fled. He had felt a flicker of sympathy for the Creature then, and also when it had been chained in the cellars. If the Creature was a fiercely intelligent genetically engineered weapon, perhaps a sense of morality had inadvertently emerged alongside its ability to kill and evade capture. Perhaps the Creature didn't want to kill them.

'We should keep going until the sun sets,' Gribbles continued. 'If there is even the slightest chance we can neutralise the Creature today we should take it. Every minute lost only increases our danger.'

'From the Creature?'

'Yes, but not only him.'

Gribbles didn't elaborate, and Tim was too weary to feel anything more than mild curiosity. His mind swam with so many unanswered questions that he didn't want to think about them anymore. He just wanted to rest. But Gribbles was determined to continue the hunt, and so on they went, once again trudging over rugged terrain towards the north-east. By now Tim was used to the views around him - the notorious bogs of Aune Mead to the east, Crane Hill in the west, the southern view of Stinger's Hill and the river Swincombe northward. He could even see the granite peaks of Sherberton stone circle, a few miles beyond which lay the main road.

In spite of his tiredness, Tim could not shake off the horrible feeling that they were being stalked. Every rustle and movement provoked nervous reactions, although Gribbles remained calm. On several occasions he indicated for silence whilst aiming the tranquiliser gun at a particular point on high ground, often towards clusters of thorn bushes or clumps of rock. But every time Gribbles eventually put the weapon down and shook his head, lamenting that he could not get a clear shot.

Try as he might, Tim could not see the Beast. He seemed too clever at hiding. But Gribbles was excellent at spotting their prey, and more than once the flicker of excitement in his eyes caused Tim to think they really might have a chance of catching him. It was only when the sun finally disappeared over the western horizon that Gribbles sighed and turned to Tim with a resigned look.

'It's too clever. We aren't going to catch him tonight.'

'So we're going to camp?'

Gribbles nodded.

Tim didn't know whether to feel pleased or appalled at this news. On the one hand he was exhausted, but his nerves were alert and on edge. Gribbles' dire warnings about the savage fate that might await them in the night filled him with dread, even though he had subsequently said the Creature might leave them alone.

Nevertheless, there didn't seem to be an alternative. He and Gribbles camped about a hundred yards from the trail in a valley close to Cater's Beam. They put up their tent by a stream and as darkness fell they lit a small fire. On any other occasion Tim would have enjoyed camping out on Dartmoor eating hot soup and bread, but he felt so scared he had to force the food down. His eyes kept playing tricks on him as he stared from their campsite out into the darkness. A thick mist had fallen, but every so often he thought he caught a glimpse of movement amid the grass, or the sight of glaring eyes in the gloom.

'Assuming we aren't horribly killed in the night, how do we know tomorrow will be any different?' Tim asked.

Gribbles frowned. 'What do you mean?'

'Even if we pick up the Creature's trail, what's to stop him from playing the same games with us? He could have us running in circles again, trying to shake us off.'

'Only if he thinks he's being followed. Our pursuit today was too blundering and obvious. If we can pick up his trail again tomorrow, we must do more than blindly follow his tracks. We need to think how he thinks.'

82

'I find it difficult to imagine what a monster that wants to eat us would be thinking,' said Tim.

'You speak of what you don't understand,' said Gribbles. 'That Creature has an intelligence and reasoning that would rival many humans, yet competing with that he has a driving, deadly animal instinct. If he is hungry, he will not think twice about killing us for food. If he thinks we are a threat, he will do the same. We should hope that our pathetic attempts at cornering him today will lull him into a false sense of security, and that he ignores us.'

'Perhaps he knows it is wrong to kill,' said Tim.

Gribbles laughed. 'He's engineered as a *soldier*. Besides, you saw what the Creature did to that sheep. He isn't going to show any mercy.'

'Then why hasn't he just killed us already?'

'I don't know.' Gribbles sat in silent thought for a moment. 'I suppose it is just possible that my experiment was less successful I thought.'

'You mean if the Creature has developed some kind of moral code, then it's because your experiment failed?'

'Let's hope it did,' said Gribbles. 'It's a faint hope, but it's the only thing we have to cling to if we wish to survive the night.'

Chapter 7: Aerial Pursuit

After they had eaten, Gribbles set up several tins on a rock a short distance away so that Tim could practise shooting. He gave him an air pistol roughly the same size as the tranquiliser gun and instructed him in how to use it.

'Hold it at arms length,' Gribbles said.

Tim held the pistol towards the tins.

'Feel the weight of the gun. Aim, and when you're ready squeeze the trigger.'

Tim fired and missed.

'Try again.'

Tim aimed and fired again. This time one of the tins was blasted from the rock.

'I hit one!'

'Excellent. Try again.'

Tim aimed again, but as he was about to pull the trigger Gribbles yelled in his ear. Tim's aim went wide and he missed.

'You have to learn to aim and shoot accurately, amid distraction, and as quickly as possible. Hesitation could mean the difference between life and death.'

'So no pressure then,' Tim muttered. He aimed and fired several more shots as Gribbles tried to distract him. But he kept missing, and by the end felt very frustrated.

'That's probably enough for now,' Gribbles said kindly. 'But you should keep practising whenever you get the chance. Those tins are only a few yards away, but in this mist the Creature could get about as near as that before you see him. And if the mist gets any thicker he'll be closer still. When you are on watch the Creature could creep up silently, so you need to be ready and watchful.'

Tim nodded. He was practically asleep on his feet and the idea of another night watching and waiting filled him with dismay, but fear of being torn limb from limb kept his senses alert.

Gribbles suggested taking the first watch, but Tim was so on edge he insisted that he did instead. The scientist reluctantly agreed and crawled inside his sleeping bag. Soon he was sleeping soundly in the tent. Tim wondered if the snoring would attract the Creature.

Whist sitting in the dark, Tim kept throwing twigs and logs onto the fire that they had collected earlier from a nearby clump of trees. But the fuel supply soon got low. As he stared into the glowing embers Tim again wondered whether his brother had recovered in hospital, and if his parents were worried about him.

Night deepened and the mist grew thicker. The wind blew cold and shrill, whirling and eddying around the boulders of the valley. The gentle, reassuring rush of the stream blended with an angry wind, making unnerving shrieking sounds. Tim recalled every single ghost story he had ever been told about the moors, and wondered what spectres or spirits haunted this part of them. He kept squinting at the dark looking for signs of the Creature, but saw none.

As the fire died, Tim paced up and down to keep warm. He knew he had to stay awake until 2am. After then Gribbles was to watch until first light. Gribbles wanted to be on the trail of the Creature as soon as light permitted, and Tim was as eager as he was for the night to be over. The danger of the Creature attacking still plagued his thoughts, and once or twice he thought he glimpsed gleaming eyes staring amid the blackness. The certain knowledge that the Beast was out there didn't help one bit, even if he was just imagining things.

The hours wore slowly on, and Tim wasn't sure how much more his nerves could take. Once Gribbles relieved him, how would he be able to sleep? He held the tranquiliser gun in his hand again, recalling the events of the previous night. If only they'd managed to shoot the

Creature then, they wouldn't be out on the sinister moors under such insane conditions. Every sudden gust of wind made him jump, and Tim kept leaping up from wherever he was sat, expecting the Creature to grab him and start mauling his body.

By 2am, Tim was a nervous wreck. He woke Gribbles and told him about the eyes he thought he had seen in the dark. Gribbles agreed that it could well be the Creature observing them, but unless the Beast was to show himself, they couldn't be sure of hitting anything in the darkness.

'Why isn't the Creature asleep?' Tim asked, just before retiring into the tent.

'He's engineered to stay awake for long periods,' said Gribbles.

'Of course he is,' Tim muttered. 'Next time you engineer one of these things, please engineer an off switch, or at the very least, normal sleeping patterns.'

In spite of his anxiety, Tim fell into sleep almost immediately. Perhaps it was the result of being on edge for so long, combined with the fact that he hadn't slept properly the previous night. However, his mind remained highly alert. As he slept the wind howled around the campsite, and Tim found himself dreaming of being attacked by the Beast over and over again. In some versions of the dream they were still in Blackthorn Lodge. In others they were on his trail and the Creature leapt out at them. It was after a particularly vivid nightmare, where the Creature had snarled viciously in his face, that Tim awoke with a sudden start.

For a second Tim thought he was still dreaming. The face of the Creature was inches away from his face inside the tent. He shook his head, thinking his imagination was playing tricks. But the Beast was still there, staring right at him with its burning eyes. It was only when saliva drooled from the razor sharp fangs that Tim realised the monster in front of his eyes was all too real.

Tim froze in absolute terror. His heart was already pounding furiously as a result of his nightmares, but to awaken and see the burning eyes of the Creature before him like this was more than he could bear. He whimpered helplessly, and as he beheld the Beast, he noticed dried blood caked into its fur. Its breath stank. Clearly it had been eating the raw flesh of some unfortunate animal, and for a moment it seemed that it had come to eat him.

In spite of his fear, Tim wondered with morbid curiosity just how the Creature would kill him. Would it sever his jugular first so he bled to death? Or would he just start taking bites out of his flesh? As the Creature continued its low growling Tim saw that it had placed its claws either side of his sleeping bag, and that they were cutting into the groundsheet of the tent. The lower legs and feet of the Creature were still outside.

The Creature stared at Tim. Tim stared at the Creature. This went on for what seemed like several minutes, although in reality it could only have been a few seconds. To his surprise, Tim found the terror gradually subsiding, although he still didn't dare to move, for fear of provoking the monster. How had the Beast managed to infiltrate their camp? Why hadn't Dr Gribbles seen it? A low rumbling noise from outside answered his question. Gribbles had fallen asleep!

At first Tim felt angry at this dereliction of duty. After all, if he could manage to stay awake, surely the least Gribbles could do was to remain alert on his watch. But as his snores mingled with the shrieking wind, Tim's mind returned to the monster in front of his eyes. In that moment he ceased to think of it as a monster. The Beast before him seemed pitiable somehow, as though it didn't know who or what it was. It had been genetically engineered, and Tim remembered how Gribbles had told him that it had human DNA. He had also referred to *it* as *he*. Tim recalled the monster from *Frankenstein*, and suddenly felt sorry for the Creature.

Incredibly it seemed that the Beast didn't want harm him, at least at present. But the more Tim looked at him, the more the Creature seemed to have a sense of pleading in his eyes, either to be left alone, or perhaps even to be rescued. Perhaps the most humane thing to do would be to put him out of his misery rather than experiment on him further. Tim decided to suggest this to Gribbles – assuming he survived this encounter of course.

To his absolute astonishment, after another few seconds the Creature withdrew, and moved back towards the entrance of the tent. He backed away from the campsite almost silently, past Gribbles as he lay slumped outside by the remains of the fire. After a minute or so Tim risked peeking out of the tent. There was no sign of the Creature.

Would he have been able to tranquilise the Creature had a gun been within easy reach? Tim rapidly concluded that he couldn't have done, as any sudden movement would probably have resulted in the Beast attacking him. It was unfortunate that Gribbles had been asleep, but he couldn't help wondering why the Creature had left them alone. Clearly he did have some sense of morality. Why had the Creature visited at all? Perhaps he was simply curious. Or did he want something and was attempting to communicate?

Tim couldn't sleep after this encounter, so was awake when the first glimmers of dawn appeared on the horizon. He woke Gribbles, knowing that he wanted to pack up their camp at first light. Gribbles was mortified that he had fallen asleep, and even angrier with himself when Tim told what had occurred.

'It's a miracle you weren't killed,' said Gribbles. 'There's no excuse for falling asleep Tim, I'm sorry.'

'Would have served me right for letting the Creature out in the first place,' said Tim.

Gribbles smiled sympathetically. 'It's no good continually beating yourself up about that.'

'If we don't fix this somehow, I'll never forgive myself.'

'Believe me, I've got a lot more to never forgive myself for.'

'That doesn't even make sense.'

'Never mind. Let's have breakfast.'

Gribbles fried some bacon and eggs which they ate on pieces of toasted bread. Afterwards, as they packed their tent away, Tim told Gribbles how he suspected the Creature had been trying to communicate somehow, and that he didn't necessarily want to hurt them. Gribbles looked intrigued, but afterwards shook his head dismissively.

'He's a genetically engineered soldier designed to kill ruthlessly and mercilessly. Believe me, he's deadly and we need to stop him.'

'But he seemed so miserable,' said Tim. 'Why do you want to recapture him anyway? If he's that deadly, surely it would be better just to kill him outright? Then your enemies won't get him either.'

'They could still get DNA from the corpse,' said Gribbles, who looked faintly disturbed at Tim's suggestion. 'Besides, it would be wrong for us to kill the Creature.'

'But you keep going on about how deadly he is.'

'Indeed.'

'Then why didn't he kill us?'

Gribbles remained silent.

'I think you know why, but don't want to tell me,' said Tim.

'There's a lot you don't know, and for your own safety you should only be told if it becomes absolutely necessary. We need to get going.'

Tim knew he wasn't going to get anything else out of Gribbles at this point, so they finished packing in silence before resuming their hunt. They followed the path of the Creature to around the same point where they had left the previous day, but picking it up again proved extremely difficult. Gribbles used his infra-red goggles to search the ground, but the heat from the Creature's tracks was much older. He also tried using the homing device, but the flashing light was intermittent, indicating the Creature was now some distance away.

'He's really trying to lose us now,' Gribbles muttered. 'Judging by these marks he is leaping considerable distances in all directions, confusing his path as much as possible. There's no real way of telling which way he went – at least, not without spending considerable time and energy. He knows this, and also that by the time we pick up his trail he'll be long gone.'

'So what do we do?' asked Tim.

'Let's head back towards Cater's Beam and see what we can see,' said Gribbles. 'Before trying to wear us out, the Creature was heading north-east, so perhaps the signal should be stronger there. To be honest, the beacon is our only real chance of finding him now.'

As they continued their journey, thick mist descended on the valley. A thin drizzle replenished the overnight dew making the ground continually damp. In these conditions Tim knew it would be difficult to spot the Creature at any distance, and it would also be easy to get lost. The hills and rocks all looked much the same in this weather, and identifying landmarks proved tricky. Gribbles used a map and compass to navigate in as straight a line as they could manage, and eventually they picked up a path heading the way they wanted to go. Tim found the going on this well-trodden route much easier after the rough terrain they had to forge their way through the previous day. They weren't following any trail as it had all but disappeared, but from time to time Gribbles identified marks and tracks on the ground that indicated the Creature had passed this way.

'It's difficult to know how recent these prints are,' Gribbles commented. 'They could have been made yesterday, but the heat from a few is more recent. This corroborates my theory that the Creature is heading north towards Cater's Beam again – albeit in a somewhat haphazard manner.'

'You mean he isn't following the path?'

'He seems to join it occasionally then leave. Perhaps he knows it would be too easy to find him if he took such a conventional route.'

'You make the Creature sound like a human rather than a...' Tim stopped short of saying the word *monster*.

'Essentially he is,' said Gribbles.

They trudged on in silence. Tim's limbs ached and he felt cold and weary. After the tension and terror of the last two nights – not to mention lack of rest – he was practically asleep on his feet. Even if the weather had been clear, he doubted he would have spotted the Creature had it been standing and roaring a few feet away.

It was just before noon when the mist finally began to clear that Gribbles suddenly halted and scrutinised the ground with a look of relief on his face. He turned to Tim and grinned.

'Recent tracks, leading away from the path directly north. It's pure luck we found the trail again.'

'Does the Creature think he's lost us?'

'Difficult to say. Judging by the obviousness of these tracks, yes. But it would be foolish to assume too much. The Creature could simply be desperate and no longer care that we are seeking him. If that is the case, we should be very, very careful. Just because he didn't kill us last night does not mean he will show us the same courtesy today.'

Tim glanced around in the clearing fog, looking for signs of the Beast lurking nearby. But there were no indications that he was present. Directly north lay the Swincombe valley and the river that ran through it. But the terrain in-between appeared uneven and boggy. After the relative relief of a proper path, Tim didn't like the prospect of slogging through the mire again, but at least they had found a clear trail once more.

As they followed this trail, they heard the unmistakable sound of a helicopter buzzing overhead. Gribbles halted for a moment with an expression of faint unease. The chances were the presence of the helicopter was entirely co-incidental, and the mist still obscured them from view in any case. But Gribbles didn't seem happy about it.

'We'd better get moving,' he muttered, casting furtive glances upward. It seemed clear enough that he feared pursuit, and that was good enough for Tim to get moving. But where could they hide on the moors? Soon the mist would clear, and if the helicopter did contain enemies, they would be spotted.

A minute or so later the sounds of the helicopter faded. Tim could sense Gribbles' relief as they continued to follow the now very clear tracks of the Creature, heading north. In this way they covered a mile or two as the fog lifted, and by lunchtime the skies were clear again. They ate a brief lunch in the shadow of boulders overlooking Swincombe valley, and far below Tim could see the rushing river snaking through the rocks and heather.

After lunch they continued their hunt as the trail led downhill into the valley. The grass was tall and filled with difficult boggy patches. In addition there were several gorse bushes that the Beast had lumbered through which were a struggle to get past. But Gribbles insisted they followed the precise path of the Creature in case it suddenly gave them the slip again.

'I wouldn't put it past him to try and lead us into tricky areas to try and put us off,' said Gribbles. 'He is much better equipped to deal with awkward terrain.'

'Do you think he realises we're following him again?' Tim asked.

Gribbles checked the homing beacon. 'No, he's still too far off. It's important to bear in mind possible strategies he might have...'

His voice tailed off as the sound of a helicopter somewhere in the south interrupted his train of thought. Gribbles and Tim both looked back up the hill they had just descended and saw, high and far off, a white helicopter crossing the skies in an eastward direction. Gribbles grabbed Tim and pulled him down into a patch of heather on their left, and it was only when they were fully submerged that he dared to peek out again.

'Keep your head down!' Gribbles whispered.

Tim wondered why on earth his companion was whispering. Even if the helicopter could see them, they certainly couldn't be heard.

'Are they enemies?'

'Very possibly. That's no police helicopter.'

'It could be anyone.'

'But it's crossed the moors twice now.'

'How do you know it's the same helicopter?'

'The sound boy, the sound. I know a great deal about avionics and the subtle variations in the noise a helicopter engine makes. Believe me that is the same helicopter. Judging by the flight path they seem to be making west to east sweeps across Dartmoor, gradually working their way northward.'

'Then they won't have spotted us.'

'Not yet. But we must be careful. And above all, we must catch up to the Creature and tranquilise him before they do.'

Gribbles turned off the homing beacon. 'We've got a clear trail to follow, but I don't know how safe it is to use the homing beacon anymore. There are ways they could trace it. I will only switch it on at greatest need from now on.'

'But how will we know when we get near the Creature?'

'We'll just have to track it the old-fashioned way - with stealth, nerve and our wits!'

The sounds of the helicopter once again faded, and Gribbles and Tim continued to follow the trail. Gribbles urged that they move as quickly as possible, since the Creature was still far ahead and at this point it was more likely that they would be spotted by the helicopter. But Tim didn't like the idea that they now had no way of knowing how close they were getting, and thought Gribbles was being a little paranoid - both about the helicopter and about the homing beacon.

As the afternoon wore on, they found two places on the trail where it appeared the Creature had rested. In one they found a mauled sheep that had been gnawed to the bone. Tim found the sight sickening, and almost threw up.

'At least it didn't eat us,' Gribbles muttered. 'Farmers won't be too pleased though.'

'Gribbles, don't you think we should warn people?' Tim asked. 'I mean, even anonymously. We could find a phone box, tell the police, and just not leave our names.'

Gribbles shook his head. 'If we tell the police our enemies will learn that the Creature is loose.'

'Surely that's not worth risking human lives? The chance that your enemies might *not* know the Creature has escaped?'

Gribbles turned to Tim, his expression fierce. 'They are now your enemies too. You have no idea what they are capable of. If they capture this Creature it will mean disaster.'

Tim swallowed hard, unhappy that Gribbles still didn't want to take him into his confidence, and annoyed that his quite logical suggestions were being disregarded. But Gribbles stormed ahead of him and refused to say another word.

They drew within about two miles of the main road that ran east through Dartmoor past Princetown and Two Bridges. It was also around here, near a small rise to the north of Swincombe valley, that the trail suddenly and abruptly turned west and then south again, back the way they came. Tim was unhappy at this development, and feared a repeat of the previous day, when they had walked in circles whilst the Creature played games with them. But Gribbles seemed less convinced this was the case, theorising instead that perhaps the Creature was unhappy at drawing so close to the main road.

After halting for a moment Gribbles looked around the valley squinting in the late afternoon sun. 'I should have brought binoculars,' he muttered. He then took the homing beacon from his pocket and sighed. 'Perhaps it *is* worth the risk...'

Gribbles switched on the beacon. The red light flashed more rapidly than Tim had ever seen. Immediately Gribbles scanned the horizon and a moment later pointed excitedly to a sharp slope on the far side of the river below.

'He's there! Look!'

Tim scrutinised the area in which Gribbles was pointing and sure enough he saw, to his amazement, the same large bulky creature he had seen in Blackthorn Lodge barrelling his way south with considerable agility. He bounded through the heather and gorse, and at a few points leapt from rock to rock almost like a gorilla.

'Can we hit him from here?' Tim asked.

'He's out of range. We need to get closer.'

Gribbles took a tranquiliser from his rucksack, loaded it, and charged down towards the river. Tim followed at a run, but kept glancing up at the Creature as it headed south. Gribbles seemed to have abandoned all idea of stealth and instead seemed like a man possessed and desperate. With all the noise they were making, Tim was concerned the Beast would look back and spot them. Indeed, if he did the Creature would have a distinct advantage, since it had both high ground and areas to hide in. By contrast, the grassy landscape which Tim and Gribbles now rushed over offered no cover at all.

But the Creature did not look back. In fact, he stopped for a moment and stared up into the sky. Tim could hardly believe their luck. Soon they would reach the river and once they were on the other side, they would surely be in range. All it would take was one shot - one well-aimed tranquiliser dart - and their troubles would be over.

Upon reaching the river Gribbles indicated for silence. They crept across on stepping stones with the utmost quiet, and Tim was surprised at the dexterity and speed with which Gribbles could move. He sprang almost cat-like to the south side of the river, and as Tim observed him approaching the Creature he couldn't help but compare the two. Perhaps something of Dr Gribbles had been engineered into the Creature. As the scientist responsible for his existence it certainly seemed likely.

Gribbles indicated for Tim to halt, so he stopped. But he kept his gaze fixed on their target, and to his surprise the Creature still hadn't budged nor looked back. He wondered if he should open his own rucksack and prepare another tranquiliser dart as a back-up plan, but he was concerned the noise might alert the Creature to their presence. Gribbles drew closer than ever, and it seemed their near-impossible task might just be attainable after all.

The Creature continued to stare at the southern horizon. Tim wondered what was bothering him, but didn't particularly care. Within seconds Gribbles would shoot him and it would all be over. The scientist raised his arm carefully and took aim. Tim's heart pounded. Gribbles seemed to hesitate and lose concentration for a moment. He stared up distractedly. Why? Tim silently urged him to stop messing around and shoot.

Sounds of a rapidly approaching helicopter suddenly provided the answer. The Creature immediately dived for cover amid some nearby gorse bushes. Gribbles stared angrily into the skies and came rushing back to Tim.

'We need somewhere to hide,' he urged. 'Quickly!'

Tim indicated some nearby heather, but Gribbles shook his head. 'No! We can't risk hiding too near the Creature, nor draw attention to it. We have to find somewhere else! Come!'

Gribbles seized Tim by the arm and practically pulled him westward, following the path of the river. After a few seconds running Tim caught sight of some boulders downstream that might provide cover, but they were already too late. The white helicopter zoomed overhead, quite low. If someone in the helicopter was looking, they would have been clearly visible.

'Damn it all!' cried Gribbles. 'I *knew* I shouldn't have switched on the homing beacon!'

Tim glanced up at the helicopter as it turned round for another pass, swooped overhead, and flew towards them. A series of rapid explosions pierced the air. To his horror Tim saw bullet impacts on the rocks and water. He had never heard machine guns before, and was astonished at how loud they were. He had also never been shot at before, and was absolutely terrified.

'Dive!' cried Gribbles, hurling Tim to the ground. As he fell he smashed his cheek on a rock amid the shingle river bank. The helicopter swooped above, merely a few feet from his head, before launching up into the sky again and turning for another ruthless attempt on their lives. Huge gusts of wind from the propellers swept through the air, and for a moment Tim wondered if a bullet had caught him.

There was no time to tend to injuries if they wanted to live. Gribbles hauled Tim up and yelled at him to run. Tim obeyed, but the malevolent presence of helicopter propellers filled him with dread. Once again the piercing sounds of white hot metal striking granite and water echoed throughout the valley as their enemies utilised their deafening machine guns. He glanced back in terror at the horrible white flying metal monster looming mercilessly behind them.

'Down!' Gribbles yelled again. This time Tim threw himself onto the ground and instinctively covered his head with his hands. Astonishingly no bullets struck them, though Tim seriously doubted they would be lucky a third time. The helicopter turned for yet another pass, and this time they would surely succeed.

Once they were on their feet, Tim sprinted flat-out for the rocks, knowing that their very lives depended on reaching cover before the helicopter caught up to them again. Blood pulsed through his veins as the terror of the attack intensified, and amid the chaos he found himself thinking of his family. He also experienced another feeling that surprised him: irritation. If he died not knowing *why* these people wanted to kill him it would be extremely annoying.

Tim suddenly caught sight of something amid the tumbled boulders that filled him with hope: a small covered alcove big enough for them both to squeeze inside. Once underneath it was unlikely that the helicopter bullets would reach them. Gribbles had the same idea as he pointed to exactly the same area.

'In there! Quick!'

Tim practically leapt into the alcove, and once inside found it provided ample cover as the uneven ground allowed them to conceal themselves beneath the sharp incline of one of the larger boulders. As he had hoped, shooting them from the helicopter would be impossible.

However, they were also trapped. A hail of bullets blasted onto the rocks as they crouched in their hiding place. Tim heard the helicopter swooping up again before it returned once more. Another round of bullets struck the entrance, but again they were not hit. It seemed they had chosen a good place to hide.

But their enemies did not give up. Although the helicopter couldn't land on account of the uneven terrain, it hovered above the river near the alcove. Tim risked a tiny peek and saw, to his horror, a man dressed in black wearing a balaclava being lowered on a wire from the helicopter onto the southern shore.

Gribbles took his tranquiliser gun and reloaded it with something different.

'What are you doing?' Tim asked.

'What does it look like?' Gribbles replied. 'We've got to defend ourselves.'

'You're going to kill him?'

'No, just stun him. The stuff we'd use on the Creature would probably kill him though, so I brought these just in case.' Gribbles indicated the new dart he had placed in the gun.

At that moment, Tim didn't feel particularly concerned for the lives of those hunting them, especially as they had just tried to kill him. He thought that he would probably have shot the man with the dart intended for the Creature.

The man in the balaclava reached the ground and pulled a pistol from his pocket. Slowly the man approached the alcove, and Tim realised he would be on them in seconds. The helicopter continued to hover above the river, no doubt so the man could return to his transport once he had carried out his grisly task.

Gribbles took a careful aim as the man stepped forward. He then squeezed the trigger.

The dart caught the man on the left side of his neck and he fell, collapsing onto the shingle. He tried to get up again but the drug went to work almost immediately and he fell down unconscious.

Tim glanced into the cockpit of the helicopter and saw the other figures inside were clearly irritated at this development. He couldn't make out their faces, but one of the remaining two men inside left his seat, and within seconds lowered himself in the same way his companion had done. His face was also masked with a balaclava, and he carried a machine gun. Once on the ground he immediately began firing into the alcove.

Tim squeezed as tightly as he could under the cover of the rocks, knowing that at any second the bullets would find him. But Gribbles had not been idle. As soon as it became clear that a second man was being deployed, he had assembled another tranquiliser dart. Risking being shot in the face, he aimed as quickly as he could then fired, striking their assailant in the neck. As before, the man fell to the ground unconscious.

Hardly daring to breathe, Tim looked out at the helicopter again, wondering what would happen next. His imagination raced with horrible possibilities. There was now only one person in the helicopter. What if they had gas pellets they could fire? What if the helicopter was equipped with flame throwers? He forced himself to calm down, telling himself he had watched too many spy movies. But such things were entirely within the realms of possibility, and these were ruthless, determined enemies.

The helicopter continued to hover. Tim glimpsed the pilot staring into the alcove in fury, seething at the outcome of their attack. But there was nowhere the helicopter could land. Tim began to wonder if they might yet escape.

A moment later, the helicopter lifted off again into the skies. Tim and Gribbles remained still, waiting until silence fell. Tim was shaking from their harrowing experience, but the knowledge that they had evaded almost certain death felt oddly exhilarating. Turning to Gribbles, he let out a huge sigh of relief. For the moment at least, they were safe.

Chapter 8: At the Two Bridges Hotel

'We need to leave immediately,' said Gribbles. 'That helicopter will be back with reinforcements.'

'What about them?' Tim indicated the unconscious masked men.

'Let's take a look.'

They emerged from their hiding place and examined their assailants. Gribbles tore off the masks; revealing one man with a bald head, and another with long hair and grizzled features.

'I don't know either of them,' said Gribbles. 'But they probably work for one of this country's covert operation forces. We'd better get moving before they come round.'

Gribbles and Tim made their way across the river and back up the other side. The skies were clear and bright, but there was no sign of the helicopter or any other enemies. In this weather they would be able to see any pursuit from quite a way off, but Tim longed for the cover of mist and drizzle, knowing that they stood a much better chance of not being detected under such conditions.

Then there was the matter of the Creature to consider. Gribbles had had him in his sights but refused to fire.

'Why didn't you shoot the Creature when you had the chance?' Tim asked.

'I heard the helicopter and didn't want to risk the Creature falling into enemy hands,' Gribbles replied. 'We can't keep searching for him now, because that helicopter will be back.'

'But we'll lose the trail.'

Gribbles frowned. 'I'd rather the Creature was loose on the moors than captured by *them*.'

'Who?'

'I've already told you, it's safer if you don't know.'

'It's *not* safer! We've just been attacked! If I'm going to die, I at least want to know why.' Tim suddenly stopped. 'I'm not moving another inch until you tell me *exactly* what is going on.'

'This is no time for arguing!' cried Gribbles, glancing anxiously at the skies. 'That helicopter could have landed nearby. Or it could fly back and catch us any minute.'

'I don't care,' Tim said stubbornly. 'Tell me who these people are and why they want to kill us, or you can find yourself someone else to go hunting with.'

'Alright, alright!' said Gribbles. 'But not here. It isn't safe.'

'Just tell me who's trying to kill us!'

'We need to get away from here first. Then I need to make a call. There's a telephone box just outside the Two Bridges hotel. That's about two or three miles away, near the road. If we move quickly we might just manage to get there without being spotted.'

'At least give me a name,' said Tim.

'It won't mean anything to you.'

'It will. It will be someone I can hate.'

'Very well. The person most directly responsible for the attempt on our lives is a man called Desmond Whitaker. Now we must get moving! We're dead if we linger here!'

Tim reluctantly followed Gribbles as he set off at a great pace across the moors. They soon struck a good path that led over the hills and along the ridges, past several areas of heather and boulders that they could hide amongst if necessary. All the time Tim kept checking the skies for signs of the white helicopter, but there were none.

'Who do you need to call?' Tim asked.

'Someone that can help us. I had hoped not to involve this person, but with the recent attack we've been left little choice.'

As usual, Tim felt infuriated at Gribbles' evasive replies. 'Are you allergic to straight answers?'

'No, but I am allergic to foolish questions from people who ought to know better than to ask!' Gribbles muttered irritably.

'What about the Creature?' Tim persisted. 'Are we going to look for it again?'

'Yes, but only after we've contacted this person to see if we can get help,' said Gribbles. 'If we're successful, we might yet stand a chance of tracking the Creature down. If not, we might as well give up now. It is vital we get these people off our back first, before attempting to locate the Creature again.'

Tim could hardly argue with that. He certainly didn't fancy trying to track down a dangerous genetically engineered creature whilst at the same time attempting to avoid assassination.

They continued north through the rugged landscape, eventually striking the West Dart River and following it to the north-west. By the end of the afternoon they came within sight of Two Bridges. The main road ran through the small hamlet of farms and farm buildings past the Two Bridges hotel and over the eponymous bridges the area was named after. Beyond the road to the north lay Wistman's Wood and the wilder areas of the northern moors.

Gribbles paused at the top of a small rise overlooking Two Bridges, considering what to do next.

'The road may be watched,' Gribbles said presently. 'Perhaps we should wait for darkness before approaching.'

'Won't the helicopter return?' Tim asked.

'Almost certainly, but there are barns and other places we might hide in. On the other hand, unless we act quickly we may find ourselves on the wrong end of a full-blown manhunt. In such a scenario, we could well be caught before the sun goes down.'

'So what do we do?'

Gribbles silently weighed their options. Tim examined the moors for signs of pursuit but there were none. The skies were clear, and there were no ominous helicopter sounds. He wondered what the Creature was doing, and whether it was just as fearful of being captured or killed by Gribbles' enemies as they were.

'We'll go down,' Gribbles said finally. 'It's risky, but not as dangerous as waiting out here. We need to do something now to get Whitaker off our backs.'

Tim and Gribbles followed the path over the hills and down to the main road. They followed a parallel trail south of the road and approached Two Bridges from the east. Near some farm buildings on north side of the road was a red phone box. Once they were about fifty yards away, Gribbles and Tim crouched behind an embankment that was thick with reeds and tussock.

'Wait here,' said Gribbles. 'I'll make the call and return.'

Tim waited as Gribbles glanced left and right furtively, before quickly running across the road. Once inside the phone box he picked up the receiver and began to make a call. Tim was unable to hear what he was saying, but he could see from Gribbles' emphatic hand gestures that he was engaged in a heated argument with whoever was on the other end of the phone.

The sun was low in the sky, and the chirping of birds in the evening light made Tim think of what a pleasant evening this would have been under ordinary circumstances. But he was tired, afraid, and at this point very lonely. He thought again of his parents and particularly Rob, who was no doubt recovering in hospital. At least, that was what he hoped.

The phone call seemed to take quite a long time. The peaceful atmosphere was occasionally disturbed by cars going past, and Tim always made sure he was well hidden as they approached. Even though he doubted that any of these motorists were looking for them, he wanted to be on the safe side. This determination to remain concealed was underscored by the sudden alarming presence of the sound he least wanted to hear – helicopter blades whirring in the distance.

Tim rushed across the road and barged his way into the phone box with Gribbles. The scientist looked at Tim in surprise, and interrupted his phone call.

'Hold on a moment…What is it Tim?'

'The helicopter's back!'

Gribbles looked out of the phone box and Tim indicated towards the south. Sure enough, the same white helicopter was approaching the Swincombe valley and seemed to be performing a low level search of the area.

Alarmed, Gribbles pulled Tim inside the phone box. He then resumed his call in an urgent tone.

'They're back. You have to do something now… I mean immediately, or we're dead… I keep telling you, they're trying kill us! … Yes… They've already made one attempt and unless you do something at once… In half an hour? We'll be waiting.'

Gribbles replaced the receiver looking grim. 'We'll have to stay in the phone box until the helicopter is gone. We should be safe enough – unless they hover next to us.'

'It looks like they're searching the area where we were hidden,' said Tim.

Gribbles nodded. 'They'll want to recover their colleagues no doubt. The problem is they'll almost certainly be able to track us.'

'So what are we going to do?'

Gribbles glanced at his watch. 'In thirty minutes we're meeting someone who will be able to divert Whitaker, at least for a while. I estimate that it will take them another hour or two at least to find us here, so we should be safe provided we aren't spotted by their aerial patrols.'

'What if they find the Creature first?'

'Right now they're more focussed on finding and killing us, but even so it's a risk we have to take, if we're to survive at all.'

Tim and Gribbles watched and waited inside the phone box. On the southern horizon the helicopter swooped and hovered, continuing the search. The thirty minute wait seemed to last forever, and on one occasion Gribbles had to pretend to talk into the receiver in order to deter another group of walkers who looked as though they might want to use the phone box. But they walked past and headed north, along the path to Wistman's Wood. The sun was low and Tim's stomach rumbled. Being in mortal peril was hungry business.

As the thirty minutes elapsed, Gribbles looked at his watch anxiously. He kept glancing up at the helicopter that continued to search above the Swincombe valley. It was slowly moving north, getting closer. Desmond Whitaker would soon discover their trail, but they had another problem.

'We need to get to the Two Bridges hotel without being spotted,' said Gribbles. 'We'll be fine once we're inside, but I'm concerned we could be seen by that helicopter if we get out of the phone box now.'

'How clearly can they see us?' asked Tim.

'I'm not sure,' said Gribbles. 'Perhaps not at all, but they're too close for comfort. It may be that they'll spot us running to the hotel, or it may be that they are looking in a different direction when we make the attempt.'

'So we're going to run for it?'

'I don't see what choice we have. I arranged to meet my contact in the reception of the Two Bridges hotel in exactly three minutes time.'

Tim looked out of the phone box towards the Two Bridges hotel - a large country building with white walls, a slate roof, and several bay windows. Well trimmed lawns and gardens surrounded the hotel, and the main entrance was about two hundred yards away along a drive;

accessible from off the main road across one of the two bridges after which the area was named.

'Shall we go now?' asked Tim.

'Not yet. Not until...'

Gribbles' voice tailed off as a land rover sped along the main road from the west. It indicated right and headed off along the drive towards the hotel, entering the car park and disappearing from view behind some oak trees. Gribbles nodded slowly.

'That's our contact. Let's wait a minute, and then when I say, walk calmly up to the front door.'

'Walk?'

'Yes. Any sudden movement could well be noticed by Whitaker's men. With any luck, if they do see us, they'll just think we're tourists going back to our hotel after a day walking on the moors. But keep your head down to minimise the chance that they see our faces.'

'Alright,' said Tim. He didn't like what was happening one bit, but even if they were spotted, it was unlikely their enemies would reach them before they could get inside the hotel. Once they were there, they were at least in a public place. But he didn't think that would deter Whitaker and his assassins. They might not attack with bullets from the air, but no doubt there were more subtle and equally lethal methods of extermination that could be used to achieve their purpose.

'How exactly is this person we're meeting going to get Whitaker to call off his search?' Tim asked.

'Never mind that now. Just remember what I said and walk as calmly and normally as possible. Don't forget to keep your head down! Once we're inside the hotel, leave all the talking to me, and do exactly as I say. Ready? And...go!'

Gribbles stepped quickly out of the phone box, strode across the main road, and then slackened his pace as he ambled up to the Two Bridges driveway. Tim followed closely, walking as casually as he dared. He stared fixedly at his feet as they crossed the bridge and strolled up to the hotel's main entrance. As they reached the door Tim couldn't resist a quick glance across the moors to where they helicopter still searched, alarmingly close by.

Inside the hotel lobby a strikingly pretty woman in her mid twenties was talking to the receptionist. She wore jeans and a leather jacket, and appeared to have just finished checking in. Gribbles went up to the woman and began speaking quietly to her, leaving Tim alone for a moment to stare at the paintings and portraits that hung on the walls. They looked old and possibly quite valuable. Outside, Tim could still hear the buzzing of the helicopter in the distance, but in here it seemed less threatening.

Presently Gribbles strolled over to Tim, and spoke in a high, unnatural voice. 'We're all checked in, dear nephew! Let's go and unpack and clean ourselves up a bit after that invigorating walk, shall we?'

The woman in the jeans and leather jacket gave Gribbles a bemused, I-can't-believe-your-undercover-acting-is-so-bad kind of look, but did her best to play along.

'Room 221, up a couple of floors,' she said coldly, looking down at their feet. 'I suggest you take your boots off first.'

Gribbles and Tim removed their footwear awkwardly. They then followed the woman up two flights of stairs to a room on the southern wing that faced back towards the Swincombe valley. The room seemed cosy and had two large beds, along with an en-suite bathroom and some very large wardrobes. Once inside the room, the woman shut the door and locked it, before fixing Dr Gribbles with a venomous stare.

'How *dare* you put me in this position!' the woman exclaimed. 'I was *this* close to getting the proof I needed to shut Whitaker down permanently. Now thanks to you he's already suspicious. He thinks *I* had a hand in keeping the Creature hidden!'

Gribbles seemed unperturbed. 'Tim Rawling, meet my daughter Emily.'

Tim was stunned at this turn of events, but before he could say anything in return, Emily started yelling at her father with even greater anger.

'I can't believe you brought a *child* into this mess! What on earth were you thinking?'

'Well, he's proved very useful,' said Gribbles. 'Besides, as I've already explained, he did have a hand in unleashing the Creature, and...'

'Oh come on off it Dad! This is your mess. It's always been your mess. What a stupid place to hide the Creature! Kids always sneak into dark abandoned buildings looking for ghosts!'

'I still think Tim bears some responsibility...'

'You just don't want to face up to yours. First you lie to me, telling me the Creature's been destroyed. Then you suddenly turn up on Dartmoor with some boy, on the run from Whitaker's assassins, and expect me to blow six months of undercover work to save you!'

'Will you save us?' Gribbles asked.

'If it's all the same to you, I'd appreciate it if you did,' Tim added, feeling small and insignificant.

Emily rolled her eyes. 'Great! Now I'm a babysitter!'

'I'm not the only one who lied to you,' said Gribbles.

'Yes, but I expect Whitaker to lie and cheat. What I don't expect is my own father to do...what you've done!'

'It was the only way to protect you.'

Emily turned to Tim. 'No doubt this is what he said to you, right? Not telling you vitally important stuff and lying in order to get your co-operation? And always under the guise of protecting or being for your own good!'

Gribbles began to get a little irritated. 'Really Emily that is most unfair. Considering the time I've spent researching and trying to find a solution to the situation with the Creature, I think I'm entitled to a little more respect.'

'It was *your* mistake Dad, don't forget that.' Emily sighed and glanced out of the window towards the south. Tim stood awkwardly, unsure what to make of this hot-tempered addition to the Gribbles' family. She seemed to be some kind of agent working undercover with Desmond Whitaker, but to what end?

'He hasn't told me it's you,' Emily continued presently. 'He just said there was an operation nearby to eliminate a couple of rogue agents.'

'No doubt he realises you wouldn't remain loyal to him for long if you knew he was ordering the death of your father,' said Gribbles.

'Don't be so sure,' Emily replied.

Tim had had enough. It was bad enough witnessing this family row, but he was tired and confused and wanted to know whether or not Whitaker's agents were about to burst into the room and gun them all down.

'I hate to interrupt,' he said, 'but I was promised an explanation.'

'You won't get one from him,' said Emily. 'Besides, he's right to a point. It *is* better that you don't know everything. But this much you might as well know: Desmond Whitaker is a very high ranking official in M16. For some time, he's been suspected of being a double agent working for the KGB. That's why they placed me under his nose to try and get proof. Whitaker is no fool. He suspects we know his true colours. I think he is planning to leave the country, but in order to return to Moscow as a hero rather than someone who blew his cover, he wants something of great value before he leaves.'

'The Creature,' said Tim.

'Well, not necessarily the Creature. Just enough genetic information from the Creature so he can return to the USSR and provide their scientists with the breakthrough they need to continue their own supersoldier programme. They are afraid of a supersoldier gap.'

'You sound like that film,' said Tim. 'You know, *Dr Strangelove*. The one with Peter Sellers playing three roles.'

Gribbles and Emily stared in bemusement. Clearly cinematic Cold War satire wasn't high on their list of viewing priorities.

'Never mind,' Tim continued, turning to Emily. 'You said you thought the Creature had been destroyed?'

Emily shot a dark look at her father. 'Yes, well that's what I thought until just under an hour ago, when I got your call. Clearly Whitaker discovered the Creature had survived before then, or he wouldn't have moved all these agents into the area. I did wonder why he assigned me to the laboratory here a couple of days ago. I assumed the whole thing was routine.'

'He suspected something, but had no proof,' said Gribbles. 'I even had his people round at the house trying to recruit me. Said the experiments were continuing nearby and that I should return and help if I could.'

'Whitaker wanted your expertise,' said Emily. 'No doubt at that point he wasn't sure if the Creature had survived or not. If he hadn't, he wanted you back on the project. We haven't had anything like the same kind of success since you left. None of the subjects survived more than a few hours.'

'We know why,' Gribbles said darkly. 'That's why I left, and that is why, as I told them, I will never return.'

'All of that is academic now,' said Emily. 'He doesn't need you. He just needs the Creature.'

Gribbles nodded grimly. 'That's why we're trying to find him before Whitaker does.'

'And why you need me to divert his agents.'

'Exactly.'

'But how will you do that?' Tim asked.

Emily sighed, and stared coldly at her father. 'By recklessly endangering my own life - par for the course with my father, as you ought to know if you've followed him this far.'

'But you'll do it,' said Gribbles.

Emily turned away and her voice dropped to barely a whisper. 'Of course I will. If there's a chance it will mean... Of course I will.'

Tim wasn't sure what Emily meant by these remarks. On the surface it seemed she was just prepared to go to any lengths to ensure Whitaker's plans were thwarted, but he wondered if there wasn't more to it than that, especially as when she turned back to face them, her face had softened somewhat.

'I'll go and make the arrangements,' Emily said matter-of-factly. She left the room, leaving Tim and Gribbles alone.

'She's not seen me in some time,' Gribbles explained. 'We had a bit of a falling out I'm sorry to say.'

'So I see. Did you used to work with her?'

Gribbles nodded. 'She went into the army for a time, but eventually the lure of lab work pulled her back. She's too much like me, even though she refuses to admit it. I got her a job in the intelligence services, and soon she had sufficient clearance to be working on top secret projects such as the one that produced the Creature. Unfortunately, once he was ordered destroyed, in my eagerness to protect the specimen, I was forced to lie to her.'

'And that's what you fell out over?'

'Not exactly.'

Gribbles said no more, and Tim knew him well enough by now to know that elaboration would not be forthcoming.

Emily returned a moment later and passed Gribbles what looked like a driving licence. 'Your name is Mr Charles White, and you are spending a holiday here with your nephew, Matthew White. His parents are abroad, and he has special permission to be out of school at this time.'

Emily handed some other papers to Gribbles. 'More details on your cover stories. You should both study them to ensure you know all the details. The tiniest slip will give you away. I'll be back tomorrow morning once I'm satisfied Whitaker's men aren't searching the area anymore. Then you can resume the search for the Creature.'

'I just hope we can pick up his trail again,' said Gribbles.

'It's the best I can do,' said Emily. 'Unless you want to go out there again and risk being shot by Whitaker's snipers?'

Gribbles shook his head.

'Didn't think so. I'll make some enquiries of my own as to the whereabouts of the Creature.'

'He's extremely dangerous,' said Gribbles.

'A bit too late for fatherly concern, don't you think?'

'Just be careful.'

Emily nodded. 'I have to go before I'm missed.'

With that, Emily left the room, leaving Tim feeling overwhelmed and utterly exhausted.

Chapter 9: The Hunt Continues

'So just how is Emily going to divert Whitaker's men?' Tim asked.

Gribbles looked out of the window and frowned. To the south a helicopter was still making passes above the moors.

'On the phone, she said she something about planting a false lead from one of their groups on the ground,' Gribbles explained. 'She knows what codes they use over the radio. It will be reported that we picked up a vehicle and headed east. Later she will say we've been spotted in Exeter. That way, the search should be diverted long enough for us to escape detection and hopefully find the Creature first.'

'I still don't understand how Emily can do all that.'

'She's working nearby, in a secret research facility in northern Dartmoor called the Sphinx building. Every day she drives along the main road outside the hotel, so it's easy enough for her to use similar radio equipment and transmit a false message from around this location.'

'What happens when they find out the message was faked?'

'Naturally, they assume they have a traitor in their midst.'

'But don't these people think they're working for the government?'

'Most of them, yes. But Emily suspects Whitaker has corrupted some of them. He will convince the rest that one of their number is a spy.'

'Isn't that dangerous for Emily?'

'She'll certainly come under suspicion. But Emily is very resourceful. If I know her, she'll plant a false trail that will have them chasing in circles for days. By that time, hopefully we'll have achieved our purpose.'

'False trails,' Tim muttered. 'Sounds familiar. Tell me, why doesn't Emily just inform her bosses about the Creature, and what Whitaker is up to?'

'Because she wants to make sure she has the evidence to put Whitaker away without alerting his suspicions. As for the Creature, there are other reasons why it would not be a good idea to inform Whitaker's overlords that the two supposed rogue agents he is after are actually you and me. Regardless of Whitaker, I'm already in a great deal of trouble for not telling them the truth about the Creature. It is also important that Whitaker's bosses do not recapture the Creature before us. Whitaker will have tried to hide the fact that the Creature is still alive from them, but that is actually to our advantage as well, at this time.'

'Why?'

'That's another thing it would be best if you didn't know.'

'Surely being arrested is better than being killed?'

'Only once we've safely recaptured the Creature.'

Tim sighed, trying to take all this information in.

'Why is Whitaker so keen to kill us?'

'Because if we get to the Creature first, his plans will be thwarted. What I plan to do will ensure the Soviets don't get any advantage in their super soldier programme.'

As Gribbles continued to look out of the window, he pointed to the southern horizon. Tim glanced out and saw the helicopter had vanished.

'Looks like Emily's message has been received and understood. Now we can look forward to dinner.'

Tim had to admit he was hungry. He also desperately wanted a shower and some rest. Gribbles walked across to the wardrobe and upon opening it found it contained fresh trousers and shirts.

'Emily thought of everything,' he said, holding up a pair of trousers. 'Looks about your size.'

After taking a shower, Tim felt refreshed though still very tired. Gribbles also changed and freshened up, and after a short rest they went downstairs to the dining room. Tim was ravenous, and the six course dinner of soup, shrimps, steak and mashed potato, apple pie, cheese and biscuits and coffee and chocolates tasted like the best food he had ever eaten. He had been worried about maintaining their cover during dinner by making sure he called Gribbles Charles, but for the most part they ate in silence.

It was only as Tim finished that he noticed one of the waiters in the dining room was watching their table closely. He had a shaved head and his eyes were dark and unwavering. Even when he caught Tim's eye the waiter didn't turn away.

Tim wanted Gribbles to finish his dinner so they could retire to their bedrooms, but the waiter continued to watch. Tim looked down at his empty plate and felt awkward. He could feel the steely gaze of the waiter, and became increasingly paranoid. What if Whitaker had tracked them down? What if this waiter was really an assassin who would murder them in their sleep?

As they left the table, Tim noticed that the waiter was still watching them closely. He whispered to Gribbles once they were outside the dining room and in the lobby.

'There was a waiter who kept staring at us.'

Gribbles shrugged. 'Perhaps he just wanted to clear our table.'

'No, I'm sure he was watching us.'

'I'm sure it's nothing to worry about.'

But Tim wasn't convinced, and that night as he tried to sleep, he kept thinking of the waiter. The bed was comfortable, and considering the conditions he had slept in the previous nights, it ought to have been a welcome relief. But instead of worrying about attacks from the Creature he was worried about a more human killer. He kept imagining scenarios where the waiter burst into their room and gunned them down in their sleep. He even wondered if Emily might have betrayed them. She hadn't exactly been pleased to see her father.

Eventually Tim could stand it no longer. Amid the snores that came from Gribbles' bed, he got up and put on some clothes. With no clear purpose in mind he silently left the room and sneaked down the stairs to the lobby. Perhaps he might find a sitting room and watch television for a bit, to take his mind off things.

As he approached the lobby, Tim noticed that the man behind the reception desk was none other than the waiter he had thought was watching them earlier. The waiter hadn't noticed him approaching, so Tim lurked out of sight behind the turning in the stairway. He then watched from above as the waiter picked up the phone and dialled a number.

The phone was answered, but Tim couldn't hear what the waiter was saying as he spoke in hushed tones. However, whatever he was saying appeared to be urgent, and from his expression and the way he was gesticulating with his hands, it was clear he was engaged in some kind of heated discussion.

Tim strained his ears to listen, but only caught odd words and phrases.

'Too late for that...'

'Can't make a move until...'

'Need all three...'

'Won't be safe...'

The waiter turned away, and it became harder than ever to hear his words. Tim thought about what he had heard, and for a minute considered going down to the reception and walking past, seeing if the waiter furtively altered his conversation or not. But if he really was an enemy agent, it would be foolish to reveal his presence. Tim thought over what the waiter had said on the phone, and realised that he could be taking what he was saying completely out of context. For all he knew, the phrases might have an entirely innocent explanation.

On the other hand, if his words did relate to their presence, perhaps it was unlikely that they would be in any danger that night. *Too late for that* and *Can't make a move until* seemed to indicate that whatever was to happen wouldn't happen until the following day. Then there was that enigmatic reference to needing all three. Who was the third? Emily? The Creature? Someone else entirely?

Presently, the waiter placed the receiver back on the phone and strode away from the reception desk. For a moment Tim thought about following him then decided against it as it would be too easy to be spotted. He trudged back upstairs and went back to bed, his head still buzzing with whether or not the waiter was spying on them. He wondered whether to awaken Gribbles or not but decided against it. No doubt the scientist would simply tell him he was reading too much into events, and there was no clear evidence that the waiter was anything more than he appeared to be.

When he did finally drop off to sleep, Tim's dreams were filled with nightmares about helicopters flying into the hotel lobby and shooting at him and Gribbles, whilst the waiter looked on smiling. Every time he awoke, he half expected to see the Creature looming over him, and more than once he could have sworn he saw the Creature's eyes watching him in the darkness. The hotel was warm and comfortable, but to Tim this made no difference. He knew he wouldn't be able to properly rest until his adventure was over, one way or the other.

The following morning at breakfast Tim didn't see the same waiter anywhere, but was temporarily distracted by the quality of the food he was served. After stuffing down an excellent full English breakfast along with plenty of cereal, toast and tea, he felt very full indeed, and the last thing he wanted to do was go chasing around Dartmoor looking for the Creature. But Emily's arrival as they were leaving the dining room put paid to any ideas he might have had about further rest.

118

'Good morning Charles,' Emily said. 'Good morning Matthew. Did you sleep well?'

'Very well, thanks,' Tim lied.

Emily indicated that they should talk outside the hotel, where they wouldn't be overheard. Gribbles and Tim followed her to the car park, where they spoke together in hushed tones.

'I've found the trail,' Emily said. 'It runs north, towards Wistman's Wood. Whitaker won't be searching the area for some time, so we've got an opportunity to look now.'

Gribbles nodded. 'Won't you be missed?'

'I've called in sick,' said Emily. She indicated a nearby Ford van. 'I know you came prepared, but I've brought one or two other things that might help us trap the Creature.'

'You're coming with us?' asked Gribbles.

Emily nodded. 'I'm not leaving you to deal with something this important by yourself, not after everything else you've managed to mess up.'

'Emily it's dangerous,' objected Gribbles.

'Well, you should have thought of that before you let loose a genetically engineered supersoldier. If it's safe enough for Tim, it's safe enough for me.'

'Alright, alright. What have you brought?'

Emily grinned. 'I'll tell you on the way.'

After getting their rucksacks and equipment, Tim and Gribbles left the hotel. Emily joined them and together they set off across the main road to the gate that led to Wistman's Wood. They took the farm track to the right of the West Dart River, and followed the path past some farm buildings on the left by the riverbank. The path then led up a short way over some rocks, gradually climbing, until it opened out onto the moors.

About a mile in the distance was Wistman's Wood - an ancient forest of dwarf oak trees.

For a moment, Tim felt as though he could almost be on holiday. The weather was bright and clear, and the morning sun shone on the rugged hills, illuminating the heather and bracken. Birdsong filled the air, and a fresh cool breeze blew down from the north-west. Sheep grazed nearby, and the occasional wild pony could be seen on the horizon. There were a few other walkers present as it was a popular path, and on the other side of the river they saw a hunting party riding through the fields and trees on horseback.

'So where did you find the trail?' asked Gribbles.

'Near the road,' said Emily. 'It zigzags all over the place, but it ends up near the southern end of Wistman's Wood. This path leads directly there, so we needn't follow the trail exactly - at least until we get there.'

Tim was pleased to be following a clear path instead of traipsing through bogs and uneven ground, even if it was only temporarily. He wondered whether they would have any more success in hunting and securing the Creature now that Emily was with them. She seemed confident, organised, tenacious and far more communicative than Dr Gribbles. Tim was particularly fascinated to hear more information about her military training, as well as her scientific background. However, her manner with her father was still very terse. Tim wondered again exactly what the nature of the falling out between them had been, but couldn't see how to enquire of it without upsetting both parties.

'Tell me Dad,' Emily asked presently. 'Are you still trying to manufacture haemomuscular enhancement compounds?'

'Yes,' Gribbles muttered. 'But with no success.'

'That's not true,' said Tim. 'They work on me, at least for a minute or so. I've got some here, look!'

Tim took out a few Hec vials from his pocket. Emily fixed her father with an accusing stare.

'So this is what it's come down to? Experimenting on children?'

'Tim doesn't mind, do you Tim?' Gribbles said, looking pleadingly at him.

'Oh, no,' said Tim, thinking Emily was giving her father a bit of a hard time. 'I actually volunteered to test them. I mean, who wouldn't want superhuman strength? A bit of Hec comes in very useful.'

Emily indicated a pocket on her rucksack. 'Well I've got some *Hec* of my own. It doesn't just work on children, and lasts a little longer than a few minutes. We've refined it quite a bit since you resigned Dad. Hardly any side effects now.'

Gribbles nodded approvingly. 'Well if we can immobilise the Creature, we'll certainly need some Hec in order to carry him back to Blackthorn Lodge. Or at least, to your van.'

Tim hadn't thought about what they might do with the Creature once they had captured him, or how they would get him back. It seemed that Emily had now come up with an ideal solution.

'Just as well you called me,' Emily said. 'If you didn't have Tim with you, I doubt you'd have even got this far.'

Emily smiled at Tim, and Tim suddenly found himself liking her a lot more.

After about half an hour of brisk walking, they came to the southern edge of Wistman's Wood. Tim stared at the trees for a moment, and wondered if the Creature could be hiding somewhere beneath their boughs. The twisted branches were interwoven with lichens and fern, and around the feet of the trees were a scattering of moss covered boulders. The forest was beautiful, yet also unusually menacing, and almost mystical. It seemed the ideal place for the Creature to be lurking, but from end to end the woods were quite small, so that perhaps seemed unlikely.

Emily and Gribbles both put on infra-red goggles, and Tim was surprised to see that she also had a homing device.

'We can't risk switching yours on or they'll find you again,' said Emily. 'However, this one should be safe enough to use. It's got a special microchip that makes it impossible to track.'

She switched on the device, and a green light flashed intermittently. After examining it for a moment Emily shook her head slowly.

'The Creature is not in the woods. We need to find and follow the trail.'

They searched the ground for a few minutes until Emily discovered fresh paw prints. The tracks led north into the woods, so they plunged under the trees to follow them. Clambering in and around the boulders proved a tricky business, especially as the stones were slippery. More than once Tim slid off and found his foot landed awkwardly, but fortunately he did not twist his ankle or sustain any serious injury.

The trees were densely packed, and picking a way through that meant they could remain on the trail was difficult. It seemed the Creature was once again leaping from boulder to boulder, though presumably not to shake off any pursuers. The trail looked quite old, but eventually Gribbles and Emily halted and stared for a moment at a large flat stone.

'The Creature rested here,' said Gribbles.

'The heat signature is bigger and much more recent,' Emily agreed. 'As recent as this morning, I'd say. The Creature no doubt spent the night here.'

Gribbles moved forward a little, scanning the ground. 'These tracks are from this morning, no question. He's still heading north.'

Tim was pleased they had found such a recent trail, but that didn't mean they were necessarily any closer to the Beast. Emily checked her homing device and it still indicated that they were some distance from their target. The Creature could move at tremendous speeds as he had been engineered with cheetah DNA, so for all they knew he could be miles away.

After another half an hour, they emerged at the north end of Wistman's Wood. The skies had clouded over a little, and the breeze was stronger and cooler. The gentle rushing of the West Dart River continued below to their left, and on the other side of the river lay the peaks of various scattered tors. Ahead of them Longaford Tor rose in the distance.

'He's still heading north,' said Emily. 'Perhaps he's trying to get to the most remote areas of the moors.'

'He knows it'll be more difficult to capture him there,' said Gribbles.

'How does he even know where he is?' Tim asked.

Gribbles and Emily exchanged glances, but it was obvious neither wanted to answer his question.

They continued north, following the Creature's trail. Their journey took them up onto some high ridges commanding spectacular views, but the clouds grew thicker and a thin drizzle of rain blew in from the west. They saw fewer and fewer walkers until eventually after about three miles there were none in sight. The tracks were still relatively easy to follow, but as before the Creature wasn't following any set path, and they often had to trample through bogs, over rocks and across uneven ground. They also often had to pause to check their direction. Thankfully there was no indication that the Creature was aware of their presence, and his trail wasn't circling back the way it had before. It continued steadily north, past the peak of Longaford Tor, and into the bleak wilderness beyond.

Presently they found another dead sheep that had been recently mauled. They also came across a Dartmoor pony that was limping suspiciously, with blood dripping from one of its legs. Emily tried to approach it but the pony reared up and staggered away, clearly not desiring any human contact.

'Poor animal,' said Emily, casting an accusatory glare at her father.

'Are we getting any closer?' Gribbles asked irritably, obviously upset at what had happened to the pony.

Emily consulted the homing beacon and nodded. 'Within a few hundred yards I'd say.'

'Then we must be stealthy and silent,' said Gribbles. 'Especially if we want to avoid the Creature spotting us and toying with us the way he did before.'

'What if he decides to kill us this time?' Tim asked.

'He won't,' Emily said emphatically.

Tim wondered what made Emily so sure, but given his own experiences of coming face to face with the Creature, he suspected she was probably correct. On both occasions he had not harmed him, in spite of the injuries that had been inflicted on his brother.

They continued to follow the trail down a steep rise into a sheltered valley with a stream that snaked through the lower regions. The valley was unnervingly quiet, and Tim wasn't entirely comfortable with how secluded and hidden it felt. The many boulders and mounds the valley contained seemed ideal places for the Beast to be lurking.

At several points during their descent into the valley, Gribbles instructed them to halt and hide themselves amid the heather or behind rocks. On the third of these occasions, he removed three sets of tranquiliser guns, loaded them with darts, and handed one each to Tim and Emily; keeping one for himself.

It was only when they were near the foot of the valley, when Gribbles yet again indicated for them to halt, that Tim saw the Creature. He was bent over the edge of the water taking a long drink by placing his face directly in the stream. The Creature was about a hundred yards away, and it was obvious he had not heard their approach.

Tim's stomach churned as they stood and watched for a moment. Gribbles crept forward a few seconds later, aiming his tranquiliser gun at the Beast. Emily watched with concern, but did not move. Tim wondered if he should stay put or go with Gribbles. He eventually decided to hide behind a rock, ready to fire his dart if Gribbles was unsuccessful.

The Creature continued to lap at the water, gurgling and growling as he did. Gribbles slowly moved closer until he could be sure of hitting his target. He aimed his tranquiliser gun and prepared to fire. After a hunt that had lasted three days, they were finally about to snare their prey.

Somehow Tim didn't feel entirely happy that they were sneaking up on the Creature like this. It seemed unfair and unsporting, even though it was utterly ridiculous to think in such terms. The only way they stood a chance was to catch the Creature unaware, and that meant catching him in precisely the way Gribbles was presently attempting.

Gribbles had been about to fire when the Beast suddenly stood up with astonishing speed and turned to face him. There was no time for Gribbles to get undercover so he shot the dart. But the Creature was too quick for him. He dodged the dart by ducking to the left. The Beast then lashed out at Gribbles with his left claw, and although Gribbles tried to move back one of the talons caught him and slashed him across the right hand side of his face.

Gribbles yelled and fell to the ground, clutching his bloody cheek. The Creature roared, and Tim was horrified once again at the sheer size and bulk of this genetically modified hybrid. The vicious fangs gleamed in the sunlight and the terrible eyes burned with anger. Tim saw a murderous fury in the Creature's face and felt sure that he was about to kill Gribbles - not because he was hungry, but out of rage.

'No!' Emily cried.

Tim hurriedly aimed his tranquiliser dart at the Creature from behind the rock. He hadn't been spotted yet, but the Beast's attention was now fixed on Emily. Surprisingly she had not aimed her tranquiliser dart but was instead beckoning to the Creature.

'Here!' Emily yelled.

'No Emily!' cried Gribbles. 'Please!'

The Creature snarled then charged towards Emily. She did not run but remained seemingly frozen where she stood, still not aiming the tranquiliser dart. The Beast roared again as he approached, but the roar was different somehow. If Tim hadn't known better he could have sworn he detected tones of anguish mingled with the Creature's fury.

Still Emily did not aim the tranquiliser dart. Tim was confused. Why was it that both she and Gribbles seemed so reluctant to shoot? It was only a tranquiliser dart after all. Why did they always seem to lose their nerve and dither at the last minute?

Tim decided he had better take a shot himself. He took aim, but as he did the Creature stopped about twenty yards from Emily. For a moment he just stared at her with a look of apparent confusion.

Emily slowly raised her tranquiliser dart and aimed at the Creature. But as she fired the Beast leapt out of the way. To Tim's horror he then lunged towards Emily and swiped at her with his claws. Emily dodged, but Tim knew he had no choice but to act immediately. He squeezed the trigger, firing his dart into the Creature's back.

The Creature immediately stopped in his tracks and roared with an anger that seemed to shake the ground. The Beast turned but before Tim had a chance to duck he had been spotted. With a terrifying leap the Creature lunged towards him, landing on top of the rock Tim had been standing behind. Tim staggered backwards, but there was no escape. The Creature launched himself onto him and his weight alone caused him to collapse.

Tim was aware of the Creature's vile breath in his face, and of the bloody, tangled, hairs of his mane. He thought he was dead for sure and that the Beast would bite his jugular or worse, but instead the Creature simply growled quietly before rolling its eyes and collapsing unconscious on his chest. The tranquiliser dart had finally taken effect.

126

Chapter 10: The Sphinx Building

For some time Tim remained on the ground in utter terror, his nerves shot and his heart racing. He could not believe he had been the one to finally tranquilise the Creature, but it seemed fitting, since he was the one that had caused him to escape. Perhaps at last his life might begin to return to normal.

'Well done Tim,' said Gribbles, staggering towards him. He clutched his lacerated face which was now caked with blood.

Emily walked across to Tim and smiled. She looked grateful, but somewhat traumatised.

'Will somebody get this great Wookiee monster off me?' asked Tim, recovering his sense of humour.

Gribbles and Emily both hauled and pulled and eventually Tim was able to get up. His back and right arm ached painfully, but he nevertheless felt a sense of pride in his achievement. He had brought the Beast down. Their hunt was a success. He did his best to look smug and like he had had the whole thing under control.

Emily tended to Gribbles' wounds using bandages from the first aid kit. Gribbles winced irritably as Emily dabbed iodine onto the deep cuts on his face.

'Don't be such a baby,' Emily muttered. 'This will help them heal much quicker, and hopefully minimise any scarring.'

'Being scarred for life isn't so bad,' said Gribbles. 'But this is. Ouch! Anyway, now we need to move him.'

'An ideal time to use these,' said Emily, producing three vials from her rucksack. Tim took one from her, eager to gain superhuman strength. He drank it down and almost choked. It burned his throat and tasted like mouldy cheese.

'That...' said Tim, '...was a vile vial.'

Gribbles made a similar expression of disgust as he drank his. 'Really, I can't understand why whoever makes these couldn't have added some flavouring. Strawberry perhaps. Or blackcurrant?'

'Most government scientists lack your eccentricities,' said Emily, gulping hers down with a very forced straight face.

'I wouldn't call taste an eccentricity,' Gribbles muttered.

They set to work moving the Creature once the serum took effect. Tim felt a great surge of warmth in his arms, legs and chest – far more than he had with the compounds Gribbles had tested on him. He was surprised to find he could lift the Creature with relatively little difficulty, although the sheer bulk meant two of them had to carry an end each. It was going to be a long and awkward trek back to Emily's van, especially as they had no way to camouflage the Beast and they would almost certainly be spotted by other walkers.

They began to trudge up the side of the valley and back along the path to Longaford Tor. The weather was cloudier than ever, and the drizzle gradually turned to heavier rain. As they came to a flatter section of the moors before the ascent to Longaford Tor, Tim felt more tired than ever, but he also felt a great sense of relief having captured the Creature.

'How long did you say he would be out cold for?' Tim asked.

'With these darts, at least five hours,' said Gribbles. 'If for some reason we are delayed, we'll fire another into him as he sleeps.'

'We must be careful about that,' said Emily. 'Ideally we would need to wait until the drug begins to wear off, or we might end up killing him.'

'I'm not sure it's wise to risk waiting for the Creature to get too wakeful,' said Gribbles. 'What's more, he'll be very bad tempered. It will feel like a very bad hangover.'

Tim silently agreed with Gribbles. He didn't want to take any chances with the Creature potentially waking up again.

'Probably the best thing to do when we get to the road is for you to go back to the hotel car park, get the van, and meet us further down the road, somewhere more secluded,' Gribbles said to Emily. 'Then we need to drive back to Blackthorn Lodge as quickly as possible.'

'Did you really mean what you said on the phone?' Emily asked. 'Is everything ready?'

Gribbles never had a chance to answer. Suddenly a group of masked, black clad, heavily armed men emerged from hidden positions all around them. They moved in rapidly and within seconds Tim and the others were surrounded.

In those two or three seconds, Tim was convinced the men in black were going to open fire and that they were all going to die. But to his surprise one of the men nearest commanded them in fierce tones.

'Put down the monster and take two steps back!'

Tim and Gribbles, who were carrying the Creature between them, did as they were instructed. The men moved closer, still pointing their weapons. As they did, the familiar sound of helicopter blades was heard from afar. Soon Tim saw the same white helicopter approaching from the south-east. It seemed that whatever diversionary tactics had been set up by Emily had at last run their course.

Tim wondered whether he would stand a chance in a fight against any of these men with his presently enhanced strength, but he knew they could just shoot him if he tried. He looked around and counted twenty four armed men, all with machine guns trained on him. Why didn't they just fire? The last time he encountered Whitaker's men they had wanted to shoot them on sight.

The man who had spoken previously yelled at them again. 'Remain completely still, or we will open fire!'

The helicopter continued to approach and eventually landed nearby on a flat area of grass. A tall, thick set, grey haired man in a blue suit stepped out and strode across to them, his expression cold and unreadable. He stared at Emily first, then Gribbles and Tim. His eyes remained on Tim for a moment before he spoke in an American accent.

'Bring them.'

After being searched and relieved of their rucksacks and other equipment, Tim, Gribbles and Emily found themselves being shoved to the helicopter and bundled inside. Ordinarily Tim would have been excited about riding in a helicopter but clearly these men did not have kind intentions. He wondered again why they hadn't been killed immediately, or whether they were to be taken to some hidden location and tortured for information.

Looking out of the helicopter Tim saw that the Creature was also being hauled by several men to a second white helicopter that was landing nearby. Once the Creature was secured inside the second helicopter took off, and at that moment the silver haired man in the blue suit joined them inside the first helicopter.

The man with the silver hair spoke briefly to the pilot, and a moment later their helicopter took off. Tim watched as the moors gradually shrank beneath them, but his view was limited by the poor weather and thick cloud. He exchanged wary glances with Gribbles and Emily, but it was impossible to communicate with them over the noise of the helicopter engines.

Altogether they were inside the helicopter about fifteen minutes heading steadily north, following the second helicopter. They then landed in an area of the moors Tim wasn't familiar with, beyond the fact that it was sectioned off from the general public for military testing. He had heard stories of unexploded mines and shells, and even a few horror stories about children who had unwittingly wandered into this private area, only to return minus a limb for their trouble.

They descended into a steep valley surrounded by tall hills, and touched down on a concrete landing area amid a military compound containing several large buildings built with reflective glass. A tall barbed wire fence ran around the compound, and soldiers patrolled the perimeter. Some of them had dogs. A single lane road led up to the main entrance, which as far as Tim could tell was the only way in or out of the place, other than by air.

Several soldiers moved up to the helicopter as it landed, training their weapons at it. Gribbles, Tim and Emily were once again robustly escorted from the helicopter out across the concrete and inside one of the glass buildings.

The spacious lobby looked no different to any other corporate building, with a reception desk and some carefully selected pieces of modern art on display. The walls were white, and the entire place had a cold, antiseptic feel, almost like a hospital.

This clinical impression was confirmed as Tim and the others were marched through a set of double doors to the left of reception. They were then escorted along a white walled corridor to a second set of double doors, and the man with the silver hair punched in a code on an electronic keypad to gain access. Their journey through the mysterious military building continued, and it soon became apparent that they were inside a large research facility, with scientific laboratories visible through doors in the windows on either side of the corridor. Tim glanced through and saw technicians and lab assistants in white coats experimenting with substances in test tubes, and other elaborate chemistry apparatus. The overall impression wasn't exactly sinister, but given what Tim knew about the supersoldier experiments, he was more than a little alarmed.

'What is this place?' Tim muttered.

'The Sphinx building,' Emily replied. 'Secret government facility. I work here.'

'Quiet!' said the man with the silver hair.

Presently they were herded into a small room with no windows. It had featureless white walls and no furniture but a metal table and half a dozen plastic chairs. In the upper right hand corner was a small, mounted closed circuit television camera.

The man with the silver hair indicated for guards to remain outside before closing the door behind them. The sound of a lock clicking shut made it clear to Tim that he, Gribbles and Emily were prisoners.

'Who is the man with the silver hair?' Tim asked Gribbles as soon as they were alone.

'No idea,' Gribbles replied. 'He's American. CIA perhaps. Or he could be...'

Gribbles stopped talking as Tim noticed Emily putting a finger to her lips. She indicated the camera furtively, and her message was clear. They should not discuss anything further, as they risked being overheard.

Emily began to search the room, looking under the tables and chairs and around the walls. Seemingly understanding what his daughter was up to, Gribbles joined in this search. Tim was puzzled for a moment, but suddenly realised what they were doing. They were looking for hidden microphones.

Eventually Emily indicated an area just below the camera. Tim noticed and saw what appeared to be a tiny microphone receiver. Gribbles seized it between his forefinger and thumb and yanked it from the wall, pulling out the wires with it.

'Now we can talk,' said Gribbles.

Emily looked irritated at Gribbles' act of vandalism. 'You do realise that American will be back any second now.'

'*If* he's American,' said Gribbles, standing carefully so the camera wouldn't see his lips move. 'For all we know he could be KGB, especially if he's in league with Whitaker.'

'Whatever happens, we must tell them nothing,' said Emily, also taking care to make sure her lips weren't seen. 'The only reason we're still alive is they want to know who else we've told about the Creature and what Whitaker is up to.'

'But we haven't told anyone,' said Tim.

'Exactly, but they don't know that,' said Emily. 'The minute we tell them the truth, we are all dead.'

Tim felt very alarmed at this thought. He glanced at his watch and realised the effects of the Hec vial he took would be wearing off by now. But as he put his hands despondently in his pockets, to his astonishment he found he still had four of the Hec vials from Gribbles. They had not been confiscated in the search.

'What will they do with the Creature?' Tim asked.

Emily stared darkly at her father as Tim asked this question. 'You tell him.'

'Well...' Gribbles said awkwardly. 'Most probably, once they've taken their DNA samples, they will destroy him.'

Although the Beast was savage and dangerous, and although the government had originally given the order for the Creature to be destroyed, Tim wasn't altogether happy about this. It didn't seem right somehow. Yes, Gribbles shouldn't have deceived them and hidden the Creature, but now it seemed wrong to just kill him. Judging by the looks on their faces, Gribbles and Emily shared that view.

Tim felt as though he was clutching at straws. 'But...well, it isn't the Creature's fault he's here.'

'Exactly,' said Emily, scowling at Gribbles.

'Well, what do you want me to do about it?' Gribbles cried, suddenly very irritable. 'I did everything I could! I hid him. I cared for him. I've been trying to find a cure, and I finally succeeded, only for...'

'Only for me to stupidly let him out,' Tim interrupted, intrigued at Gribbles' sudden reference to a cure.

'Which he didn't do on purpose,' said Gribbles, surprisingly coming to Tim's defence.

'Just like you didn't create the Creature on purpose,' Emily muttered.

'You know I didn't!' Gribbles yelled, angrier than ever. 'Besides, you know as well as I do that we've just spent the last three days trying to get him back! I know I made a mistake Emily, but God knows I've spent every waking minute since trying to put it right!'

'Well, there seems little point in keeping the truth from Tim any longer,' said Emily. 'You might as well tell him who the Creature really is, especially as we're all going to die.'

'Don't say that,' said Gribbles.

'It's the truth! They won't allow witnesses to live, and Whitaker will be able to make up any story he likes.'

Gribbles nodded sadly. 'I'm afraid it's true Tim. I'm sorry you got dragged into all of this.'

'I don't care,' Tim said defiantly, though he certainly didn't feel brave. 'Just tell me what you mean about who the Creature is.'

Gribbles cleared his throat. 'The Creature is my fellow scientist Dr Eric Hunter. He was diabetic, and in a horrible mix-up one of his insulin syringes got confused with one of the experimental drugs containing a mixture of cheetah DNA and other genetic enhancements that we were testing on mice at that time.'

Tim gasped in horror. The idea that the Creature had once been a human shocked him to his very core. He could only stare aghast at Dr Gribbles as he elaborated on his story.

'I hadn't worked with Eric before, but he had a very promising career before him as an up and coming researcher, and this was his first government contract. Although he expressed some reservations at the morality of what we were attempting, he was a very brilliant man who proved to be the ideal laboratory companion. We bounced ideas off one another and he had many superb notions that advanced our experiments a great deal. We successfully created various versions of the haemomuscular enhancing compound, and we had some degree of success with the supersoldier serums we were creating. The problem was that these serums were proving to be irreversible. We wanted to create a supersoldier army that was genetically programmable but also controllable, so that once these supersoldiers were unleashed; they could be recalled once their task was completed.'

'So they could be changed back into humans?' Tim asked.

'Precisely,' said Gribbles.

'But that's impossible!' cried Tim. 'People can't just mutate backwards and forwards like that! It sounds like *The Incredible Hulk* or something.'

'A crude analogy, but it provides a reasonably good idea of what Project Centaur was all about. The only difference being, unlike Bruce Banner's emotional instability, it was meant to be entirely within our control. Don't look so surprised! There are mutations in life all the time. Look at viruses. They cause humans to become weak and ill for a time, until the antibodies fight the virus and they regain their strength. The serums Dr Hunter and I worked on were exactly like viruses, only instead of attacking the body they enhanced it; causing the temporary mutations that would provide the necessary qualities for a supersoldier. Experiments on animals were in advanced stages, and it was hoped that human trials would follow.'

Tim had got so used to Gribbles' unorthodox testing methods that this idea appalled him less than it would have done a few days previously.

'Human trials? On who exactly?'

'Oh, military personnel. They wouldn't have known exactly what they were getting into of course, other than that it was an opportunity to serve their country in the war against the spread of Communism.'

'But the tests never got that far,' Emily interjected.

'Indeed,' said Gribbles. 'That was when disaster struck. After Dr Hunter was accidentally injected with the experimental serum, he mutated into the Creature.'

Gribbles paused for a moment, his expression full of remorse.

'It was *so* foolish of me - *so* careless to leave the syringes lying at his workstation like that without telling him, without labelling them, without any indication of warning whatsoever. I had simply intended to use them on mice during our next tests, but before doing so decided to take a break. I went to find a coffee, thinking Dr Hunter was already in the canteen. But I was mistaken. We missed one another, and he returned to his workstation. I had failed to notice the insulin syringe he had previously prepared and left on his desk to remind him to inject himself - for he had recently been diagnosed as diabetic. It was very difficult to tell the difference and...well, you can guess what happened.'

'Did you see this?' Tim asked Emily.

Emily nodded. 'I worked for Project Centaur as a lab assistant. I didn't have such high-level clearance at that point, but I knew some very important research was taking place, and I had made several educated guesses as to what it was. Both Dad and Dr Hunter had dropped hints to me, but nothing prepared me for what I saw when he injected himself that day.'

'You were there?'

'I was assisting Dr Hunter at the time he injected himself. It was horrible. He started screaming, and his face burned red as though he had an extremely high fever. He was sweating profusely, and fell to the ground, seemingly in agony. The pain was so bad he couldn't even speak. I raised the alarm, and Dad was there a moment later, but by then it was too late. He had already started to change. Hairs sprouted from his neck. His muscles bulged, and his eyes changed colour and shape. His mouth and nose started to bleed profusely, and horrible claws grew out of his hands, piercing his skin.'

Even though Emily described this appalling transformation very matter-of-factly, Tim could tell that she had been deeply traumatised by the experience. She spoke in clipped tones, as though glossing over the horror of what had occurred.

'A brief examination of Dr Hunter's work station confirmed the worst,' Emily continued. 'So we had no choice but to place him in protective custody, for his own safety. After all, he was in a furious rage, tearing the laboratory apart. He smashed equipment, desks, chairs, glass windows, and at one point attacked me.'

Emily rolled up her sleeve and showed a large scar that ran down the lower length of her arm to her jugular vein near her hand.

'I doubt he intended to kill me, but in his rage the Creature slashed at me with his claws. This more than anything proved Dr Hunter was no longer in his right mind. And yet, I believed that something of Dr Hunter must still be in the Creature.'

'Buried very deeply,' said Gribbles.

'Maybe that's why he didn't kill me,' said Tim.

'Perhaps,' said Gribbles. 'Dr Hunter's condition appeared to be irreversible. But I knew there must be an antidote so I immediately set about looking for one. Unfortunately, once the government heard about the accident, they became uneasy and ordered Project Centaur to be terminated. All the records and evidence of our work was to be destroyed, including the Creature.'

'And you were all too happy to comply,' Emily muttered in an accusatory tone.

'Well obviously I had to make it appear that way, or they would have suspected what I was up to,' said Gribbles, sounding rather hard done by.

'You knew perfectly well how I felt. I could have helped you! You couldn't trust your own daughter?'

'I had my reasons for deceiving you.'

Emily scoffed. 'Don't tell me you did all this because it had to look convincing.'

'No. I did all this to protect you, as you are my daughter.'

This frank admission seemed to take the wind out of Emily's sails a little, but she still couldn't help a retort.

'This is the problem with you Dad. You think keeping people in the dark is somehow going to protect them. Well, it didn't work with me - or Tim for that matter!'

Tim was hardly in a position to disagree, but nevertheless felt a bit sorry for the old scientist. Gribbles had, in his own way, simply been trying to be a good father. Of course, his lies had meant estrangement from Emily, as it was clear from their exchange that her protest at the government's order to exterminate Dr Hunter had been what caused the bust-up between them. It must have been very difficult for Gribbles to appear to tow the line at the cost of alienating his own daughter. Yet the sheer unfairness of the order to liquidate Dr Hunter made Tim think that Gribbles had acted entirely properly.

'We can't let this happen,' said Tim. 'To the Creature. I mean Dr Hunter. We can't let them kill him.'

'More than that,' said Gribbles. 'We can't let them take DNA samples. Somehow we have to stop them.'

'Because you think Whitaker is KGB?'

Gribbles was silent for a moment. Emily stared at her father and nodded slowly.

'I know that look,' she said. 'It means you're still not telling us everything. What else is going on here that we don't know about?'

'Project Centaur was just the beginning,' Gribbles answered slowly. 'I had suspicions, and before I resigned - indeed, before Dr Hunter's accident - I heard some very strange rumours about where things might lead should our experiments prove a success. But I was blinded by my own scientific ambition. Now I am paying the price, and I fear many others will pay it too, if we can't stop Whitaker.'

'What are you getting at?' Emily asked.

'This Sphinx facility, for one thing,' said Gribbles. 'Why build it here? What is it about north Dartmoor that makes it vital to have a research centre this secluded and cut off?'

'Secrecy?' Tim suggested.

Gribbles shook his head. 'It would be far easier just to use existing secret laboratories elsewhere in the UK. The island of Rhum off the west coast of Scotland for example has long since held a top secret government base for this kind of research. But this place is new.'

'That's true,' said Emily. 'It was only finished around six months ago.'

'And since the area was already under military jurisdiction, that made it all the more convenient,' said Gribbles.

'Perhaps that's why,' said Tim.

'No, that is incidental,' said Gribbles. 'I smell a rat. Something else is going on here. Something big enough to warrant CIA interest as well as MI6. I now only wish I had chosen somewhere else to hide with the Creature. I fear his incarceration here will prove disastrous.'

As usual Gribbles wasn't elaborating on his mysterious mutterings, but before Tim or Emily got a chance to get something more coherent out of him, the door suddenly opened. Two black clad guards armed with machine guns stepped into the room, and between them strode a third figure.

The visitor was a six foot man in his late forties, impeccably dressed in a dark grey suit. Not a single one of his black hairs was out of place, and his sunken eyes were shrewd and calculating. He smiled coldly, and as he entered hummed a few bars of Mozart's *The Magic Flute*. Gribbles and Emily both stared grimly at the new arrival.

'Tim,' said Gribbles. 'Allow me to introduce Desmond Whitaker.'

Chapter 11: Desmond Whitaker's Secret

As the door shut, Desmond Whitaker stared at each of his prisoners in turn, as though assessing them carefully. For a few seconds he didn't speak. Tim could tell just by looking at Whitaker that he wasn't a man who could be easily outwitted. *Slippery* was the word that sprang to his mind. With a scheming eye Whitaker nodded slowly at Tim, before finally addressing him.

'The curious boy who discovered too much,' he said. 'Curiosity is a two-edged sword Tim Rawling. They say it killed the cat, but the truth is the cat died because it was stupid. How stupid you are remains to be seen.'

Whitaker turned his gaze to Emily. 'On the other hand, Emily Gribbles I must say I'm very disappointed in you.'

'I'm disappointed you didn't tell me the supposed rogue agents you were hunting were my father and an innocent boy,' Emily retorted.

'And how would you have reacted to the news I wonder, discovering we were attempting to permanently silence your own kin? Oh, the little charade you played by pretending you weren't speaking to him! But I knew once you discovered your father had hidden the Creature your allegiance would shift.'

Whitaker looked to Gribbles 'As for you Archibald Ernest Gribbles, I'm disappointed that you couldn't see the bigger picture.'

Tim was surprised at hearing Dr Gribbles referred to by not only his first but his middle name too.

'Why didn't you join the new project Archie-E?' Whitaker continued, punching Gribbles in the arm in a playful manner. 'A mind as brilliant as yours could have great fun in such a venture.'

'I'm not interested in your projects,' Gribbles replied. 'If you're going to kill us you'd best get it over with.'

'Ah, but as you will no doubt have surmised, I can't kill you. First, I've got to find out just who you've told about recent events.'

'We won't talk,' said Emily.

Whitaker chuckled to himself. 'You of all people should know how persuasive my methods can be. Of course you'll talk. The real question is will you have permanent brain damage afterwards?'

Tim swallowed hard, trying to look brave.

'However, there is no need for such unpleasantness. At least not yet. It is entirely possible that you may all make it through this experience alive, in return for a little co-operation.'

'What do you want?' asked Gribbles.

'Put simply, I want you Archie-E. I want you to come and work on the new project. Don't answer yet! At least let me tell you about it. Allow me to give you a tour of our facilities, and show you the discovery.'

At the words *the discovery* Tim's interest was piqued.

'What about us?' Emily asked.

'Oh, you can come as well,' said Whitaker. 'You know too much to live in any case, so I don't object to you learning a little more. Besides, if you're smart, there may yet be a way for you to survive this, as I have already indicated.'

Whitaker glanced up at the broken microphone and tangled wires beneath the surveillance camera.

'I expected nothing less from old hands like you and Emily,' Whitaker continued. 'However, if I just signal the camera thus...'

A second later the door opened and two men entered. One was the silver-haired man in the blue suit. The other was a bald headed man in the same black clothing as the guards, but instead of a machine gun he simply had a handgun attached to his belt. His face was hard and cruel, and his eyes flickered with a barely suppressed glee.

'This is Colonel Clover,' said Gribbles, indicating the bald man. 'He's a member of an elite special forces unit called the Vulture Squad. More secret and deadly than the SAS or other such groups, they carry out unpleasant but necessary missions that no-one wants to officially sanction. Their unit was named after vultures, because like those birds, they strip away dead flesh and thus cleanse, preventing the spread of disease and unpleasantness. One particular disease they want to prevent is the plague of unnecessary information. At present there is a great risk that what you know could become public knowledge. If that risk exists then Colonel Clover will eliminate it. All he will require from you are the names of those you have passed information on to, and so the disease can be halted in its tracks.'

'You're insane,' said Gribbles.

'You of all people know such distinctions are relative,' said Whitaker. 'I can assure you that Colonel Clover will find out what he wants to know, whether you co-operate or not.'

The sadistic glint in Clover's eye left Tim in no doubt that this was the case.

'On the other hand, there is a more pleasant alternative,' said Whitaker, indicating the man in the blue suit. 'This is Randy Jayne, of the CIA.'

'Randy Jayne?' said Gribbles, his expression one of amusement and disbelief.

'Jayne has a great deal of experience in brainwashing. Indeed, for many years he has successfully used the technique with assassins and other assets used by the CIA. He can remove your memories of this place, the Creature, and anything else we need you to forget. I am sure you will agree that is a much happier outcome than torture and death.'

'You can't just wipe our memories!' cried Gribbles.

'I don't include you in this plan Archie-E,' said Whitaker. 'Hopefully, by that point you'll have agreed to work for us. Indeed, I'm sure you will once I show you the discovery. But Emily and Tim must not remember what they have discovered, for reasons of their own safety.'

Tim didn't like the sound of brainwashing one bit. Somehow it seemed even worse than what Colonel Clover might do to them.

'Why is the CIA here?' Emily asked.

'You can't uncover something this big without involving your good buddy Uncle Sam,' said Jayne, smiling in a manner that Tim found rather sickening.

'Where is the Creature?' asked Gribbles.

'Somewhere safe,' said Whitaker. 'We've already taken the DNA samples we need. Afterwards we had planned to destroy him.'

'You can't do that,' Emily blurted out. 'My father can reverse the genetic effects of Dr Hunter's mutation.'

Whitaker looked astonished, and turned to Gribbles. 'Is this true?'

Gribbles appeared irritated at his daughter's outburst. Evidently he had intended to keep this information secret.

'I would like to run more tests first,' Gribbles said unconvincingly. 'But essentially yes, I am now confident I can reverse the condition.'

'Well then, I think the answer to our problems is simple: you agree to work for us, and in return we allow Dr Hunter to return to his human form. Of course, we will have to come up with a convincing cover story, as he was officially declared dead.'

'It would be easy enough to manufacture a story saying that he lost his memory,' said Jayne. 'I could even subject him to treatment that would make him believe he had lived another life somewhere, for the necessary period of time.'

Emily looked between Whitaker and her father doubtfully.

'How do I know you'll keep your word?' said Gribbles.

'My dear Archie-E, you don't. But you have no choice but to trust me. We could kill the Creature, your daughter and this boy right now, and then brainwash you into working for us. It would be far more difficult and messy, but we could do that if necessary. However, I would much prefer that you aided us willingly, and that Emily and Tim could return to their lives with no knowledge of this unfortunate business. Dr Hunter will also be restored. In short: everybody wins.'

Gribbles didn't look convinced.

'I do hope you'll see sense Archie-E,' Whitaker continued. 'Think of poor Tim's parents, and how disappointed they will be to hear news of his demise.'

'Are you still spying on them?' Tim suddenly demanded.

'I haven't been spying on them,' said Whitaker, apparently in genuine surprise. 'Why should I spy on your parents? They know nothing.'

'I saw them!' Tim cried. 'Men in a van outside our house. They came and questioned them.'

Whitaker looked baffled and shrugged. 'I have no idea Tim. I honestly know nothing about this.'

'Well if you aren't spying on them, who is?'

Whitaker shrugged. Tim looked to Gribbles in confusion, and was surprised to see he was indicating for him to keep silent. Whitaker noticed this too, and began to chuckle quietly.

'I think your friend Dr Gribbles might know more than he's telling.'

'Your parents are safe,' said Gribbles, with a reluctant sigh. 'They won't be harmed.'

Emily stared at her father and shook her head as though he had sunk to a new low. As for Tim, he couldn't believe his ears. '*You* spied on them?'

'I hired some people I trust to *appear* to spy on them, and to protect them. There was no other alternative. I needed your help and couldn't risk you returning to them. Besides, given who we were dealing with, it was a wise precaution. They could easily have been captured and used as leverage against you.'

'Oh, that is most unfair,' said Whitaker. 'You must take me for a monster.'

144

'You *are* a monster,' said Gribbles with complete conviction and sincerity.

Tim was so appalled he couldn't speak. Gribbles had deliberately deceived him in order to gain his assistance in tracking down the Creature. He had even gone so far as to lie and say his parents were being spied on by Whitaker. Tim felt furious, especially given how much he had worried about his parents in the interim.

Whitaker stared at Dr Gribbles, and nodded slowly. 'You and I do not differ in our methods as much as you pretend. Like you, I occasionally have to make decisions for the greater good. I have no desire to harm you, but I will if it means the information you have learned does not fall into the wrong hands.'

'*For the greater good* is an expression that falls too quickly and easily from the lips of people like you,' said Gribbles. 'Yet it is true that I am guilty of using that precise excuse. Had I not, the Creature would never have existed in the first place.'

'Then you accept my offer?'

Gribbles said nothing. He was obviously considering what Whitaker had said, but he still looked dubious. At this moment Tim didn't trust Whitaker or Gribbles, especially after what he had learnt about his parents. But trusting Whitaker was even more of a stretch, especially as Emily had been assigned to investigate him by those who thought he might be a Soviet spy.

After much consideration, Gribbles finally spoke.

'Let's see this discovery.'

Tim, Gribbles and Emily were escorted by Whitaker, Jayne, Colonel Clover and some guards from where they had been imprisoned along several white corridors. They then took a lift which required a key card to operate it. Whitaker used his, and the lift descended several floors below the ground floor. To access the lowest level, Whitaker typed in a code on a wall panel. Tim watched closely and noted the code that was punched in: 300366.

The lift doors opened into a small lobby area with another set of double doors that had two guards posted either side. Whitaker typed in the same code and the doors opened, leading onto a vast mezzanine walkway which overlooked a huge pit.

Tim gasped. A great ceiling had been constructed over the top of the pit above their heads, but the digging was still continuing in the earth below. Teams of archaeologists clad in anti-static plastic garments were gingerly unearthing and removing several sets of bones. Ladders led up to other levels, and Tim could see various laboratories and storage areas beneath him. But by far the most astonishing feature of the pit was what lay at its centre: a great skeleton stretched some thirty feet across. It was vast, as though it had once belonged to a giant human. The skeleton had not yet been removed from the ground, but most of its bones were clearly protruding, leaving Tim in no doubt what he was seeing.

'That can't be real!' Tim exclaimed.

'Oh, it's definitely real,' said Whitaker. 'We believe it's a crucial missing evolutionary link.'

Gribbles stared hard at the skeleton, frowning uncertainly. Whitaker noticed this, and misread Gribbles' expression.

'This isn't a hoax I assure you,' said Whitaker.

'Oh I know that,' said Gribbles. 'It's buried much too deeply, and no doubt you will have verified that the bones are real. But what makes you so sure it's an evolutionary missing link?'

'Well, what else could it be?' said Jayne.

'If it's a missing link, why all the secrecy?' asked Emily. 'Why not just announce the discovery?'

'Because of the tests we did on the bones,' said Whitaker, with barely suppressed excitement. 'You see Archie-E, these bones contain fascinating genetic material. They are not entirely human.'

Tim thought that was obvious, but kept his mouth shut as Whitaker continued to explain.

'In the genetic material acquired from this missing link, we have discovered a species of prehistoric humanoid far stronger, far more agile and potentially far deadlier than anything we could engineer ourselves. The supersoldier programme just took a quantum leap.'

Gribbles stared at Whitaker with a horrified expression. 'You want to reverse-engineer one of these things from preserved DNA and use them as supersoldiers?'

'Actually, it was our American cousins who first made that suggestion,' said Whitaker, indicating Jayne. 'It was codenamed Project Minotaur, and became the natural successor to Project Centaur. But all tests so far have failed for one reason: we have gaps in the DNA sequences extracted from the bone marrow, and human DNA doesn't seem to fill those gaps properly. We need something more robust, given that this seems to be an evolutionary off cut of some description. Otherwise, the mutation collapses.'

'Just so I understand this correctly,' said Tim. 'You take DNA from this giant missing link thing, try to recreate it in a lab, then you find there are missing ingredients in your recipe. You then try to use human DNA to replace these ingredients, but human DNA isn't strong enough. Then you hear the Creature that Dr Gribbles was supposed to have destroyed is not only alive but on the loose. So you recapture him – well, actually you let us do the dangerous bit and recapture him – then you hope to use his DNA to provide the missing ingredients for your supersoldier giant missing link thing.'

'An accurate if colloquial summary,' said Jayne.

Tim could hardly believe his ears. 'Does this strike anyone else as one of the most insane ideas of all time?'

'You don't even know what that thing is,' said Emily, indicating the skeleton. 'Messing with human evolution like this could be extremely dangerous. What makes you think you'll be able to control the results of your experiments anymore than Dad could control what Dr Hunter turned into?'

'It hardly concerns you,' said Whitaker. 'Especially as you and Tim aren't going to remember any of this.'

'Tell him about the other bones,' said Jayne.

'There are others,' said Whitaker. 'Other bones we found that belonged to various species of animal that as yet we have been unable to identify. The curious thing is that they seem to be hybrid creatures, like half dog half bird, that kind of thing. This entire area seems to be a repository for evolution's rejected concepts – a kind of missing link graveyard.'

'So why try to recreate rejections?' Gribbles asked.

'With the knowledge we have now, and some experimentation, perhaps we can bring a stability that didn't exist back then. It's the only logical answer. Otherwise, nature wouldn't have rejected these creatures.'

'Six digits,' Gribbles muttered, staring at the giant skeleton. 'The skeleton has six digits.'

'Another evolutionary aberration,' said Jayne.

Gribbles shook his head. 'No.'

'What do you think it is?'

'Just think about this for a moment. What is the probability that so many hybrid creatures and this giant all decided to lie down and die together in exactly the same place? For this to have happened, there must have been some kind of evolutionary rejects officer who herded these unfortunate creatures here and told them they weren't good enough to make the evolutionary grade. No, something else happened. Something far more sinister, I fear.'

Whitaker smiled indulgently. 'What is your hypothesis, Archie-E?'

'Nephilim.'

Tim had no idea what Gribbles was talking about. Nor it seemed did Jayne.

'I'm sorry... Come again?'

But Whitaker began to laugh. Emily rolled her eyes wearily. 'Very funny Dad.'

'I'm completely serious,' said Gribbles. 'The giant skeleton has six digits, exactly like the Annakim in the book of Joshua. The book of Enoch speaks of these ancient giants and hints that they created hybrid creatures akin to the skeletons you discovered. They were just as heavily into genetic research as you are Desmond.'

'Are we talking Sunday school stories here?' asked Jayne.

'Not exactly,' said Whitaker. 'The book of Enoch isn't even in the Bible.'

'No, but the apostles clearly thought highly of it. Jude directly quotes from it.'

'For heaven's sake Archie-E! We're men of science not superstition!'

'As a man of science I must consider the evidence,' said Gribbles. 'And the evidence here points at something akin to what I have just described, rather than to evolution.'

Jayne and Whitaker burst into hysterical laughter. All this talk of giants and Bible stories had somewhat confused Tim, so he asked the obvious question.

'What is so funny?'

'I'm sorry Tim,' said Whitaker. 'I should let you in on the joke. You see, the Bible talks about fallen angels breeding with human women and creating a race of hybrid offspring that were giants called Nephilim. Archie-E here thinks we've found a Nephilim skeleton.'

149

'If we have, I can't understand why you find this funny,' said Gribbles. 'Enoch speaks of what these unspeakable beings did. They caused chaos and misery on the Earth, afflicting mankind with unspeakable cruelty. They tormented and killed millions of people and animals, not to mention their unspeakable experiments in creating monstrous animal hybrids.'

'So in fact they were quite like you,' said Emily, in a somewhat accusatory tone.

Tim looked down at the gigantic sinister skull, staring into the vast empty sockets that would once have housed great eyes. Could it really be true? Was this giant once a tyrant that unleashed unspeakable horrors across the world?

'Fairy tales,' said Whitaker. 'If those Bible stories were true, they would have been corroborated elsewhere.'

'They are corroborated elsewhere,' said Gribbles. 'For example most Greek myths have their roots in events that occurred in this First Age of the Earth. The Nephilim oppressed the people and were treated as gods amongst races as diverse as the Aztecs, Sumerians, Egyptians as well as the ancient Chinese, Toltec and Nordic cultures. There are stories of them in legends of every continent including the United Kingdom, Europe, Africa, Asia, Australasia and both North and South America. That makes it more than a co-incidence, more than just a few verses in the Bible and the Apocrypha. These beings were hugely powerful, oppressive and impossible to resist - and you!' Gribbles pointed accusingly at Whitaker. 'You want to bring them back. Tim is correct. This is one of the most insane ideas of all time.'

'My dear Archie-E,' said Whitaker. 'You cannot have scruples based on such flimsy evidence. Besides, we have technologies that can keep any potentially dangerous effects of these experiments well under control. Suppose we do accidentally engineer a vengeful Nephilim giant we can't control? Well, then we just shoot it in the head.'

150

Gribble shook his head. 'You're an arrogant fool Whitaker. You're tampering with things you cannot possibly comprehend.'

'You mean I'm a scientific researcher? That's funny I thought you were one too. It seems I was mistaken.'

'Project Minotaur is a disaster waiting to happen,' said Gribbles. 'Desmond, you must stop this now, before it gets out of hand. Do not mingle that skeleton's DNA and that of the Creature. You could unleash destruction on the world the likes of which it hasn't seen in thousands of years.'

Whitaker sighed. 'It's getting late. I'm running out of patience. Your answer please, Archie-E. Will you agree to my terms?'

'If you mean, will I help you spawn a race of genetically engineered demon giants, then no.'

Jayne seemed annoyed. 'Damn it all Gribbles! I've read your file. You're an atheist! You don't believe this stuff!'

'Perhaps not,' said Gribbles. 'But I do believe that the kind of control you are attempting here simply isn't possible, and I want no part of it.'

Whitaker began to get angry. 'You realise by your words you are condemning yourself, your daughter and this boy to death?'

'You didn't intend to let them live,' said Gribbles. 'At least be honest about that. You simply hoped that by getting me here to see this skeleton that my scientific curiosity would override any sense of morality.'

'Oh Archie-E, I had every intention of honouring my promise,' said Whitaker. 'But this is your last chance. If you do not do agree to join me, I will have no choice but to put a bullet in Tim's brain, right before your eyes.'

'No!' cried Emily.

Whitaker turned to Colonel Clover. 'Shoot the boy.'

Colonel Clover took the handgun from his belt and clicked the safety off. Tim could hardly breathe he was so scared, but somehow he managed to mutter a few sarcastic words at Desmond Whitaker.

'Really got the *not-a-monster* thing down to a tee, haven't you.'

'Dad!' Emily cried. 'For pity's sake!'

Clover pointed the gun at Tim's head.

'Alright!' cried Gribbles. 'Alright! I'll do it!'

Chapter 12: A Desperate Plan

Whitaker smiled. 'Didn't think you'd have the stomach to see the boy you dragged into this business executed right in front of you,' he said.

Colonel Clover put his gun back in its holster and Tim found he was able to breathe again. For now at least, it seemed there had been a reprieve.

'I'll join your project,' said Gribbles. 'But I want Emily and Tim taken away from this place at once.'

'Not so fast,' said Whitaker. 'At this point I believe you would say anything to save them. As a gesture of good faith, I want you to start work immediately on blending the DNA extracted from those bones with that of the Creature. We have all the equipment you need here.'

Gribbles visibly swallowed.

'Jayne, perhaps you would be good enough to conduct Dr Gribbles to the Creature?'

'Follow me,' said Jayne.

Jayne left with Dr Gribbles and two guards. Whitaker then turned to Emily and Tim.

'Well, this is where it ends for the pair of you. Colonel Clover will escort you back to your quarters. In time, Jayne will be along to remove the necessary memories so you can both return to your normal lives – assuming Dr Gribbles co-operates of course.'

Whitaker gave a nod to Colonel Clover, and a moment later Tim and Emily were being bundled back towards the lift. They were escorted to the upper levels and back towards the room where they had been imprisoned.

Tim had a sudden but definite instinct that Whitaker had betrayed them. There was no way they were going to be allowed to live. All they really needed Dr Gribbles for was to oversee the blending of the Creature's DNA with the giant's DNA. As Gribbles had been the one to create the Creature, his expertise was invaluable. They on the other hand were expendable loose ends. All that talk of brainwashing was nonsense. Tim knew it in his gut. They had to do something at once, or they would be killed.

But what could they do? Colonel Clover was armed, and there were two guards with him, both carrying machine guns. Any fight they started would result in them being shot. Tim looked around the white corridors and wondered if there was any chance of making a break for it through the doors, but as far as he could see they all led to laboratories with no other exits. There were some emergency staircases, but these required the use of key cards or codes.

With no conceivable way of escape, Tim fumbled around in his pocket, until his hand closed on the vials of Hec that Whitaker had failed to confiscate. In that moment, he came up with a desperate plan. The chances were that it would fail, but it was surely better to die trying to escape than just blindly accept that they were going to be killed. Steeling his nerves, Tim chose his moment carefully, just as they were approaching the room they had been shut inside earlier. He then suddenly collapsed to his knees and pretended to start crying.

'No!' Tim wailed. 'Don't kill us! Please!'

'Get up!' Clover yelled.

Tim remained on his knees. 'I don't want to die! Please! I don't want to die!' He thought about a Disney film that had made him cry when he was younger as he said this, in order to act convincingly and produce real tears.

'I don't believe this,' Clover muttered.

Tim buried his head in his hands, and as he did, quickly and discreetly swallowed the contents of a Hec vial.

Clover sighed irritably, and bent down to grab Tim. As he did Tim suddenly seized his arm and flung Clover with astonishing force back against the other two guards. All three of them fell to the ground.

154

Immediately understanding what Tim had done, Emily rapidly grabbed the handgun from Clover's belt and pointed it at the mass of arms and legs that were Clover and his men.

'Move and you're dead!'

Emily looked and sounded like she meant it. Evidently Clover believed her as he did as he was told, though he stared at Tim with a mixture of incredulity and fury.

'Take off the guns, and push them aside!' Emily continued.

After disentangling themselves, the two guards slowly removed their weapons and pushed them away. Tim went to pick them up. They were Uzi 9mm machine guns, and surprisingly heavy. He also grabbed the key card from Clover's pocket.

'What do we do with them?' Emily asked Tim, still pointing the gun at Clover's head.

'I hadn't thought that far ahead,' said Tim. 'Ideally we need to tie them up and hide them.'

'Get up!' Emily said, indicating Clover and his men. 'Slowly!'

Tim could scarcely believe how well his desperate plan had worked out. Clearly neither Clover nor his guards had expected him to suddenly develop extra strength and attack them.

After a quick examination of the corridor that ran parallel to the one they were on, Tim found a storage cupboard filled with stationary. They herded Clover and his men inside then tied them up and gagged them using a great deal of masking tape. It was a surprisingly tiring task, and by the end Tim felt quite exhausted. All the time Emily trained the handgun on them, but Tim didn't think Clover and his men would have tried anything anyway. From the looks on their faces they were familiar with Hec and its effects. Luckily they didn't seem to be aware that this particular variation wore off in minutes.

After they had finished tying up Clover and the guards, they took some masking tape with them, in case they needed to do the same to anyone else.

'Where to now?' Tim asked, as they shut the cupboard. 'It won't be long before the alarm is raised.'

'We need to find Dad and the Creature,' said Emily. 'I suggest grabbing some white coats so we blend in a bit more, but then we need to return to that pit. We can use your key card to get down, but what about the pass codes?'

'300366,' Tim replied. 'I watched closely when Desmond Whitaker keyed it in.'

Emily grinned. 'Excellent. Let's get going.'

'What about these?' Tim asked, indicating the machine guns. 'They're heavy.'

'I'll take one,' said Emily, and slung one around her shoulders. She placed the handgun in her belt and strode off towards the lift. After putting the second machine gun around his shoulders with some difficulty, Tim followed. It took some time to find white coats, but they eventually found a few inside a cloakroom, and took a pair. They concealed the weapons beneath their coats, and in spite of the resultant bulges looked a lot less conspicuous than they would have appeared otherwise.

They reached the lift, and shortly afterwards successfully used the key card then entered the six digit number that authorised them to reach the lower floors. Emily clicked the safety off her handgun, and took a deep breath.

'There were guards outside that door, remember? Just follow my lead, and point that gun at them when I say so. But don't fire it whatever you do.'

Tim nodded nervously, and sure enough when the lift doors opened, they came to the same lobby and double doors. The two guards either side stared at them in surprise, but before they could make a move, Emily thrust the handgun in their direction. Tim did the same with his machine gun, feeling rather ridiculous. He wouldn't be able to fire this weapon even if he wanted to.

'Make a move, and you're dead!' said Emily. 'Very slowly, take your guns out of their holsters and drop them.'

The guards did as they were told.

'Kick them towards him.'

The guards kicked the weapons towards Tim, and Tim picked them up. Afterwards he once again found himself busy tying them up with masking tape. He glanced anxiously at the ceiling, but there were no surveillance cameras that he could see. However this time there was no convenient cupboard to place their prisoners inside. They would have to leave them where they were, so it would only be a matter of time before they were discovered.

After keying the code into the door, Tim and Emily rushed towards the mezzanine floor, doing all they could to remain hidden. There was no-one visible to either the left or right of the walkways, but there were still several men below uncovering the gigantic bones.

Gribbles had been escorted along the left walkway, so Tim and Emily hurried along in that direction. They came to a staircase and walked down as confidently as they dared, knowing that they would almost certainly be observed by the people below, or from the other laboratories that were visible from the side of the pit. Tim could scarcely believe how well their plan had gone so far, but now they had a real problem. Where was Gribbles? They could hardly ask for directions, and already they were getting odd glances from some of the other members of staff.

After about fifty yards, they came to a white walled passageway that led off to the left. There was a set of blueprints pinned to the wall near the entrance – a map indicating where various rooms and laboratories on the lower levels were located in relation to the pit. It seemed the area was still very much under construction, as many of the passages and tunnels did not link up or appeared to be unfinished. However, from glancing at the map, Tim and Emily were able to take an educated guess as to where Gribbles and the Creature might be.

Emily traced their route on the map with her finger. 'If they came in this direction, they are almost certainly heading for the large laboratory a short distance along this corridor. There aren't any others in this direction, and unless they have completed these passages marked *under construction* that head back east, there would be no logical reason to come this way if they were heading for the laboratories on the other side of the pit.'

As a working theory it was as good as any, so Tim and Emily continued along the tunnel. From examining the blueprint they knew they would come to a large laboratory area around the corner to the right. Sure enough, as they turned the corner they saw it through a large set of windows on the left hand side – a vast area filled with glass screens, plastic sheeting, medical equipment and staff clad in protective clothing. In the centre the sedated Creature had been strapped down to a metal table, and Dr Gribbles stood next to him. A short distance away Desmond Whitaker and Randy Jayne watched avidly.

Tim and Emily watched as Gribbles took blood samples from the Creature. Some he injected into test tubes which he placed in centrifuges. Others he placed under slides on a microscope, and occasionally invited Whitaker to examine them. At other times he took test tubes and syringes from cold storage units and did other tests, combining them with various other unknown chemicals.

All the time Whitaker watched Gribbles like a hawk. From the look on Gribbles' face Tim could see he was a man under serious duress. Gribbles was combining the Creature's DNA with that which had been extracted from the giant bones, and it was against his better judgement. But he had done this to save their lives, or at least to buy time. Now it was down to them to rescue him and the Creature, and also to prevent the experiment Whitaker was attempting. Gribbles' dark premonitions about Nephilim and tyrannical giants had seriously unsettled Tim, and he was determined to do all he could to stop these terrifying ancient creatures from becoming a reality again.

But he had no plan. How could they possibly get Gribbles and the Creature out from under the noses of Whitaker, Jayne and the other scientists? Tim thought over the problem, and as he did he heard Emily take the machine gun out from under her white coat and click the safety catch off.

'Tim, cover me,' she said.

Tim was confused. 'Cover you?'

'Hold your machine gun with both hands at arms length, point it at some of the machinery inside the lab, and shoot. Stand as far back as you can, or you'll get glass in your eyes. Oh, and don't forget to take the safety catch off.'

Emily grabbed the machine gun that was around Tim's neck and clicked off the safety catch before giving him a final piece of advice.

'Try not to shoot anyone. They may well deserve to die, but I don't know that you could live with the consequences of knowing you killed somebody.'

Tim had no chance to argue with her or even think about what he was doing. All he knew was that a second later a deafening volley of machine gun fire pierced the air as Emily shot the glass outside the laboratory. She then threw herself into the room through the broken window and fired her weapon, shooting up equipment and glass screens as she went.

Immediately a blaring alarm sounded and red lights flashed in the corridor. Tim knew he had no choice but to do as instructed, so he aimed his Uzi 9mm and began to fire at some of the machines and equipment inside the laboratory. Fortunately as soon as Emily opened fire Jayne and Whitaker dived for cover, as did the other laboratory assistants. Several guards were rushed into positions to return fire, but amid the confusion they had yet to perceive a target. Tim continued to shoot, which caused the guards to take cover whilst Emily advanced towards her father and the Creature. The gun felt heavier than ever, especially as he was holding it at arms length. The weapon also kept recoiling, which meant Tim had a job to keep forcing it down into position and not shoot the ceiling.

Tim watched incredulously as Emily charged through the laboratory to where the Creature lay strapped down. She then ducked to avoid being shot by the four guards who were now firing back at her. With incredible skill and dexterity she rolled over and systematically fired bullets into each of their legs, one by one. Each guard fell to the ground clutching their wounds in pain, and the immediate threat was thus eliminated. Upon seeing this, Whitaker and Jayne fled the laboratory via a door further along the corridor from Tim. They continued into the distance, raising the alarm.

Emily wasted no time. Amid the blood, glass and smoke she charged towards her father and seized him by the arm.

'Get up Dad! We need to take the Creature and get out of here!'

Gribbles stared in amazement at his daughter but wasted no time. He unstrapped the restraints that held the Creature. He then hurriedly drank some liquid from a test tube and passed another to Emily. She drank the mixture, and a second later Tim understood that they had both taken a Hec serum, as between them they hauled the Creature off the surface from where he had been tied down. After grabbing a small package containing syringes, Gribbles and Emily ran from the laboratory out to where Tim was waiting.

Though he felt utterly terrified, Tim couldn't help but smile at the tenacity of Emily's plan. Although her scheme had been incredibly reckless, sometimes it seemed that subtlety and cunning were overrated. Sometimes straightforward violence was far more effective.

'Drink this,' said Gribbles, handing Tim some Hec.

Tim drank the Hec then asked the obvious question. 'How are we going to get out of here?'

'One thing at a time,' said Gribbles. 'First we have to destroy this place.'

'How are we going to do that?' asked Emily.

Gribbles smiled. 'Follow me.'

As they ran through the corridor and back along the walkway, Tim and Gribbles carried the Creature between them. A few guards from the other side of the pit spotted them and began to open fire. Emily fired back, and Tim was surprised to see that she was an astonishingly good shot. In all cases she managed to put them down by merely shooting them in the legs.

'We must hurry,' said Gribbles. 'There will be many more to follow, and they will shoot to kill.'

They rushed out to the lift again, past where the guards they had bound with masking tape were still tied up and struggling to get free. Tim used Clover's key card to activate the lift, and they went up a couple of floors, but were still in the lower levels of the facility. With alarms blaring in their ears they rushed along another set of corridors upon leaving the lift. Emily led the way, and every time they were confronted by guards she opened fire before they had a chance, shooting them in the legs. Even though these men were out to kill them Tim couldn't help but feel sorry for them, as they were reduced to writhing in bloody pain as they ran past. Tim was also amazed at Emily's military skills, although given her background this ought not to have been such a surprise.

Eventually they came to an area marked with radiation warning signs, and several other doors that required Clover's key card to access. They then entered what appeared to be a large weapons storage area with many sealed metal crates. Some were marked as ammunition supplies, others as rifles, handguns, machine guns, rocket launchers and so forth. A few members of staff were present, checking clipboards as though in the process of a stock take.

'Out of here now, or you're dead!' Emily cried, firing her machine gun into the air.

The terrified staff immediately did as they were told and rapidly filed out from the room. Gribbles and Tim placed the still unconscious Creature against the wall. Gribbles then pulled out a large crate that looked different to the others and opened its electronic seal using Clover's key card. It was only when Tim noticed the radiation warning on the crate that he suddenly suspected what was inside. His instinct was confirmed seconds later as a conical shaped device was revealed, bearing an electronic counter.

'That's a nuke!' Tim exclaimed.

Gribbles grunted an affirmative and immediately began unscrewing the tip of the device as Tim gaped in stunned disbelief.

'You can't be serious!'

'I am,' Gribbles replied firmly. 'This is a tactical nuclear weapon kept here as a failsafe in case the base needed to be destroyed in a hurry. Detonating it underground will bury these lower levels and contaminate them with radioactive material to ensure they cannot be dug up again for many, many years.'

'But a nuclear explosion like that could destroy everything for miles around!'

'It will be contained,' said Gribbles.

Emily shook her head. 'Dad this is insane! Think of the fallout and danger to local populations, not to mention the damage to the environment.'

'Oh Emily, do some research! Tactical weapons don't cause widespread destruction. The blast radius for a small one like this is less than a mile. Only the levels beneath the ground will be irradiated. The surface will experience minimal contamination and even then only within about half a square mile. Besides, the alternative is unthinkable! Better a small nuclear explosion and containable damage than to allow the continuation of a genetic experiment that could unleash creatures capable of destroying the Earth as we know it!'

Tim found this rather difficult to swallow. 'How did everything get so apocalyptic all of a sudden? I understand you don't want secret formulas to fall into the hands of the Soviets, but we've gone from that to global annihilation! It's ridiculous!'

'Life is ridiculous,' said Gribbles. 'Surely if your experiences have taught you anything, they have taught you that.'

Tim felt completely unable to take in what was happening as Gribbles continued to set the detonator on the tactical nuclear warhead.

'Don't you need to enter a load of secret codes to get that thing to work?'

'Of course. But I know how to bypass them.'

Tim looked at Emily uncertainly. 'Really?'

'Sadly he's not joking,' said Emily.

'I thought genetics was your thing?'

Gribbles sighed irritably. 'I'm allowed to have more than one *thing* surely? Nuclear warhead electronics is a hobby of mine.'

'A hobby, I see,' Tim muttered sarcastically. 'Not a huge difference between that and collecting stamps...'

'Will we have enough time to reach minimum safe distance?' Emily asked.

'I cannot adjust the length of the countdown,' Gribbles replied grimly. 'It's pre-set, and once initiated the bomb can't be defused.'

Tim didn't like the sound of that. 'Isn't there a red wire to cut or something?'

Gribbles shook his head. 'Too many films…'

'But they will surely have allowed a few minutes…'

Suddenly the alarm sirens changed in tone. They became higher pitched, and were accompanied by a loud recorded voice.

'Warning: Nuclear device activated. Detonation in T-minus fifteen minutes. Evacuate. Evacuate.'

'That's done it!' said Gribbles. 'We've fifteen minutes to get out of here and reach minimum safe distance.'

At that moment, Whitaker, Jayne, Clover and at least twenty guards burst into the room. Tim, Gribbles and Emily were immediately seized and bound together with the same masking tape that they had used on Clover and his men. They did a very efficient job, and by the end of it Tim was on the floor with his knees bundled up to his chin, unable to budge an inch.

Clover held up a roll of tape in front of Tim's face and smiled. 'Two can play at that game, Tim Rawling.'

Whitaker turned to Gribbles. 'Once again, I'm very disappointed in you Archie-E.' He reached into Gribbles' coat pocket and removed the syringes he had taken from the laboratory.

'You might have caused this facility to be destroyed, but thanks to you we have what we need: the blended DNA samples. I am sure these will prove very useful. Obviously we are now going to kill you all, but before you die, I wanted you to know your efforts to stop me were in vain.'

Whitaker suddenly struck Gribbles across the face with his fist. Blood dribbled from the corner of Gribbles' mouth as he stared back defiantly.

'You and your pathetic superstitions,' Whitaker hissed. 'You're no longer a scientist. You're no better than one of those religious maniacs you always said you hated so much – standing in the path of mankind's progress.'

'You aren't about to progress,' said Gribbles. 'You're about to plunge us back thousands of years into the darkest era of human history.'

Whitaker shrugged. 'Well, if I am you won't be there to see it.' He stood up and addressed Emily, shaking his head. 'It was your futile antics that led to this. Such a waste.'

Finally, Whitaker turned to Tim. 'And you proved a lot less smart than I gave you credit for.'

'It's a pleasure to disappoint you,' Tim said, his defiance sounding hollow. In truth, he was more terrified than ever.

'I think we'll gag you all, in case you somehow conceive an escape plan,' said Whitaker. Clover smiled sadistically and put tape across their mouths. 'We reap what we sow,' Whitaker added, addressing Tim directly. He stared coldly at him.

'I'm wondering whether I should personally murder you with my own hands. I can imagine I might find it pleasurable. However, such things are more Clover's line of work. Besides, it's cleaner and simpler with the paperwork if you were just unfortunate enough to be caught up in the blast. And on that note, I shall bid you all farewell.'

Whitaker left the room. Jayne, Clover and the other guards followed, and some of them carried the still unconscious Creature between them. Tim and the others remained bound and helpless. The sirens continued to blare, and the automated voice continued to foretell their imminent death.

'Warning: Nuclear device activated. Detonation in T-minus twelve minutes. Evacuate. Evacuate.'

Tim struggled against his bonds but it was no good. They were too tight, not to mention the fact that he was sitting back to back with Gribbles and Emily, both of whom were also struggling in vain.

A minute passed. Tim began to sweat, and once again his heart pounded with fear. But despite the seriousness of their predicament, he suddenly felt a strange sense of resignation. They had done all they could. Besides, if the myths and legends about the Nephilim were true, and Gribbles was right about the terrors Whitaker was about to unleash on the world, perhaps there was also a higher power who might yet devise a way to release them.

'Detonation in T-minus eleven minutes.'

By now Whitaker, Clover, Jayne and the guards, scientists and other staff would have left the building. Since they were right next to the bomb, at least they would be vaporised instantly. Tim had heard horrible stories about the gruesome and painful deaths suffered by people caught further out from the epicentre of a nuclear device blast radius.

But Gribbles and Emily hadn't given up. They were still fighting to get free. Tim joined in the struggle once more, but no longer thought they stood a chance of actually escaping. He watched the red electronic counter on the warhead grimly as the last minutes of his life ticked away, all the time pulling at the rolls of tape that kept him cruelly fixed in place. Something about the situation made Tim want to laugh. It all seemed so utterly ridiculous - like a crazy nightmare that had the impertinence to make itself real.

It was only a few seconds later, as his wrists were raw from tugging at their bonds, that he saw the door of the room open. At first, he thought he was hallucinating. He blinked several times in amazement, but in the end there could be no doubt. Several men in military uniforms charged into the control room and cut their bonds. Clearly these were not men under Clover's command, but who were they?

A moment later, Tim saw the face of the last person he expected to see amid the soldiers. He gasped, and as his gag was removed exclaimed in complete astonishment and disbelief at the sight of his brother.

'Dubbler!'

Chapter 13: Dubbler's Adventures

'What are you doing here?' Tim cried as he stared at his brother. He was still injured where he had been attacked by the Creature, and had bandages in various places.

Rob grinned. 'You wouldn't believe me if I told you.'

'Who are you people?' asked Gribbles.

'No time to explain!' cried a man with a familiar looking face. 'This device can't be stopped! Where's the Creature?'

It took Tim a second or two to realise who the mystery man was: the suspicious waiter from the Two Bridges hotel.

'Whitaker took him,' said Tim.

'We need to get out of here now,' said Rob. 'Follow me.'

'Detonation in T-minus ten minutes.'

The automated voice re-focussed everyone. Since Tim didn't want his immediate future to involve a deadly radioactive explosion, he ran behind Rob and the man from the Two Bridges hotel as they bolted out of the weapons storage room. Gribbles, Emily and the others followed.

They ran along several corridors, down at least three flights of stairs, and out into a tunnel cut from the rock that appeared to lead back towards the archaeological dig where the skeletons had been uncovered.

'This is the way out?' Emily asked dubiously.

'Trust me,' said the man from the Two Bridges hotel.

After reaching the pit with the giant skeletons, Rob and the man from the Two Bridges hotel crossed it rapidly, eventually reaching a small, barely noticeable fissure in the rock that opened in the lower section of the pit. It was narrow, but just big enough for a human to squeeze through.

'Detonation in T-minus seven minutes.'

One of the soldiers shoved a torch into Tim's hand as they ran into the crack in the rock. He switched it on to see that the rocky tunnel widened out almost immediately, but the ground was uneven. It rose sharply and the going was tough, but Tim knew they had less than seven minutes to get to safety before the nuclear weapon exploded.

The entire party rapidly ascended through the tunnel, and after what seemed like a huge climb it began to twist left and level out a little. At this point Rob and the man from the Two Bridges hotel picked up the pace a bit. Tim glanced back and heard the grunts and pants of Dr Gribbles behind him. Further back he saw Emily.

Tim ran faster than he had ever run before, climbing and leaping over every rocky obstacle. He banged his head a couple of times on the lower parts of the tunnel, but the blinding pain was secondary to his urgent desire to escape being caught in the blast wave. The nuclear flames would no doubt surge through these passages, incinerating everything in their path. How much time did they have left? For all he knew, it could be mere seconds.

Presently the tunnel climbed again, more steeply than ever. Tim reckoned they must have come at least a half a mile already, but tactical nuke or not, that might not be enough distance. Morbid fears preyed on his mind, and he began to wonder what would happen if Gribbles was wrong. What if the bomb was more powerful than he thought?

Presently they reached an opening in the rocky ceiling. The man from the Two Bridges hotel shone his torch up briefly, illuminating a rope ladder.

'Climb!' he said simply.

Tim didn't need to be asked twice. He hurriedly followed Rob up the ladder, ascending the vertical shaft. After about thirty rungs the ladder came to an end, and he pulled himself up into a large cavern with rotten timbers on the floor and ancient beams supporting the roof. Puddles of muddy water were dotted around the ground, and the sound of dripping echoed in the blackness.

'An old tin mine,' Rob explained. 'Agent Saunders says we should wait here for the explosion.'

'Agent Saunders?'

'He was keeping an eye on you in the Two Bridges hotel.'

As they spoke, the others speedily climbed up the rope ladder into the tin mine tunnel. Saunders, Dr Gribbles and Emily followed, gasping for breath.

'Detonate the charges,' Saunders instructed.

Two soldiers pressed switches on remote control devices. Muffled thuds and the sounds of a cave-in far away could be heard.

'We laid charges earlier, in case of pursuit or worse,' Saunders explained. 'I only hope its enough to protect us.'

'Won't the force of the nuclear explosion collapse the mine?' Tim asked.

'It might,' Saunders admitted. 'But we've only got a few more seconds before...'

At that moment, there was a much louder muffled thud. Tim felt a violent shudder as the ground shook. The water in the puddles rippled and the rocks around them trembled. Dirt and mud from the ceiling began to dislodge, and as Tim glanced up he saw the rotting beams of wood rattling. He squeezed his eyes shut, waiting for the floor to stop shaking.

'It's alright,' Saunders said presently. He took a Geiger counter out of his rucksack and began checking the tunnel for radiation. After a moment he turned to Dr Gribbles.

'We're safe.'

Tim breathed a sigh of relief, but Gribbles didn't look particularly impressed.

'That's good to know. And now I require an explanation. Who are you people and why did you rescue us?'

The scientist's tone was almost accusatory. Tim couldn't understand why. It seemed the height of ingratitude to question their rescuers, especially as one of them was Rob.

'We're here because Agent Gribbles didn't report,' Saunders explained.

'I didn't get a chance,' said Emily. 'And don't call me Agent Gribbles. I'm not an agent.'

'You agreed to spy on your boss, Dr Whitaker,' said Saunders.

Emily sighed. 'Yes, I suppose so.'

'That makes you an agent, even if it doesn't say so on paper. You failed to report. Your last known position, at the Two Bridges hotel, was given to us by your superiors. I went undercover there immediately, and was surprised to find none other than Dr Gribbles present, under an assumed name with an eleven year old boy posing as his nephew. I knew Dr Gribbles wasn't working on government projects any longer, so why was he suddenly in the Two Bridges hotel behaving like a spy?

'At one stage we even suspected you might be secretly working for Dr Whitaker, in spite of being asked to spy on him. But that didn't explain Tim's presence. Nor did it explain the sightings of the monster. Gradually we put two and two together. It seems the experimental beast from Project Centaur was still alive, and that Dr Gribbles had covered up its existence. Dr Whitaker had learnt the monster still lived, but had not reported the matter further. Instead, he used his own considerable resources, including people who were loyal to him, to begin his own hunt for the Beast.'

Saunders turned to Gribbles.

'When you left the hotel to track down the Creature, London ordered that you and the Creature be detained. We moved in to arrest you, but Whitaker got there first and took you to the Sphinx facility. We knew about his research there, including Project Minotaur, and that the presence of the Creature could mean a great scientific breakthrough. If there was ever a time when Whitaker would make a break for the Soviet Union it would be now, especially as he might already have suspected we were on his trail. We discovered these tunnels and a way into the facility. The tunnel was blocked, but a few well placed charges cleared the obstructions, and soon we managed to enter the Sphinx building in the lower levels. Imagine our surprise when we got there only to discover a panic as a nuclear device was activated.'

'After that, we had barely minutes to track you down,' said Rob. 'Luckily, Saunders had a blueprint of the base, and knew where the nuclear device was kept. It was his intention to try and deactivate it then search for you, Emily, Dr Gribbles and the Creature. Well, you know the rest.'

'No we don't,' said Gribbles. 'How on earth did you get involved? You were supposed to be in hospital.'

'I didn't get very far,' said Rob. 'The ambulance was attacked on the road. I don't remember much as I kept falling unconscious as a result of the painkillers the ambulance staff gave me, but there was a large black van that appeared alongside us on the dual carriageway. I heard the sound of raised voices, and I think the men in the van were pointing guns at the driver and telling him to pull over.

'The driver accelerated and sounded his siren. At that point I heard gunfire and the ambulance skidded all over the road. For a couple of minutes we swerved around the traffic being chased by the van. I could see it through the back windows. There were men inside dressed in dark uniforms, and they were carrying automatic weapons. They looked like Special Forces or something. Obviously the medics in the back of the ambulance were very frightened.

'Anyway, they kept shooting, and in the end some police cars joined the chase. The ambulance driver swerved off the dual carriageway at the next slip road with the black van and police cars in pursuit, and at that point I heard the sounds of a helicopter above us and more gunfire.'

Tim listened in fascination to his brother's story. It seemed he had experienced more than his fair share of adventures too.

'Were you scared?' Tim asked.

'Terrified, but what could I do? I'd just been attacked by a genetically engineered monster so wasn't really in a fit state to try and escape. The helicopter landed in front of the ambulance to block it, and at that point I noticed the police cars had blocked off the road at the dual carriageway end to make sure no-one else got involved. It seemed the police weren't chasing the black van at all but instead had been recruited to assist them! I remembered what Dr Gribbles said about the police, and how they couldn't be trusted.

'Anyway, I think I blacked out at that point, because the next thing I remember is men in dark uniforms opening the back of the ambulance and being carried on a stretcher out into the early morning light. I was carried into the helicopter and vaguely remember it taking off. After that, one of the men took a syringe and injected something in my arm. I don't remember anything else after that.'

'What about the ambulance men?' Tim asked. 'Were they killed?'

'I don't think so. I was later told it was explained to them that I was a threat to national security and that was why it was urgent that I be taken from them. I think that was what the men in the black van had tried to convey to the ambulance driver, but he didn't believe them, hence the big chase.'

'It's a miracle no-one died,' said Emily.

'My thoughts exactly. But I think the ambulance driver had good instincts. I awoke in what I was told was a safe house somewhere in the Crown Hill area. I discovered the people who abducted me worked for a man called Whitaker, and that he was very keen to learn all I knew about Dr Gribbles and the Creature. Because of my injuries, I was aware I wouldn't be able to resist torture, but they had something else in mind. They injected me with sodium pentothal, and after that I found myself telling them all I knew. One thing about sodium pentothal – it gives you the worst headache imaginable afterwards. You don't see that in James Bond.

'Anyway, I never met this Whitaker, but I was aware having told them what I knew that I would have served my purpose. I was worried they would kill me, but that was when Saunders and his men appeared.'

'We'd been made aware of the incident with the ambulance and the helicopter,' Saunders explained. 'The operation had been cleared by Whitaker, which made us suspicious. We were aware that Agent Gribbles...'

'Emily!'

'...was undercover trying to prove Whitaker was a double agent. But as I mentioned she had failed to report. We also knew from the police that a teenage boy had been captured by Whitaker's men, but we didn't know why. However, we knew the locations of the safe houses in the area, so London ordered us to rescue the boy.'

'He means me,' said Rob. 'Saunders and his gang posed as rogue mercenaries during the operation.'

'Why?' Tim asked.

'Well, we couldn't pose as KGB, as that would make Whitaker suspicious. So we posed as mercenaries acting on behalf of another interested party.'

'Interested in what?'

'The Creature.'

'Wait! Sorry, I'm getting completely lost. Why pose as anyone at all? You're all on the same side, surely? You're all working for MI6.'

'In theory yes, but Whitaker is a high-ranking spymaster with many people and resources directly under his command. If the other powers

174

at MI6 are suspicious of him, they have to use their own people to investigate, which means placing people undercover with him, and having us pose as mercenaries would deflect suspicion.'

Tim found all this subterfuge was giving him a headache. 'OK, so there are now basically two rival MI6 groups: one led by Emily's bosses, the other led by Whitaker. And you lot rescued my brother because you want to know why he was kidnapped by Whitaker?'

'Correct,' said Saunders. 'But Rob refused to tell us anything at first.'

'Good for Rob,' said Gribbles.

'We learnt who he was, but his parents and brother seemed to have disappeared.'

'Mum and Dad are safe,' Tim said to Rob. 'Dr Gribbles hired bodyguards to look after them.'

Rob looked confused.

'I'll explain later,' said Gribbles. 'Go on Saunders.'

'In the meantime, I went undercover at the Two Bridges hotel,' said Saunders. 'It was only at that point, after discovering Dr Gribbles and Tim, that we made the connection with Rob. We confronted Rob with the facts, and he agreed to help, but only if he was allowed to come with us...'

'You just want the Creature for yourselves,' Gribbles interrupted. 'If we hadn't been captured, you would have taken him.'

'We didn't want the monster to fall into the hands of someone who was potentially a Soviet spy,' said Saunders.

Gribbles stared suspiciously at Saunders. 'He's not a monster. He has a name: Dr Eric Hunter.'

'What are you going to do with him if you find him?' Emily asked.

Saunders sighed. 'Look! I'm not the bad guy. At least I got Rob the medical attention he needed and took care of him!'

'Took care of him? You brought him right back into harms way!' cried Emily.

'I insisted they did,' said Rob. 'After all, my brother was in danger.'

'It seemed the right thing to do,' said Saunders. 'He knew more about the Creature than we did, amongst other things.'

'You still haven't said what you want him for,' said Emily. 'What are your orders?'

'We've been ordered to recover the Creature, nothing more,' Saunders insisted.

Emily stared coldly at Saunders. 'You're lying.'

'If you insist on being paranoid, you're entitled to your delusions. Quite honestly, I expect a little more thanks from someone who has just been rescued from a nuclear explosion.'

'What will Whitaker do now?' Tim asked.

'Try to leave the country,' said Saunders. 'We were tracking him, but that little stunt of yours with the nuclear device may cause him to slip through our fingers.'

'Surely after a nuclear explosion London would send in troops to shut down Whitaker's operation,' said Emily.

'Of course. No doubt those fleeing are being arrested and interrogated about Whitaker's plans as we speak. But Whitaker is slippery. So are Clover and Jayne. I fear they may elude us.'

'The detonation was necessary to prevent unleashing even worse terror on the world,' said Gribbles. 'But it will all be in vain if we don't recapture Whitaker. He has Dr Hunter and syringes containing DNA that could give the Soviets the edge in the race to create a supersoldier army.'

'And we can't afford a genetically engineered monster gap, is that what you're saying Dr Gribbles?'

'What I'm saying, Agent Saunders, is that unless we stop him, the world as we know it will cease to exist.'

Saunders looked confused for a moment. 'Isn't that stretching the point a little? We aren't talking nuclear secrets here.'

'No Saunders,' said Gribbles. 'We're talking something potentially far worse. Something so bad it almost consumed mankind in the terrors of the Earth's First Age.'

Saunders rolled his eyes. 'Alright. Well, one crisis at a time. We've just rescued you from being incinerated in a nuclear blast. Next stage: we need to stop Whitaker.'

'No, *you* need to stop Whitaker,' said Gribbles. 'These are innocent children, and it is my fault they got involved in this.' Gribbles indicated Tim and Rob. 'I'm taking them home.'

'Now wait just a moment Dr Gribbles,' said Saunders. 'I'm in charge of this operation, and frankly we need the help of everyone here.'

'Including Tim and Rob?' Emily asked.

'No, but they can't be released until they've been debriefed.'

'You make it sound like we're prisoners,' said Tim.

'We should be allowed to help,' said Rob.

'You've been very useful to me so far,' Saunders admitted. 'And I understand Tim was the one who tranquilised the Creature, but it isn't right to put you in harm's way any longer.'

'I agree,' said Gribbles.

'No,' said Tim. 'You can't just ditch us now. If you do, we'll go to the press and tell them everything we've seen. On the other hand, we'll co-operate fully on two conditions.'

'What conditions?' asked Saunders.

'We help you get Whitaker, and then Dr Gribbles gets the Creature.'

'Whatever for?'

'Dr Hunter's life is presently a living hell,' said Gribbles. 'I've invented a technique to revert him to human form that was ready to be tested, but I didn't get the chance before he escaped.'

Saunders considered for a moment. 'Very well. I have your full co-operation, in exchange for which you get the Creature once Whitaker is in custody.'

'I still don't like the idea of Tim and Rob being in harm's way for a second longer,' said Gribbles.

'You didn't seem to mind when we were hunting the Creature,' said Tim. 'Besides, it's really my fault Dr Hunter escaped, so I need to help get him back.'

Gribbles nodded reluctantly. 'Very well.'

A moment later, Saunders and the others led Tim, Rob, Dr Gribbles and Emily along the passages of the abandoned tin mine. The roofs of the tunnels appeared very unstable, and at several points they had to watch their footing to avoid plummeting into shafts that plunged down hundreds of feet. The mud and watery puddles made the going difficult and messy, and Tim was relieved when after ten minutes they finally caught a glimpse of sunlight.

Once outside, Tim looked out across the moors. They stood near the top of a steep hill facing north. The rugged Dartmoor landscape appeared as it always did amid the drizzle, grey skies and rocky tors, but Tim guessed the peculiar cloud about two miles away on the horizon was a result of the nuclear detonation.

'Are we really safe here?' Rob asked.

'According to Dad,' Emily replied doubtfully.

One of Saunders' men started sweeping the area with a Geiger counter and nodded in their direction.

'He seems to think so too,' Emily muttered.

Tim glanced over to Dr Gribbles, who was in the middle of an animated discussion with Saunders a few feet away. He couldn't quite make out what they were saying.

'I don't trust Saunders,' Emily said in an undertone to Tim and Rob. 'I know he agreed to your terms, but he seems a fairly by-the-book type. I think he has orders to detain Dr Hunter at all costs. They won't allow us to go back to the laboratory to try and fix this mess.'

'He's been good to me so far,' Rob whispered back.

'You shouldn't trust anyone in this business,' Emily replied. 'Tim, has Dad been completely open and honest with you?'

Tim knew he couldn't answer that question positively. Emily smiled grimly.

'See what I mean?'

'Then we shouldn't trust you either,' said Tim.

'Everyone has their own secrets and agendas,' said Emily. 'Even me.'

'What's your agenda?' asked Rob. He stared at Emily in a way that suggested he had finally noticed she was quite pretty.

'Trying to keep you out of trouble.'

Rob shrugged nonchalantly, obviously trying to look cool. 'Oh, I don't know. Being in trouble is quite fun.'

Tim rolled his eyes at his brother flirting. Looking across to Gribbles and Saunders, he saw they were continuing their discussion, but after a minute or so Gribbles walked away, leaving Saunders to use the radio. He wondered what they had been talking about, and whether or not Emily was correct. Would Saunders renege on their deal? Would he betray them for the sake of following orders?

A moment later, Saunders put the radio away and addressed everyone present.

'They're sending a helicopter for us. London has moved against Whitaker's people and captured several who were fleeing from the bomb. Of course, most of these are innocent parties, but they will still question everyone to try and get a lead on where Whitaker might have gone.'

'Then they've lost him?' asked Gribbles.

'Unfortunately, yes. The Creature is also missing, though we assume Whitaker has him. It's now our number one priority to track Whitaker down before he leaves the country. We're pursuing all possible leads, but so far we've drawn a blank...'

'What about the homing beacon?' Tim asked suddenly. 'Dr Gribbles planted a homing beacon inside Dr Hunter. That's how we managed to track the Creature down in the first place.'

'Of course!' cried Gribbles. 'Whitaker doesn't know about the homing beacon. All we need to do is scan for the right frequency. I just need to create a new tracking device and with a process of trial and error it should lead us straight to him!'

Chapter 14: The Farmhouse

Saunders immediately contacted his superiors by radio, and let them know how they could track the Creature. A few minutes later, a helicopter landed at the foot of the hill with the disused tin mine. Saunders led Tim and the others inside, and soon they were flying above the moors.

Tim looked out at the darkening skies feeling utterly exhausted after all their adventures. As the sun set in the distance, he knew he would not be able to rest until Whitaker and the Creature had been found. He stared for a moment at the plume of smoke that rose from where the Sphinx facility had stood, wondering if the giant skeletons that lay buried there would ever be found again. Given what Gribbles had feared, he hoped not.

The helicopter headed south, and after ten minutes of flying over Dartmoor and the Crown Hill area of Plymouth, landed at the airport. From there Tim and the others were immediately escorted by land rovers to a farm on the outskirts of Meavy, a small village north of Plymouth on the edge of the moors.

'This is your base of operations?' Rob asked as they stepped out of the land rover into the farmyard. Tim looked around curiously. It appeared no different to any other farm in the area, with barns, stables, pig pens, and cattle sheds.

'We were investigating Whitaker,' Saunders replied. 'So obviously that meant discretion.'

Saunders led Tim and the others into the farmhouse. There was a large warm kitchen, a sitting room with a great fireplace and a dining room on the ground floor. However, upstairs the rooms were filled with ammunition, weapons, military uniforms, and radio equipment. One large briefing room contained a great map of Dartmoor and the surrounding areas pinned to the wall.

'What are these?' asked Tim, picking up a brown object resembling a small Easter egg, only much heavier. There were several of them on the table.

'Disguised stun grenades,' Saunders replied. 'They contain a gas that will disorientate most people for around thirty seconds. Just pull out the small pin in the top section and boom!'

Tim examined the stun gas grenade, and eventually found the pin. It was well hidden. He smiled, impressed. They really did look like Easter eggs, but it wasn't Easter.

'Wrong time of year for these,' said Tim.

'They're leftovers from an operation earlier this year,' said Saunders. 'Believe me, they did their job well.'

After being invited to sit down, Tim, Rob, Emily and Gribbles were left alone for a moment as Saunders tried to get some news as to whether or not Whitaker had been located. Outside the sun finally disappeared and it began to grow dark.

Rob questioned Tim at length about his adventures, and between them they brought each other up to date with their respective experiences. Rob was particularly impressed at how Tim had tranquilised the Creature.

'Do you think they'll have found him already?' Tim asked.

'I wouldn't be surprised,' said Emily.

'I don't trust Saunders,' said Gribbles. 'In fact, I'm going to find him. If they've got the Creature cornered, I need to know about it straight away, in case they do something foolish.'

Gribbles left the room.

'Wow, no-one trusts anyone around here,' said Rob.

'As I've already told you, if you want to survive, that's the way you have to think,' said Emily.

'I used to want to be a spy,' said Tim.

'Don't. Trust me, it's not fun.'

'I thought you were a scientist,' said Rob.

'I am a scientist, but... Well, let's just say I have my reasons for doing what I'm doing. I want Whitaker behind bars as much as anyone.'

'What did Whitaker do to you?'

Emily shifted uneasily. At first she didn't look as though she was going to reply, but eventually she spoke.

'The short version is Whitaker ordered the death of the man I was engaged to.'

'You were going to get married?' Rob asked, in a tone that simultaneously suggested sympathy and that the man in question was very lucky indeed.

Emily nodded. There was an uncomfortable silence. Presently a tear rolled down her cheek which she hurriedly brushed away.

'I can't believe I'm telling you this,' said Emily, looking up at Rob and smiling. 'It's not something I usually talk about. There's no point in going into details, except to say that it was unfair and wrong, and obviously I hate Whitaker for it. When I heard he might be working for the Soviets, I immediately agreed to spy on him. It was a chance for revenge.'

'Surely Whitaker wouldn't want you close to him after he ordered the death of your fiancee,' said Tim.

'He didn't know about our relationship. No-one did. Not even Dad, until afterwards. Anyway, do you want to see him?'

Emily reached into her pocket and took out a small photograph, which she passed to Rob and then Tim. It showed a very handsome young man in a leather jacket standing next to a motorbike. Emily was next to him with her arms wrapped around his neck. She looked a lot happier.

'Well, I've just been given a fresh reason to hate Whitaker,' said Rob, handing the photo back to Emily.

Emily smiled and to Tim's surprise took Rob's hand in hers, gripping it tightly. Rob seemed a little taken aback, but not altogether unhappy. Tim however found the whole situation very awkward so changed the subject rapidly.

'Your Dad has some people protecting our parents. Can they be trusted?'

'Knowing Dad, I doubt it,' said Emily. 'They're probably hired thugs. But I don't think you need be too worried. Dad may know some dangerous criminals, but they're *his* criminals, and they'll do what he tells them.'

'Actually I'm quite pleased Mum and Dad are safely out of the way,' said Rob. 'They wouldn't be able to cope with any of this.'

'No-one should have to cope with this,' said Emily. 'This whole thing would never have happened if Dad hadn't tried to play God in the first place.'

'I think he's sorry,' said Tim. 'He's trying his best to put it right.'

'But he might not be able to put it right. Being sorry doesn't make a difference now.'

Tim shook his head. 'I think it does. If your Dad wasn't sorry he wouldn't care what happened to the Creature, and he wouldn't have bothered to bury those skeletons or try and stop Whitaker leaving the country.'

'I suppose you're right,' said Emily. 'It's just... Well, I'm tired and irritable and quite honestly I've had enough. It's not easy having a mad scientist for a father. In fact, it's downright exhausting.'

'He's not mad, not really,' said Tim. 'But I can understand why people might think that.'

'I can see he's rubbed off on you at least,' said Emily. 'No doubt stalking a genetically engineered creature across Dartmoor has forged something of a bond between the two of you. But don't be fooled. Dad is crazy and dangerous, perhaps now more than ever.'

184

At that moment, Saunders entered the room with Dr Gribbles.

'We've got them,' said Gribbles. 'We've used the frequency to triangulate their position north of here, near Tavistock. Roving trackers confirm the location, and we're about to move in.'

'We are, you aren't,' said Saunders. 'Dr Gribbles, I must insist you remain here with the others.'

'I don't see why we can't come too,' said Gribbles.

'It may be dangerous,' said Saunders.

'That didn't stop you taking Rob with you when you raided the Sphinx facility,' Emily pointed out.

Gribbles eyed Saunders suspiciously. 'Are you going back on our deal? You promised the Creature would be left to me.'

'And he will be I assure you, Dr Gribbles, but Whitaker is armed and dangerous, and we can't risk civilian casualties on this operation. You are to remain here, and we will bring the Creature to you if we find him.'

'What are we supposed to do in the meantime?'

'Given the hour, I would get some sleep. There are plenty of bedrooms on the floor above this one.'

Tim stared at Saunders in disbelief. In spite of everything he had gone through, he was being told it was bedtime.

'Unacceptable,' said Gribbles. 'I gave you that frequency to track him. At the very least, I insist on accompanying you.'

'With respect Dr Gribbles, you aren't in a position to insist on anything. You have deceived Her Majesty's government with respect to Project Centaur, and could be charged with High Treason. As it is, we have been more than fair with you and promised that the Creature will be returned to you once we find it. That in itself is more than I ought to have promised. You should consider yourself extremely fairly dealt with.'

'So why don't you want us to come with you?' asked Tim. 'I can't believe it's because you are actually concerned for our safety.'

'There have been enough violations of protocol in this affair,' said Saunders. 'From now on, we are playing it safe. There will be very serious repercussions if any of you are injured or killed, especially the children.'

Tim didn't like being referred to as *the children*, as though they were little more than infants. But in the end there was nothing they could do. Try as they might they could not persuade Saunders to change his mind, and so they had no choice but to remain at the farmhouse and await the outcome of the attempt at intercepting Whitaker and the Creature.

Saunders and his men left a few minutes later, leaving Tim alone with Rob, Dr Gribbles and Emily. With little they could do in the meantime, Dr Gribbles showed Tim and the others the radio room where they had tried to triangulate the position of the Creature in conjunction with the roving trackers. When Gribbles checked the frequency again with his newly built tracking device he discovered the Creature still hadn't moved.

'Perhaps he's resting,' said Tim.

'That seems the likeliest explanation,' said Gribbles. 'On the other hand, there is no guarantee Dr Hunter is with Whitaker. For all we know he could have escaped again.'

'I think there may have been some sightings from members of the public if that were true,' said Emily. 'Especially if he's near Tavistock.'

'I wonder,' said Gribbles. 'He's trained to evade detection, and that in itself makes me doubt...'

Gribbles' voice tailed off. He stared for a moment at the radio equipment and the latitude and longitude position that had been scribbled down on the notepad next to it.

'Something's wrong,' Gribbles said presently. 'The Creature is intelligent, and is engineered for survival. He wouldn't go to a place where he would be easily spotted. Tim, remember how much trouble we had tracking him down on Dartmoor? I can't believe he's made it this easy for Saunders.'

'Well clearly he has,' said Rob. 'He's following the frequency you gave him.'

'I know,' said Gribbles. 'But something's not right. I can sense it.'

Tim and the others debated the Creature for some time, and whether or not Saunders would successfully capture him. Whilst they discussed the matter Gribbles took apart pieces of the radio equipment and began to build something else.

'What's that?' Tim asked.

'If I can get it to work, another homing device,' said Gribbles. 'Could be useful.'

In the end they grew tired, and decided in spite of everything to try and get some rest. After saying goodnight Tim and Gribbles walked up the stairs to the top floor, leaving Rob and Emily behind, as they were still chatting together. Tim had become irritated with Rob's very obvious attempts at impressing Emily.

They each found a small bedroom on opposite sides of a corridor near the top of the house. Feeling utterly exhausted, Tim climbed under the duvet fully dressed, and was asleep almost as soon as his head hit the pillow. But his dreams were filled with uncertainty and dread. Again and again he experienced running from the underground explosion at the Sphinx facility, only this time the nuclear blast wave caught up with him. He woke with a start several times, all within an hour of having fallen asleep. His mind simply could not rest, and when he wasn't dreaming of being caught in the bomb blast, he dreamt of Saunders and his men as they converged on Whitaker. In his dream Tim saw them closing in on what appeared to be the Creature, only to find it was merely the Creature's skin that had been stuffed with sawdust.

Tim felt disturbed at the thought that Saunders might have been sent on a false trail, and yet again awoke with a start. But this time his awakening had been caused by a handgun pressed against his cheek. Tim nearly cried out, but a gloved hand covered his mouth and he couldn't breathe. Unsure whether he was still dreaming or not, Tim struggled, but firm hands held him in place. His assailant placed gaffer tape over his mouth and bound his hands with strong cords. The sensation of the ropes cutting into his wrists convinced him that this was no longer a nightmare but a new horrifying reality.

The intruder dragged Tim from his bedroom out onto the landing. There Tim saw Dr Gribbles, who was also bound and gagged. The men who had captured them wore dark outfits and Tim recognised some as security men who had been with Clover at the Sphinx facility.

After staring at Gribbles in alarm, he heard cries from the floor below. It seemed Emily and Rob had also been captured. The intruders roughly escorted Tim and Gribbles down the stairs, all the way to the ground floor and into a large empty cellar.

The cellar had tall walls built from large stones and seemed to have been abandoned for some time. Tim was reminded of the basement in Blackthorn Lodge, but this cellar was smaller. Inside they found Rob and Emily bound and gagged. They had already been forced on wooden chairs at gunpoint, and there were two more chairs waiting. At the far end of the cellar stood Colonel Clover.

'Vladimir doesn't like loose ends,' said Clover.

Tim was puzzled. Who was Vladimir? Tim remembered how Whitaker was possibly a Soviet double agent. Was Vladimir his contact?

'Given everything you've seen, we have to make sure you remain silent,' Clover continued. 'This is the second time we've had to go to the trouble of making your deaths look like an accident. This time however, we will succeed. We can't set off any bombs, but a house fire will do the job nicely.'

Gribbles struggled against his bonds, but Clover's men held him firmly in place. Tim did a quick count. There were five in total, including Clover.

'The smoke will probably kill you before the fire,' Clover continued matter-of-factly. 'And not as painfully as I would have liked, given all the trouble you've put us to. Still, you'll die. You've only got yourselves to blame for interfering.'

Clover indicated for Tim and Gribbles to be placed on chairs next to Rob and Emily, where they would no doubt be tied down.

Tim frantically thought over their options. There was no chance of overpowering five men, all of whom were armed with handguns, especially as their hands were tied. But if they were to make a break for it they had to do so now, before they were tied to the chairs. Glancing around the room he saw nothing that could possibly aid their escape, until his eyes settled on a large grey rugby ball shaped object in the far top left hand corner of the room behind Clover. Tim identified it immediately and at that moment had the beginnings of a desperate plan.

The previous summer, Tim and Rob had accidentally disturbed a wasp nest when picking blackberries. It wasn't an experience he was likely to forget given how many stings he sustained, nor was it an experience he wanted to repeat. But given their circumstances, the large nest in the corner of the cellar could prove the diversion they needed in order to escape.

The problem was how to wake the now sleeping wasps. He needed to aim a projectile of some kind at the nest to break it open. How could he do that, given that he was gagged with his hands tied behind his back?

Even if he could disturb the nest, there were five enemies in a confined space, all of whom were carrying firearms. The likelihood of making it out uninjured and alive was virtually zero. But it was a choice between that and being trapped in a house fire. As Tim and Gribbles were thrust towards the chairs, Tim caught Gribbles eye and urgently indicated the wasps nest with a movement of his head. Gribbles saw the nest, and his eyes widened. He nodded rapidly at Tim, indicating approval of his crazy idea.

As Gribbles was thrust onto a chair, Tim realised that he had mere seconds to act. On the floor nearby he caught sight of an old leather football covered in cobwebs. It had lost much of its air, but a well aimed kick just might...

Tim suddenly twisted his arm and broke free from the man who was shoving him towards the chair. Clover barely had time to open his mouth before Tim ran to the football and kicked it up into the air. At first Tim thought he had kicked too hard. His aim was off and the ball bounced off the ceiling. But it bounced at the exact angle needed for it to strike the nest.

Within a second, the air filled with buzzing angry wasps. Clover aimed his gun but the stinging insects covered him. Desperately, Tim charged towards Clover and head butted him in the stomach, sending him flying to the ground.

Looking back Tim saw that Emily had leapt up to take advantage of the confusion. She performed two flying kicks with considerable speed and dexterity that sent two of their captors crashing across the room. Yet again Tim was astonished at Emily's fighting skills, and the example she set was immediately followed by Rob and Dr Gribbles who hurled themselves at the other two men amid the swarm of wasps. They fell to the ground overwhelmed.

Unfortunately, Tim was also overwhelmed. He could feel the wasps landing on him and stinging all over his face and neck. They also crawled into his clothes and stung his back, arms and legs. It was particularly nightmarish as his hands were still bound. As he felt wasps flying into his hair and stinging his scalp, he yelled aloud, but his cries were muffled by the gaffer tape.

Clover and his men fired their weapons. The gunshots were ear-splittingly loud amid the vicious buzzing of wasps. Realising they had no choice but to run for it, Tim pelted up the stairs. He heard the others following, but a sharp cry from Emily told him that she had been hit.

As soon as he reached the top of the stairs, Tim waited for Gribbles, Emily and Rob to rush through before slamming the cellar door on their pursuers. But one of Clover's men was close behind, and his arm got caught in the door. Rob, Gribbles and Emily held the door in place with their backs as the man tried to push it back, whilst Tim ran off, desperately trying to come up with a plan of what to do next.

His first thought was to rush to the kitchen and find a sharp knife. Once there, he found a knife rack and took one with some difficulty, before manoeuvring it into place with his fingers and using it to cut his bonds. All of this took around a minute, and judging by the muffled grunts and groans coming from nearby, the others were still doing all they could to keep their captors in the cellar by leaning against the door.

Once his hands were free, Tim tore the gaffer tape from his mouth and frantically ran his fingers through his hair and all over his body to get rid of the wasps. He then grabbed a frying pan from a nearby pan stand, and rushed back to where the others still held back Clover and his men. Several wasps had flown through the crack and were mercilessly stinging Gribbles and the others, although that was nothing to what Clover and his men were no doubt experiencing.

Tim ran up to where the man's arm remained trapped in the door and pounded his fingers with the frying pan. The man immediately withdrew, and the door slammed shut. Seeing the key was in the lock, Tim turned it then used the knife to cut the bonds of the others. Once they had torn the gaffer tape from their mouths, they rushed out into the kitchen to get away from the wasps that had swarmed up from the cellar.

'We need to get out of here now!' cried Rob.

'Emily needs help!' Gribbles cried, indicating his daughter. She was bleeding from where a bullet had caught her in the shoulder. Gribbles rushed out of the kitchen and emerged a few seconds later with a medical kit and a handgun.

The sound of gunfire told Tim that Clover and the others were shooting their way out of the wasp infested cellar. Gribbles and the others fled the farmhouse. Tim grabbed a handful of stun gas grenades on the way out, just in case.

They fled towards a silver BMW car that was parked nearby. It was unlocked, but there were no keys in the ignition.

'I'll take care of this,' said Gribbles as he began to hotwire the vehicle. Tim got into the front seat, and Rob helped Emily into the back. After a few seconds Gribbles managed to start the car, but at that point Clover and his men emerged from the house, firing guns.

'Get down!' cried Gribbles, as the car reversed away from the farmhouse with a loud wheel spin. Tim and the others ducked as gunshots filled the air. The sound of smashing glass resounded in the night air as bullets hit the windscreen.

Gribbles turned the car and zoomed off into the darkness. Only when Tim sensed they had sped onto the main road did he dare to get up again. The gunfire faded into the distance. For the moment it seemed they were safe.

Chapter 15: Confrontation at the Quayside

Tim glanced at his watch. It was just after midnight. By now Saunders would have found Whitaker and the Creature. Or would they?

'How did Clover find us?' Tim asked.

'I was wondering the same thing,' said Rob, as he dressed the wound on Emily's shoulder using the medical kit Gribbles had picked up.

'Saunders,' said Emily. 'I reckon they hadn't found the Creature at all. It was a trap set by Whitaker, and Whitaker probably got the information about our whereabouts from him.'

'Saunders wouldn't have given us up willingly,' said Gribbles. 'They would have tortured him, or used sodium pentothal.'

'I'm not so sure,' said Emily. 'I still don't trust him. He may not be working for the Soviets, but he only cares about his own agenda.'

'So you think Whitaker captured Saunders and his men?' asked Rob.

'Or killed them,' said Emily. 'Either way, we need to contact London and update them. Look out for a phone box.' She rubbed her arm. 'Damn these wasp stings!'

'We won't have much time,' said Gribbles. 'Clover will be on our tail. For all we know they could be tracking this car.'

'We should ditch it,' Emily agreed. 'But after I make the call to London.'

After driving back to the Crown Hill area of Plymouth, Gribbles pulled over near a red phone box, and Emily got out. Tim and the others watched as she used the telephone, looking around anxiously for signs of pursuit. So far there were none, but Tim kept eyeing the car distrustfully, wondering where a homing device might be hidden. Although he was exhausted after their narrow escape from Clover he felt more alert than ever – albeit in considerable discomfort from having sustained so many wasp stings.

After a minute or so Emily returned looking grim. 'Saunders and his men found a device transmitting on the same frequency as the Creature, and as we suspected they were captured by Whitaker. He tortured them, and Saunders gave us up. But afterwards Saunders managed to escape and inform London.

'There is some good news: amid his capture Saunders managed to find out that Whitaker – who's real name is Vladimir Tarkovski – is going to leave the country in the early hours of the morning with the Creature and the blended DNA samples. Clover is working with him and will be joining him, but apparently Jayne claims he didn't know Whitaker was KGB, and is now working with us to try and recapture them.'

Tim was astonished at this news. 'They're overlooking that he was working with Whitaker?'

Gribbles laughed. 'Tim, as long as people are useful to governments, they always overlook their crimes. Think of all the Nazi scientists who went over to the Americans and the Soviets after World War II.'

'Does Jayne know Whitaker's escape route?' asked Rob.

'No,' said Emily. 'But I don't believe him. Nor do the powers that be. They're still interrogating him.'

'I think Jayne *was* working with the Soviets,' said Tim.

'So do I,' said Emily. 'But even with our testimony, there's no proof. London has already made a deal with him in exchange for full co-operation, and in the interests of Anglo-American diplomatic relations.'

'I rest my case,' muttered Gribbles.

'How is Whitaker going to leave the country?' asked Tim.

'According to what Saunders overheard, there's a Soviet submarine lurking somewhere in the English Channel. We don't know exactly where yet, but the coastguard and navy have been alerted.'

'Without more precise information, he will almost certainly escape,' said Gribbles.

'So we have to find Whitaker to get the Creature and DNA samples back, whilst evading Clover and his men,' said Rob. 'Where do we start?'

Gribbles thought hard for a moment. 'If they know about the homing device in the Creature, they have probably found a way to disable it. That would explain why they were able to divert Saunders. Because of this, we have no leads. Whitaker and Dr Hunter could be anywhere, and will escape this very night, unless...'

Gribbles' eyes flickered. Tim had known the scientist long enough to tell a brilliant but no doubt highly dangerous plan had just occurred to him.

'We need to get captured again.'

Emily looked appalled. 'You cannot be serious!'

'Not all of us,' said Gribbles. 'In fact, probably only one of us. I'm not saying it isn't dangerous. But this is too important. Dr Hunter and those DNA samples cannot fall into Soviet hands. We must get them back, even if it means one of us has to risk our lives. That person should be me.'

Tim stared at Gribbles. Even by his standards, the plan seemed completely crazy.

'How does you getting recaptured and probably killed help us find Whitaker?' asked Rob.

'I will tell them I am fed up with the West and intend to defect to the Soviets. It's a long shot, but I think I can make it sound plausible. After all, I do have a grievance or two with the British government. I will tell them I have vital secrets, but that I will only talk to Whitaker. After that, hopefully they will take me to him. All you have to do is follow us at a distance.'

'They would see us,' said Emily.

'Not if you track me with this,' said Gribbles, taking the homing device he built earlier from his pocket. There were two parts to it − a small electronic chip the size of a pen top, and a larger tracking mechanism with a display panel that looked like a small sonar screen.

'I will swallow this chip then all you have to do is track me. A small green dot will appear on the screen if I am within a twenty mile range. As you move towards me the green dot will eventually get to the centre of the screen. At that point, you will have found me. But keep your distance and wait until I have stopped before moving in. Obviously, you'll need a vehicle, and there isn't time to call for backup so you'll have to steal one.'

'We can't steal a car!' cried Tim.

'Didn't your father ever teach you how to hotwire a vehicle?' asked Gribbles.

Tim and Rob rolled their eyes. Clearly Gribbles parenting methods differed somewhat from their parents.

'I'll get us a car,' said Emily. 'But I still don't think Clover will believe you, especially if he finds you sitting here like bait.'

'I'm a good liar,' said Gribbles. 'Besides, we can make it look convincing. I can say I forced you out of the car at gunpoint, and knew they would track me down, so just waited.'

'Won't they want to know what happened to us?' asked Tim.

'More importantly, won't they want to kill us?' asked Rob.

'Well, yes, but even if I'm supposedly defecting, they wouldn't believe that I'd shoot my own daughter. I can insist that they leave you alone as one of the terms of my defection.'

'They sounded fairly determined to kill us and make it look like an accident,' said Tim.

'In the end, all they really care about is escaping to Moscow. I think it was me they most wanted to kill, as I'm the one with the knowledge of genetic research that can threaten their programme. If I can convince them I'm going to defect, they won't want to assassinate a potentially valuable asset. Leaving the rest of you alive would be neither here nor there, in spite of whatever personal grudges they might have.'

'It's too dangerous,' said Emily. 'Dad, they'll shoot you!'

'We have to risk it,' Gribbles insisted.

'No, there has to be another way.'

'The more we sit here arguing, the more likely it is that they'll find us here and kill us all!' cried Gribbles. With that, he swallowed the electronic chip.

'Dad, please,' said Emily. 'Can't we call for help, capture Clover and his men, and find out where Whitaker is that way?'

'Clover won't give up his location,' said Gribbles. 'Then we lose Whitaker, the DNA samples, and Dr Hunter. Surely you don't want that?'

Emily shook her head. 'No… But there has to be another way.'

'There isn't.'

Emily looked as though she might cry. In spite of everything, Tim could see that she was very fond of her eccentric father.

'Alright,' she said finally. Emily hugged Dr Gribbles. 'Please be as convincing a liar as I know you can be.'

The scientist grinned. 'Trust me.'

Tim, Rob and Emily took the tracking device and got out of the car. The night was deep, clear and colder than it had been previously. The stars shone overhead, but were dulled by the orange glow of streetlights. Cars passed along the road, and as they walked around a corner to a residential street, Tim cast one glance back towards Dr Gribbles in the BMW. Gribbles smiled as he disappeared from sight.

Emily immediately set about finding a suitable vehicle to steal, eventually settling on a blue Volkswagen Polo. Using a hairpin she picked the door lock and got into the drivers seat, before hotwiring the car. Tim glanced around nervously, hoping no-one was watching from the nearby houses. The last thing they wanted was to be reported to the police.

'Shouldn't we call London again and ask for their help?' asked Rob.

'Not yet,' said Emily. 'They're already searching for Whitaker, and might have leads of their own. We need to be sure we've found Whitaker and the Creature before letting them know.'

Emily started the car and indicated for the others to get in.

'Should we risk driving out of the road yet?' Rob asked.

'We should check Dad's location,' said Emily, turning on the tracking device. A bleeping noise indicated it was working, and the green dot was moving slowly south.

'He's on the move,' said Tim.

Emily nodded. 'I just wish we could tell if he was still alive or not. For all we know they've shot him and are disposing of the body.'

'I'm sure he's fine,' Rob said unconvincingly.

'Your Dad is a good liar,' said Tim. 'I believed him when he said our parents were being watched by Whitaker's men, so I'm sure he'll be able to persuade Clover he wants to defect.'

Emily still didn't look completely convinced, but nevertheless drove away a minute later. They followed the green dot on the tracking device, driving towards Plymouth but eventually turning west on the dual carriageway that headed for the Tamar Bridge and Cornwall. The roads still contained quite a lot of traffic in spite of the fact that it was past two o'clock in the morning, so Tim doubted Clover would spot any signs of pursuit. But they would have to be careful, especially once they got off the dual carriageway.

After about twenty minutes, the green dot began to move south again, and it became clear that Clover's vehicle had left the dual carriageway. Emily took the next exit and winced. Her wound was still very painful.

'You shouldn't be driving,' said Rob, indicating her shoulder.

'No-one else can,' said Emily. 'And we have to find Dr Hunter.'

'I can drive,' Rob muttered. 'At least, I know how to.'

'Have you had lessons?'

'Not yet.'

Tim suppressed a giggle. He could tell his brother wished he was just a little bit older.

They continued in silence for a while, driving along main roads that led towards the dockland areas of Plymouth. The green dot continued to move, and Tim wondered again whether Gribbles had been successful in convincing Clover that he wanted to defect. It was an outrageous plan, but Tim still had hope. For one thing, he thought it probable they would have stopped somewhere less populated to dispose of the body if they had murdered Dr Gribbles.

Presently the green dot came to a halt. Emily stopped the car outside a large warehouse in the docklands and there they examined the tracking device.

'By my calculations, he's nearby; about three hundred yards south,' said Emily.

Tim looked out of the window. Beyond the warehouse lay the quays where trawlers and other merchant vessels had docked.

'Perhaps he boarded one of the ships,' said Rob.

'We'll find him,' said Emily. 'But we need to be careful. Before we call for back-up we need to verify Dad is with Whitaker and the Creature. We can't be spotted. Otherwise, this will all have been for nothing.'

Slowly and cautiously Tim, Rob and Emily got out of the car and crept around the walls of the tall warehouse towards the quayside. The night was cool and silent. Gloomy shadows were cast amid the narrow alleys at the sides of the building. Tim glanced nervously up at the window panes, imagining faces watching them.

As the quayside came into view, Emily indicated for them to hide behind a pile of crates. Tim peeked through a crack and saw two men about seventy yards away. They wore dark clothes and stood on the quay between two large fishing vessels.

'That man with his back to us looks like Whitaker,' Emily whispered. 'Their position is more or less correct, according to the tracking device.'

Tim squinted, trying to see if it really was their enemy. Certainly the build was correct, and he was about the right height. But they could only be sure by seeing his face. If it was Whitaker then Dr Gribbles and the Creature would be nearby.

A moment later, the men stopped talking and walked off in separate directions. One boarded the vessel furthest from them whilst the man who they thought might be Whitaker turned towards them, revealing his face at last.

He was not Whitaker.

'I don't understand,' Emily whispered, as the other man walked out of sight. 'They must be around here somewhere. The reading says they should be right over there.' She pointed to the space where the men had stood, between the two ships.

'What if there's a boat down there, out of sight?' Tim whispered. 'What if they're already aboard, and are just waiting for Whitaker to show up?'

Emily glanced at the tracking device and nodded slowly. 'They aren't moving, so perhaps that's why. We should wait here, until Whitaker turns up.'

'Why don't I sneak across to see if there is a boat down there?' asked Tim.

'Too dangerous,' said Emily. 'You could be spotted – either by Clover or by Whitaker if he suddenly turns up.'

Tim pointed to a large dockland crane on their right, overlooking the ships. 'I could climb up there to get a better look and stay out of sight easily enough.'

Emily thought this over for a minute, but Rob didn't sound keen on the idea.

'I don't know Dubblety. If they see you...'

'We have to risk it,' Tim interrupted. 'Otherwise, for all we know this could be another false trail, like what happened with Saunders.'

'I doubt this is a false trail,' said Emily. 'But you're probably right. We should check.'

Rob sighed. 'I should go.'

'No,' said Tim. 'I'm smaller than you. And I've always been a better climber. All I need to do is climb up the side of the crane's leg, out of sight, and I should get a view of what's between those two ships.'

'Alright, but be careful,' said Rob.

Tim crept out from their hiding place, ducking behind some large oil drums and other crates that were stacked nearby before reaching the foot of the crane. Once there he climbed carefully onto its metal frame, choosing the leg nearest to the back facing the warehouse. Tim tried to remain as hidden as possible, but as he climbed he realised that if someone looked directly up at him, he would be spotted.

Steadily he ascended. The quayside was eerily quiet, and Tim felt unnerved. Up here the salty air blew gently in his face, carrying with it the unmistakable odour of ships and the sea. As he climbed his view of the two fishing vessels improved, until he was able to see clearly between them. Once he was at about twenty-five feet, Tim spotted a small tug that lay moored between the larger ships. There was no one on deck, but a light shone from inside the bridge. It seemed likely that Dr Gribbles and Clover had hidden aboard, and that they were waiting for Whitaker.

Tim was about to climb down and report what he'd seen, when footsteps echoed somewhere to his right. He glanced down and saw a shadowy figure approaching. Soon the face of the new arrival was visible and there was no mistaking him. Desmond Whitaker. He halted next to the tug, glanced at his watch, and stood waiting.

Tim stared down at the others who remained hidden behind the crates. They had spotted Whitaker and were looking up at Tim in alarm. Obviously it was time to call for back-up, but they wouldn't leave without him. He had no choice but to attempt climbing down anyway, hoping that Whitaker wouldn't see him.

Whitaker took a two-way radio from his pocket and spoke into it in Russian. Tim's blood ran cold. So Whitaker *was* a Soviet spy! From the response Tim caught the word *Vladimir*. He could see the others urgently indicating that he should climb down, but a sudden fear of discovery gripped him. If they were seen they would certainly be killed.

Tim willed his arms and legs to respond, but they would not move. A large white van approached to his right. It was reversing and stopped just short of where Whitaker stood and a moment later four men emerged. The back doors of the van opened, and inside Tim saw a great metal cage with an electronic keypad lock. To his astonishment, the Creature was inside, grunting and snarling.

'We ran out of sedatives,' one of the men said to Whitaker in English. 'That thing is awake now, and getting less drowsy all the time. If you want to take it with you you'll have to sedate him again.'

'What's the code to open the door?' asked Whitaker.

'Five-five-eight-nine-eight-one,' said another man with a Russian accent. 'But you can shoot Creature with tranquiliser dart from outside.'

Whitaker stood at the cage considering carefully. 'We have the syringes with the blended DNA. This Creature is too dangerous to take on the submarine. We'll have to kill it.'

At that moment, Tim noticed a man emerge onto the deck of the tug. He climbed up a ladder onto the quayside, and when he stood in the light, Tim saw it was Clover.

'Colonel Clover,' said Whitaker. 'What of this defector you spoke of?'

'He's inside,' said Clover. 'I don't trust him. I think it's a trick.'

'Almost certainly,' said Whitaker. 'But he is desperate to stop us escaping with the Creature and the DNA. At this point he'll try anything.'

'So we should kill him?'

'Not yet. There is a slim chance he might be telling the truth. If so, we would be foolish not to take him with us. A mind like Dr Archibald Gribbles could prove very useful. We will test his loyalty. Bring him up here!'

One of the men climbed down to the tug between the fishing ships. Whitaker produced a handgun from his pocket and loaded it with bullets. A moment later, Dr Gribbles was escorted from the boat and up onto the quay.

'So you want to defect to the Soviet Union?' Whitaker asked.

'That's correct,' said Gribbles.

Whitaker laughed. 'After all your turgid moral speeches; your delusional rants about good and evil, do you honestly expect me to believe that? You would no more defect than cut off your own arm!'

'It's the truth.'

'It was a lie, to attempt to buy time and locate the Creature.'

'I have my reasons for wanting to defect.'

'But you're forgetting something Archie-E. I was the one who caused those reasons, not the British government. You have no reason to turn against them. For a master of deception even you have to admit that's a little thin, to say the least.'

Gribbles remained silent.

'Well, there is one way to prove your loyalty.'

Whitaker handed Gribbles the gun whilst the other men trained their weapons at him. Gribbles looked up at Whitaker in confusion.

'Shoot the Beast.'

Tim gasped, horrified. He knew he would have to act quickly, but what could he do?

'Go on!' Whitaker urged. 'Shoot the Creature. We aren't taking it with us.'

Gribbles looked shocked. 'But he's very useful to you! Do you know how much research...?'

'We have the DNA,' Whitaker interrupted. 'Besides, there are no more tranquilisers and we can't risk keeping him caged and conscious aboard a submarine all the way back to Soviet territory. We have to kill the monster. *You* have to kill the monster. It is the only way you can prove your loyalty.'

As Gribbles continued to argue the value of the Creature, Tim watched feeling helpless. He glanced down at the others, who were still gesticulating wildly, indicating that he should quietly climb down. Still Tim could not bring his arms and legs to move. They seemed frozen with terror. The hopelessness of the situation felt overwhelming. There were at least six of the enemy below, no doubt armed. By contrast, Tim, Rob and Emily had no guns, and were outnumbered. Gribbles at least had a gun, but how could a prisoner, two children and an injured woman possibly outwit them; much less recapture a savage genetically engineered creature?

The Creature.

Tim put his finger to his lips and gestured to the others to remain calm. A crazy and desperate plan had occurred to him, no doubt the result of being around Dr Gribbles too much. It was almost certainly doomed to failure, but it was the only hope they had. He would have to act immediately, so there was no time to call for back-up even if he could creep back to the others undetected. There was no time to even inform them of his plan. He would simply have to go ahead regardless.

With his reckless plan formulated, Tim found he was able to move his arms and legs again. Now he had an idea of what to do, he needed to come up with a diversion. He reached into his pocket and found the stun gas grenades he had taken earlier. This seemed an ideal time to use them.

Very carefully, but as quickly as he could, Tim climbed back down the crane leg. Below Gribbles continued to plead with Whitaker to keep the Creature alive, but he was rapidly loosing the argument. Emily and Rob stared at Tim expectantly, but he didn't go back to them. Instead, Tim crept rapidly along the quayside to the right, ducking behind oil barrels and crates, before pulling the pin from one of the stun grenades and throwing it as far as he could away from Whitaker and his men.

An explosion pierced the calm. Tim saw a cloud of white gas erupt from where the grenade had struck, further along the quayside.

Immediately, four of Whitaker's men ran to investigate the explosion. Tim ran back in the opposite direction until he reached the Creature's cage. Gribbles caught sight of him and smiled. Whitaker turned and stared in disbelief, but had no time to react further. Tim grabbed the second grenade and threw it at Whitaker's feet.

The explosion knocked the Soviet spy to the ground. As the stun gas blasted in his face, and the faces of the others who remained with him, Tim wasted no time. Putting his hand over his mouth and nose he ran up to the electronic keypad on the Creature's cage and typed in the code he had overheard earlier: five-five-eight-nine-eight-one.

The cage door swung open, and with a savage roar the Creature burst into life from within. Tim barely had time to duck before the beast Dr Hunter had become came bounding out, catching Whitaker with a savage right hook. Tim heard his cry and glimpsed the bloody slash marks across his cheek where the claws had torn his skin. Whitaker fell to the ground in agony.

But the Creature didn't stop there. With a horrifying roar he turned on Colonel Clover. Clover raised his gun to fire, but was still disorientated from the stun gas. The sound of gunfire erupted in the night, but his bullets went wide. The Creature snarled and charged him, striking him a terrific blow in the chest. Clover immediately lost his balance and fell into the sea between the two fishing vessels.

By now the men who had rushed to the first gas grenade had realised they were investigating a diversion, and ran back along the quayside. Instinctively Tim fled towards the place where Emily and Rob lay hidden. Behind him he heard gunshots, and with a thrill of horror realised the men were shooting at him. But as he glanced back he saw them suddenly dive for cover. Dr Gribbles had recovered from the effect of the stun gas, and now fired the handgun to cover Tim's escape. Next to him was an unconscious man, the one who had been sent back onto the tug to retrieve him. It appeared in the confusion Dr Gribbles had successfully knocked him out.

But then Tim saw the Creature lumbering furiously towards him – a mass of matted hair, bloodied claws and snarling fangs. Even at this distance, he could smell the foul breath of the Beast, and fresh terror gripped his heart. He had let the Creature out. Now it was coming for him. The Beast made no distinction between the humans in its vicinity. All were a threat.

'Tim!' Gribbles cried in horror.

Tim ran as fast as he could, but it was no use. The Creature charged after him, and he knew it was only a matter of time before he was caught. Thinking he was done for, Tim began to resign himself to his imminent death, and hoped the Beast would kill him quickly.

At that point Tim saw Rob and Emily run out from behind their hiding place to the left of the crane. Rob turned and began to shout to the Creature.

'Here! Here!'

The Creature turned in confusion and began to chase Rob and Emily instead. Tim didn't know what to do. Having unleashed the Creature they now had to get him under control again, but how? Looking around desperately, he caught sight of Gribbles retrieving the blended DNA syringes from Whitaker's pockets. The Soviet spy was still on the ground moaning in pain.

'The Creature,' said Gribbles. 'Tim, we have to stop him!'

With that, Dr Gribbles ran after the Beast. Tim followed, clueless as to how they had any chance of saving Rob and Emily, not to mention themselves. They might have prevented Whitaker from getting away, but they would all die at the hands of the Creature.

'How can we stop him?' Tim cried.

'Honestly, I'm out of ideas!' Gribbles yelled back.

Ahead, Tim saw the Creature had caught up with Rob and Emily. He grabbed Rob by the arm and cast him aside like a rag doll. Rob slammed into some nearby crates in what looked like a very painful landing. Considering he had already been savaged by the Beast only days previously, Tim dreaded to think what new injuries his brother had sustained.

But now the Creature turned his attention to Emily. He snarled, but as he drew closer, the Creature seemed to calm a little. Emily looked up at the Beast, and Tim was surprised she did not look afraid. Tears rolled down her cheeks, but her face seemed more sympathetic than fearful.

'Emily, keep away from him!' cried Dr Gribbles.

Emily didn't respond. She just stood there, watching the Creature as he moved closer. Dr Gribbles ran to them, and Tim followed. He couldn't understand why the Creature seemed less aggressive with Emily. Perhaps he was still groggy from being drugged. But such questions hardly mattered in the face of their hopeless predicament. Without tranquilisers they couldn't stop the Creature, but if the Creature ran, they would have to track it down amongst a busy city. They now had no way of tracking the Beast, and there could easily be civilian casualties along the way.

Gribbles seemed to be thinking the same thing. As he reached firing range of the Creature he raised his handgun. Emily saw what he was doing and yelled in protest.

'Dad! No! You can't do that!'

'It's the only way,' said Gribbles. 'We can't risk the Creature getting loose in the city. Innocent people will die.'

'But he's a person!' cried Emily. 'It's Dr Hunter! Could you really shoot him in the back?'

'There's no other choice!'

'Dad, please. I'm begging you. There has to be another way!'

'I'm sorry Emily. I've run out of ideas.'

'Look, he's fine now. He's not hurting anyone!'

It was true. For a few seconds the Creature had remained poised in front of Emily, snarling quietly but looking in front and behind, watching Tim and Gribbles as they approached, and glancing ahead to where Rob loitered uncertainly.

But at that moment the Creature roared once more. Dr Gribbles raised his gun and took aim.

'I am truly sorry,' Gribbles muttered sadly, as he put his finger to the trigger.

'Dad! No!'

Chapter 16: The Flight to Blackthorn Lodge

In the split second before Dr Gribbles had a chance to fire, the sudden sound of a rapidly approaching helicopter filled the air. Gribbles took his finger off the trigger and looked up. The Creature snarled and ran towards him, but before he could reach Gribbles, he suddenly fell to the ground as if he had tripped. Tim expected the Creature to get up again but he didn't move. It wasn't until he saw the tip of a tranquiliser dart poking out of his neck that he realised the Beast had been sedated.

A great light illuminated the quayside and Tim looked up to see a rapidly descending helicopter just above them. He ran to one side as the helicopter landed, and as it did, he noticed two snipers with tranquiliser guns. One he recognised immediately: Saunders.

Saunders and the other sniper rushed out of the helicopter, along with half a dozen other armed agents in black uniforms. Several vehicles screeched to a halt near the place where Whitaker lay injured, and within seconds another half dozen armed agents had rushed to the quay, evidently to secure the area.

After checking the Creature was completely unconscious, Saunders ran up to Tim and Gribbles, smiling in a faintly smug manner.

'That's the second time I've rescued you from a tight spot, Tim Rawling,' said Saunders.

'Oh, he was doing alright without you,' said Gribbles, as Rob and Emily joined them. 'Tim deserves a great deal of credit. Without him, we'd probably all be dead by now.'

'From what I saw, Tim foolishly released the Creature and it nearly killed you all as a result.'

In spite of Saunders' timely intervention, Tim didn't like his condescending tone. But he could hardly be anything less than grateful. Looking back along the quay, he saw that Desmond Whitaker, Colonel

Clover and the rest of his men were already in custody. Saunders' agents had moved fast.

Saunders insisted that Tim and the others stayed put whilst Whitaker and the other prisoners were escorted safely away. Over the next hour there was a great deal of rushing to and fro whilst Tim and the others were forced to wait exactly where Saunders found them. They were given hot tea and refreshments, but otherwise could only pace up and down to alleviate the boredom. Tim was exhausted, but also anxious. They had to get Dr Hunter to the laboratory so Gribbles could attempt to turn him back into a human. The longer they had to wait, the more uneasy Tim felt, especially as he watched the sedated Creature being placed inside the helicopter a few feet from where they stood.

In the end, a full two hours passed before Saunders returned. The first signs of dawn appeared on the horizon as he spoke.

'I'm sorry you've been kept here. With a case this serious, involving double agents, classified government secrets and so on, we have no choice but to seal the area off until all traces of what occurred have been removed, and a plausible cover story can be devised...'

'How did you know we were here?' Tim interrupted. 'We didn't have time to contact you.'

'After Emily called London, we sent someone to make sure you were safe. As they approached they saw Clover talking with Dr Gribbles and immediately realised something was wrong. The matter was reported, and soon we had a tail on Clover, which eventually led us here. It seems you also followed them.'

'I pretended I wanted to defect,' said Dr Gribbles. 'But it was a ruse so the others could follow. We hoped the trail would lead to Whitaker and it did.'

Saunders stared in disbelief. 'They believed *you* wanted to defect?'

'Not really. But I know Whitaker. He's greedy. He couldn't risk letting an opportunity like that slip through his fingers. After all, I am the most widely recognised scientist in my field.'

'And the most modest,' said Emily.

'What about the Soviet submarine?' Rob asked. 'It's supposedly waiting somewhere in the English Channel.'

'After Whitaker fails to show up, it will probably head back to Soviet waters,' said Saunders. 'But we've got vessels checking the area, just in case.'

'Anyway, alls well that ends well,' said Gribbles. 'You've got Whitaker, Clover and his men, so hopefully you won't need Emily for any more dangerous undercover work.'

'You'll all be needed for de-briefing,' said Saunders. 'I'm afraid you'll have to stick around for some hours yet.'

'But we have to get the Creature back to my laboratory at once,' said Gribbles. 'That was our deal. I've developed treatments that should return Dr Hunter to his human form.'

Saunders sighed heavily. 'That won't be possible. I'm sorry."

'I knew it!' Emily spat furiously. 'I knew you couldn't be trusted.'

'Now wait a minute!' cried Saunders. 'I just saved your lives!'

'What about his life?' cried Emily, indicating the Creature.

'Sorry Miss Gribbles, but I have my orders. The Creature is to be transported back to London immediately.'

'Why?'

'All I know is that I have to make sure he gets there.'

Emily nodded slowly, her eyes burning with rage. 'They're going to kill him.'

'Miss Gribbles, I hardly think...'

'They're going to kill him! You knew that all along! You used us! You used us to get to Whitaker.'

Tim's heart sank. In spite of Emily's warnings, he couldn't believe Saunders was going back on his word.

'Look, I'm sorry,' said Saunders. 'But orders are orders.'

'To hell with your orders!' cried Gribbles. 'This is a human being! I am taking him back to my laboratory whether you like it or not.'

Saunders pulled out his handgun. 'If you attempt to do that Dr Gribbles, I will be forced to shoot you.'

Gribbles laughed. 'You wouldn't.'

Saunders clicked the safety catch off his gun. Gribbles stared into his eyes and nodded.

'Actually, I believe you would.'

'Enough!' Emily cried. 'Saunders, Whitaker is the enemy, not us. Let us try and save Dr Hunter. You know it's the right thing to do.'

'I'm sorry Agent Gribbles, but I have very clear instructions...'

'I am not an agent!'

'You have no choice but to co-operate. We can't let you have the Creature. He is government property.'

Emily was beside herself with fury. 'Government property? Dr Hunter is person like you or me!'

'What Dr Hunter has become is a failed experiment that needs to end!' Saunders yelled.

'So you're going to kill him,' said Tim.

Saunders glared at Tim as though he was something nasty that he had accidentally stepped in.

'I mean we are going to deliver that thing to the proper authorities so it can be properly disposed of.'

A chorus of protest rose up from Tim, Rob, Emily and Dr Gribbles, but in the end it was Dr Gribbles who managed to shout loudest.

'Agent Saunders, there is a difference between a moral order, and an immoral order. The orders you received regarding the Creature are immoral. If you hand Dr Hunter over to be disposed of, you will be complicit in murder. Dr Hunter will be killed, and that is something you will have on your conscience for the rest of your life.'

'Since when are you an expert on conscience?' Saunders exclaimed. 'You're the reason that thing exists in the first place. You agreed to participate in these godforsaken experiments, and you have the nerve to lecture me about morality?'

'I have the nerve to say what is right,' said Gribbles. 'Yes, I've made mistakes. Now I want to make amends. If you let me take Dr Hunter back to my laboratory I can cure him. He will return to human form and no longer be a threat to anyone.'

'That's not going to happen.'

'If you claim to be against these experiments, why do you work for a government that undertakes them? Why not allow us to have mercy on this poor man and bring him back from the hell that he is suffering?'

'We too plan to end his suffering.'

'Don't you dare try and justify this! This is a human being!'

'I have my orders.'

'Damn you Saunders! Don't make me do this!'

'Do what?'

Gribbles suddenly pulled out the handgun he had in his pocket and smashed Saunders across the face. Tim gasped in shock as the agent stumbled and fell, clutching his bloody, broken nose.

'Quick!' cried Gribbles. 'Follow me!'

Tim ran after Gribbles as he rushed towards the helicopter where the unconscious Creature had been placed. Immediately other agents drew their weapons and gave chase, but upon reaching the cockpit Gribbles aimed his gun, forcing them to halt.

'Get back! All of you!'

The agents halted, but kept aiming their weapons.

'Come on Dr Gribbles!' cried one of the agents. 'No-one wants this.'

Gribbles ignored them. 'Tim! Rob! Get inside quickly and strap yourself in!'

Tim and Rob ran into the helicopter and did as they were told. Tim could scarcely believe this turn of events, and wondered if they would all end up in prison as a result. But he agreed with Gribbles. Allowing Dr Hunter to be destroyed would be tantamount to murder, and after everything they had been through he was determined that would not happen.

'Emily, take this and cover me!' Gribbles handed his daughter the gun, which she continued to point at the other agents whilst her father started the helicopter engines. As the blades whirred into life, Saunders picked himself up.

'You won't use that,' Saunders said to Emily.

Emily aimed at Saunders' left arm and fired. He fell to the ground, moaning and clutching the wound.

'Yes I will,' Emily retorted. 'Only my aim is a bit off at the moment, because of my shoulder injury. You were lucky the bullet only hit your arm Saunders. It's less than you deserve.'

The other agents had Emily in their sights, as she backed into the helicopter still pointing her gun. Seeing that she was inside, Gribbles took the controls and lifted off. Tim watched nervously as the agents on the ground kept pointing their weapons at the helicopter. Once they were high enough, Emily lowered her gun, closed the door and ducked.

A volley of bullets impacted on the metal hull. Tim felt the helicopter bank sideways as it flew above the docklands.

'Stay down!' cried Gribbles.

Over the next few seconds, the firing ceased. Tim, Rob and Emily put on headsets so they could talk to one another above the noise of the helicopter blades.

'Are we safe?' asked Rob.

'For now,' said Gribbles. 'But they'll probably try and intercept us before we can get back to Blackthorn Lodge.'

'I didn't know you could fly a helicopter,' said Emily.

'Flying lessons is one of the many things I did after you stopped talking to me,' said Gribbles. 'I had to alleviate the boredom somehow.'

Emily grinned then looked down at the Creature. Her smile melted. 'Not long now Dr Hunter,' she muttered.

Tim watched the Creature curiously, and wondered whether Dr Gribbles would succeed in transforming him. What would the real Dr Hunter be like? Would he be angry with Gribbles? Would he even remember his actions whilst he was the Beast? Only now did the full horror of Dr Hunter's sufferings occur to Tim. He felt all the more desperate that they should reach Blackthorn Lodge, and that the treatments for the Creature would be a success. By helicopter it wouldn't take long, but as the early morning light began to illuminate the city below, it became apparent that their journey wouldn't be that simple.

'Two helicopters at eleven o'clock,' said Gribbles. 'They might be taking an entirely unrelated early morning flight, or...'

Tim looked out of the window. The helicopters approached rapidly, and he just had time to notice they were military grade with machine guns on either side of the cockpit before they opened fire. Tim, Rob and Emily all ducked once more as bullets smashed into the hull. Gribbles put the helicopter into a steep dive to avoid the hail of gunfire, before finishing his sentence.

'...or they might be trying to shoot us down.'

Risking a glance out of the window, Tim saw the helicopter gunships swoop round for another attack.

'Hold on tight!' cried Gribbles, as he hurtled the helicopter down at an even steeper angle towards the dual carriageway below. Tim thought he might be sick, and almost was when Gribbles suddenly levelled out.

Staring in disbelief, Tim saw they were only a few feet off the ground, skimming the surface along the road whilst veering left and right to avoid oncoming traffic.

'Dad, you'll kill us!' cried Emily.

'If we fly this low, they can't shoot at us,' said Gribbles. 'They won't risk civilian casualties.'

Tim looked up and sure enough the pursuing helicopters kept their distance, but still hovered above their location. However, given that they were banking left and right with cars speeding at them, there was a serious chance they would be killed in a collision.

'Couldn't we at least fly on the other side of the road?' Rob asked. 'That way, the cars are going in our direction.'

'No,' said Gribbles. 'They could drive army vehicles behind us with rocket launchers.'

'But on this side, they could send them towards us,' said Tim.

Gribbles shrugged. 'At least we'll be able to see them coming.'

Cars honked their horns and their occupants stared incredulously, as the helicopter continued to zoom along the dual carriageway. At one point Gribbles carefully manoeuvred underneath a pedestrian bridge. But they were dogged at every step by the gunships, ever present about two hundred feet above their position.

As they reached the Plympton turnoff, Gribbles pulled the helicopter up a little, but maintained a relatively low height to discourage their pursuers from firing again. However, that didn't stop the relentless pursuit. Gribbles soared above housing estates and buildings in the Plympton area and continued in a direct line towards Cromwell Hill. He was forced to climb a little higher to prevent crashing into trees and it was over these wooded areas that their pursuers opened fire once more. Yet again Tim and the others ducked out of sight of the windows as bullets smashed into the side of the helicopter. One window shattered, and Tim felt tiny shards of glass collapsing onto his head. He peeked up at Dr Gribbles in the cockpit as he brushed the fragments from his hair.

'They've hit the fuel line!' cried Gribbles. 'Luckily we haven't much further to go, but we'll have to land within a minute or so, one way or the other.'

'Can we land?' asked Rob.

'The lawns at Blackthorn Lodge are big enough for one helicopter,' said Gribbles. 'Our friends will be forced to land in the street, which should buy us a little time.'

'Won't the house be watched?' asked Emily.

'I doubt it. They know where we live, but I kept Blackthorn Lodge very secret.'

Tim hoped Gribbles was right, but either way it seemed to matter little. They would know about the house as soon as they landed.

The fierce gunfire continued until they were once again over a residential area. Tim glanced down and saw a few bewildered faces staring up at the low-flying helicopters. He thought how it must seem utterly surreal to witness an aerial chase directly above their houses.

After a few more seconds, Tim heard the engine splutter and choke. The blades slowed. They were out of fuel and about to crash.

'There!' cried Gribbles, indicating a house and grounds below. Sure enough, Tim recognised Blackthorn Lodge. It looked no less sinister from the air, and part of him still wondered if there were ghosts haunting the place.

They landed seconds later on the back lawn. Gribbles turned immediately to Tim and Rob. 'Drink these!' he cried, passing them Hec vials. 'You'll need to carry Dr Hunter inside.'

Tim and Rob did as instructed and a moment later hauled the Creature from the helicopter. Emily disembarked ahead of them, pointing her handgun at the two other helicopters that still hovered overhead. Tim glanced up and noticed their doors had opened. Snipers were moving into position.

'Run!' cried Tim.

Carrying the Creature between them, Tim and Rob ran across the overgrown lawn around the house towards the front door. Ear-splitting gunfire followed, and Tim heard bullets passing dangerously close. They slammed into the bricks of the house. Splinters of stone flew through the air, and one struck Tim in the cheek. Putting his hand to his face he felt a trickle of blood, but this was no time to pause and assess injuries. They had to get inside the house, or they would be killed.

Emily fired back at the helicopters, and Tim thought he heard a cry from above. He glanced up briefly and saw one of the snipers clutching his shoulder. It appeared Emily had hit him. But the sniper from the other helicopter opened fire, and it seemed unlikely they would reach the front door alive. There was no hope, unless…

Tim felt in his pocket and realised he still had one more stun gas grenade. He threw it up into the air towards the helicopter with the sniper that was firing at them. It exploded well short of their pursuers but a great cloud of gas blocked the sniper's view, providing the cover they needed to reach the front door. Tim heard the helicopters move away, and as he glanced back he saw that as Gribbles predicted they were landing in the road.

A few seconds later, Tim, Rob, Emily and Gribbles were inside the dusty old house, gasping and panting in the hallway. They continued to rush inward, along the corridors and towards the door to the cellars.

'Will you have time to change Dr Hunter back before they get here?' asked Rob.

'No,' said Gribbles. 'It's a delicate operation, and I need time.'

'We don't have any more time!' cried Emily.

218

'There *is* something we could try to slow them down,' said Gribbles. 'It's a desperate, dangerous move, but it's the only chance we have of bringing Dr Hunter back.'

'Everything I've done since meeting you has been desperate and dangerous,' said Tim. 'Why should this be any different?'

'Very well,' said Gribbles. He grabbed a couple of torches that he had left outside the cellar and passed them to Tim and Rob.

'Get Dr Hunter to the laboratory beneath the cellar and wait for me there.'

'What are you doing?' asked Emily.

'Just do as I say!' cried Gribbles.

There was no time to argue, so Tim, Rob and Emily continued down into the cellars, carrying the Creature with them. They reached the trapdoor and climbed down into the lower tunnel with some difficulty, especially as they had the unconscious Dr Hunter with them. Once inside the lower tunnel they continued past the generator room towards the laboratory and opened the door. Rob looked around and discovered the light switch, but couldn't turn on the light. They used torches to find their way, and Tim stared once again in awe at the peculiar equipment the room contained. The test tubes, cables and other scientific paraphernalia were still present, as well as the great machine that looked like an airlock. The smell of the place had not improved.

'We need to put Dr Hunter inside the machine,' said Emily.

Tim opened the door of the airlock-type device and then he and Rob placed the still unconscious Creature inside. Tim examined all the dials and switches on the side of the machine, and wondered how Dr Gribbles would be able to use it to return Dr Hunter to human form.

Presently they heard footsteps in the passageway outside, and the sound of the generator starting up. It seemed Dr Gribbles was about to join them. A moment later the single electrical light bulb above their heads flickered into life.

'You'd have thought with everything else he built your father could have put in some better lighting,' Tim commented.

Emily was about to reply when the sound of several muffled but nevertheless loud and extremely violent explosions filled the air, followed by the horrifying noises of collapsing bricks and wood. The ground shook and Tim fell to his knees. The overhead bulb flickered on and off for a second, and Rob and Emily stared at one another in alarm.

'What was that?' said Tim.

A few seconds later, Dr Gribbles entered the room. He was covered in dust and appeared very out of breath.

'That should give us another half an hour at least,' said Gribbles.

Emily stared at her father dubiously. 'Dad, what have you done?'

Gribbles smiled and his eyes widened in a slightly manic way.

'I've blown up Blackthorn Lodge.'

Chapter 17: The DNA Replacement Pod

Tim stared open mouthed at Dr Gribbles. In spite of the many crazy things they had done together, he wondered if perhaps the scientist had finally gone too far.

'We're buried beneath the rubble,' Dr Gribbles explained. 'It will take them a while to sift through it all and find us, by which time we'll hopefully have finished what we need to do.'

'Is setting off a bomb your answer to everything?' cried Rob. 'You could have killed us all! How is being buried alive a good idea?'

'Oh, we can get out easily enough,' said Gribbles. 'There's another passage that leads out beneath the garden and emerges near the gate. The entrance is covered in undergrowth so they won't find it unless they know exactly where to look.'

'Assuming your little fireworks display didn't collapse the tunnel,' said Rob. 'If so it could take days to dig us out!'

'Yes, well let's hope it doesn't come to that,' said Gribbles.

Rob stared disapprovingly at the scientist.

'Look, we needed time!' cried Gribbles. 'This was the only way. Assuming the machine works, the process should reverse itself fairly quickly. But we can't have Saunders and his goons bursting in on us prematurely.'

'He's right,' said Emily.

'Shall we get on with this?' said Tim, who didn't see how arguing made any difference to their predicament.

There was little else to be said, so in spite of Rob's irritation at Gribbles' reckless actions, they proceeded with trying to turn Dr Hunter back into a human being. Gribbles positioned the unconscious Creature carefully inside the machine, and with some difficulty wrapped a white sheet around his body.

'Why are you doing that?' asked Tim.

'To preserve Dr Hunter's modesty, in case we are successful,' Gribbles replied.

The scientist sealed the door. The machine hummed gently, and Tim watched as peculiar gases were vented into the Creature's face. Dr Gribbles adjusted dials and looked anxious.

'This is a DNA Reversal Pod, or DRP,' said Gribbles. 'There will be a bit of trial and error. It's a case of finding the right mixture of oxygen and the other compounds needed to reverse the genetic process.'

'What other compounds?' asked Emily.

'They're a kind of virus,' Gribbles explained. 'It's engineered to strip away certain kinds of DNA, so that only human DNA remains. Of course, in the wrong hands it could be twisted into a horrible weapon, and if I've made a mistake in my calculations...'

'We have to take the risk,' said Emily. 'If not, he'll be killed anyway.'

Tim watched in fascination as Dr Gribbles and Emily worked together; flicking switches and dials, trying to get the right mixture of oxygen and other gases. Emily had a look of intense concentration on her face, and seemed completely consumed with ensuring the success of their plan. Tim knew there was nothing more he or Rob could do to help. They could only watch and wait to see if the experiment worked.

'I think we've done it,' Gribbles said presently. 'The balance looks about right. We should activate the DRP now.'

Tim and Rob exchanged uneasy glances. 'Perhaps we should wait outside the room,' said Rob.

'No, you'll be safe enough here,' said Gribbles. 'Just wear these.' He tossed them a couple of pairs of dark blue tinted goggles. He and Emily put on a pair each and a moment later they stood at the side of the DRP near some switches and a large lever.

'When this valve reads one hundred, turn the lever,' Gribbles said to Emily. 'Don't turn it before, or Dr Hunter could implode.'

'That would be messy,' Rob whispered to Tim, as they put on their goggles.

Emily nodded to her father and began to stare intently at the valve. Dr Gribbles turned a switch and the DRP came to life with a low hum. The hum built gradually, and soon Tim could see the needle on the valve Emily was watching begin to climb. Inside the machine, a dim light around the Creature grew brighter, and soon became almost blinding. Tim was glad of the goggles, and even with them on began to think he might need to look away.

The light continued to increase in intensity, and the humming got louder and more high-pitched. The machine began to shake. Dr Gribbles hurriedly examined its outer casing, as though worried it might suddenly explode. Given what had happened up to this point, Tim had no reason to feel reassured. For all he knew the DRP could fall apart and blast them into a million pieces.

The valve continued to climb. Emily held on to the lever tensely, awaiting the right moment to turn it. Dr Gribbles continued to make adjustments to other switches, but the shaking of the machine got worse. Soon the DRP wobbled violently like an old washing machine on high spin. The light became dazzling, the humming ear-piercingly high pitched. Tim squeezed his eyes shut and put his fingers in his ears.

'Now!' cried Dr Gribbles.

Tim heard the loud clunk of the lever being shoved into place. At that moment the shaking stopped. A searing heat emanated from the DRP, and Tim wondered how the Creature could possibly survive without being incinerated. Dr Gribbles cried aloud in pain. He had inadvertently touched the casing of the machine, which had suddenly heated up. Now his hand was badly burnt.

Gribbles and Emily backed away from the DRP. As they did, the machine exploded in a hail of flame and metal. The door flew off its hinges and blasted across the room, narrowly missing Tim and Rob's heads and embedding itself in the wall. Everyone was thrown to the ground. Pieces of hot wire and metal were scattered. The DRP, such as it was, lay in ruins surrounded by a great cloud of smoke.

At that moment, the light went out. Amid shock of what had happened, Tim noticed the generator was no longer humming its familiar hum. Everyone coughed, and eventually Gribbles managed to speak.

'The generator fuses must have tripped. I need to reset them.'

Tim heard the scientist staggering around in the gloom, groping around trying to find the door. Presently he felt someone grab his arm.

'Careful! That's me!'

'Sorry! Sorry!'

'Is that you Tim?' asked Rob.

'No that's me!' Emily replied somewhat indignantly.

'Just stand still for a moment!' cried Gribbles. Tim heard him leave the room and fumble around in the darkness outside. A moment later tinkering sounds came from the generator room. Tim didn't particularly enjoy being plunged into darkness, especially as he was concerned about what would happen if they couldn't get the light working again. For one thing, there was the Creature to consider. Surely amid that explosion and general racket they had either killed him, or else he wouldn't remain sedated for much longer, and they were all in serious danger of being mauled.

After a minute or so the light came back on. The smoke gradually cleared, but in the midst of the carnage lay the Creature. He was covered in the white sheet, still unconscious.

Despite the danger Tim moved closer to the Beast. There was something different about him. It wasn't until he was standing right next to Dr Hunter that Tim suddenly realised what was happening.

The Creature was shrinking.

Somehow, Dr Hunter's body mass was being reduced. Muscles seemed to get smaller. Hairs got shorter. The eyes had turned brown. Fangs reverted to what appeared to be human teeth. Much of the hair and fur seemed to fall from the body and disintegrate. Claws and paws were becoming hands and feet. A rapid and miraculous transformation was taking place - a transformation that was turning Dr Hunter from beast back into the man he once was.

'It's working,' Emily exclaimed in a whisper. She fell to her knees at Dr Hunter's side and watched as the transformation continued. Over the course of about three minutes Tim observed the Creature become a man once more, and he couldn't help laughing. Not because it seemed absurd - which he thought it might, considering the transformation was like something out of a fairy tale - but because between them he and Dr Gribbles' had succeeded. In spite of their mistakes they had set things right. They had triumphed. Feeling exhausted, he looked up at Dr Gribbles who grinned at him in silence.

When Tim turned back to Emily he saw tears pouring down her cheeks. With great affection she reached down to the ground and stroked the face of the man who lay there. As Dr Eric Hunter slowly came to, Tim watched him curiously. There was something very familiar about this man. He was tall, handsome and muscular with intense but kind eyes. Dr Hunter stared up at Emily with the look of a desperately thirsty man being offered a drink of water. But it was only when he smiled that Tim suddenly realised where he had seen Dr Hunter before.

He was the man in the leather jacket on the motorbike that Emily had shown a photograph of earlier: Emily Gribbles' fiancé.

Dr Hunter finally spoke. 'Emily?'

'Eric,' Emily whispered in relief. 'Eric...'

Tim watched as Emily and Eric embraced. Emily wept gently as Eric held her in his arms.

Dr Gribbles walked across to Tim and Rob, and quietly escorted them from the room to the passageway outside. 'It's best if we give them a moment alone,' he said.

Chapter 18: Who went to prison, and who didn't

Gribbles and Tim talked excitedly about what would happen next, but Rob was unusually quiet. He just stared at the floor as they spoke, alone with his thoughts. Tim wondered whether his brother wasn't just a tiny bit jealous of Eric now that he wasn't a monstrous hybrid beast anymore.

'Will you rebuild that DRP machine?' Tim asked Gribbles.

Gribbles shook his head. 'Too dangerous. If it fell into the hands of militarily ambitious governments, we'd be in serious trouble. It's best that it remains destroyed, along with these.'

Gribbles took the DNA samples Whitaker had created from his pockets. Hurling the test tubes onto the floor, he smashed them and ground the liquid and shards of glass into the dirt with his feet.

'It's finally over,' said Gribbles. 'Thank you Tim. Thank you Rob.'

'What about Saunders?' Rob asked suddenly. 'He's not going to be very happy about what we did.'

'It's too late for them to do anything,' said Gribbles. 'Eric Hunter can no longer be listed as officially dead. We've created a big bureaucratic problem for the government, which I can't say is likely to weigh heavily on my conscience. Still, it's time we went to face the music. I'll take full responsibility. If someone ends up going to prison, it will be me.'

Tim and Rob immediately protested, saying how they all had an equal hand in escaping from Saunders, but Gribbles would have none of it. 'You both got into this by accident,' the scientist insisted. 'I on the other hand have to answer for what I have done, even though the outcome has been favourable for us.'

They returned to the room where Eric and Emily stood together, and as they entered Emily spoke.

'Tim, Rob, I'd like you to meet my husband-to-be, Dr Eric Hunter.'

Eric turned to them and smiled. 'Thank you, Rob. Thank you, Tim. Emily's told me so much about what you did to help me. Without you, I would still be that horrible creature.'

Tim shrugged. 'It was nothing.'

Eric noticed Rob's shoulder. 'I understand I injured you Rob. I'm sorry.'

'We've all been injured for one reason or another,' said Rob, indicating Tim and Gribbles' faces, and Emily's arm. 'Besides, you couldn't help it. You weren't in your right mind.'

'What was it like?' Tim asked. 'Can you remember anything?'

'Very little,' said Eric, his eyes darkening. 'Just rage. Blind rage. It's like remembering a nightmare from childhood. There was this horrible feeling of being constantly hunted.'

'Well, we did hunt you,' said Tim.

'Tim was the one who caught you,' said Gribbles. 'And the one who set you free to maul Whitaker.'

'I can't say I'm too sorry about that, since he ordered I should be killed,' said Eric.

'Nor am I,' said Emily. 'But if it wasn't for Dad hiding you away, you really would be dead.'

Dr Gribbles extended a hand to his former colleague. 'Eric, I'm sorry for everything.'

Eric shook Dr Gribbles' hand firmly and smiled. 'That's fine, but I could do with some proper clothes. Emily tells me even though I'm legally dead, I still have my motorbike.'

'Somehow I couldn't bring myself to sell it,' said Emily. 'Now I know why.'

Eric and Emily hugged each other again. For a moment there was an exhausted silence. Then Tim decided things had got far too sentimental.

'So how do we get out of here?'

Dr Gribbles led them to an area of the floor with a great flagstone. Using a crowbar he lifted it, revealing a ladder into a dark passageway below. Gribbles descended into this new tunnel first, followed by Tim, Rob, Emily and Eric. The passageway was cut from granite and ran for a couple of hundred yards before leading to a steep set of steps. Gribbles led them up and out, pushing aside the foliage covered flagstone that covered this secret way into the house.

They emerged blinking in the morning sunlight tired, dishevelled, and covered with dust. Tim stared incredulously at the pile of rubble that lay where Blackthorn Lodge once stood. The twisted heap of beams, plaster and brick were being picked through by several men in hard hats. Several agents were stationed around the perimeter, and Saunders himself stood at the gate conversing with local police. His injured arm was in a sling.

Saunders caught sight of Tim, Gribbles and the others the moment they emerged. Immediately several police surrounded them and placed them in handcuffs. When Eric Hunter asked exactly what he was being charged with, Saunders indicated the white sheet he was wearing and muttered something about it being see-through and indecent.

But Tim no longer cared. Whatever happened now, they had prevented the British, American and Soviet governments from having a potentially deadly genetic weapon. They had also successfully rescued and restored Eric to his true form, brought him back to Emily, and in turn brought about reconciliation between her and her father. Prosecutions for assault, firing on British agents, stealing government property and so forth seemed a small price to pay.

One month after Eric Hunter had been restored to human form, Tim cycled along Cromwell Road on his way to the park to meet up with some of his school friends. The days were getting colder, and golden leaves filled the lanes as autumn set in.

Upon passing the ruins of Blackthorn Lodge, Tim recalled the aftermath of his adventure on the day Dr Gribbles had destroyed it. Not for the first time, he felt amazed he had survived at all.

After extensive questioning, Saunders and the other government agents agreed to drop all charges against Tim, Rob, Eric and Emily. Tim later found out this was because Eric had agreed to keep quiet about what really happened to him, and instead tow the line regarding the cover story the government put out: namely, that he had been suffering from amnesia and was stranded abroad somewhere in South America. It wasn't a very convincing lie, but it was enough to paper over the far more unbelievable truth.

The other condition of their release was that Dr Gribbles agree to work for the government on another secret project. Gribbles initially refused, but when he discovered what the secret project was, he couldn't resist accepting. The excuse he gave for agreeing was that he wanted to make sure this new technology wasn't misused, although Tim could see from the glint in Gribbles' eyes that he was very excited about whatever this top secret project was. In spite of the way the government had treated him, Gribbles seemed happy to once again be doing what he loved best.

Desmond Whitaker, Colonel Clover and the other Soviet spies stood trial for High Treason, though the reasons why remained top secret. All were found guilty and sent to prison.

Tim and Rob remained good friends with Dr Gribbles, Eric and Emily. After the charges were dropped, Gribbles arranged for Tim and Rob to be reunited with their parents. But Tim's Mum and Dad seemed merely irritated by their experiences, and their chief concern was getting back to work as quickly as possible, in spite of the fantastical nature of Tim and Rob's adventures. Tim and Rob had been strongly discouraged from giving the full details in any case, as the government wanted to bury all trace of Project Centaur and Project Minotaur. Saunders told Tim and Rob in no uncertain terms that the government would deny all knowledge of genetically engineered creatures and the like, so there wasn't really any point in trying to convince their parents that such things had existed.

Eric and Emily were married a fortnight after Saunders let them go, and Tim and Rob were guests at the wedding. It seemed to Tim that his brother got over his infatuation with Emily easily enough, especially as he was presently visiting one of his other girlfriends. All things considered, everything had turned out well in the end, although Tim had made a mental note to never again open locked doors to rooms that might contain monsters.

It was as he rode his bike past Blackthorn Lodge and onto the pathway beyond that a familiar gang of boys rode into view from the opposite direction, blocking his path. Tim stared darkly at Jake Buxton, Carl Ledger and Gary Price as they dismounted from their bikes, waiting to see what they would do or say next.

'You're in for it now, Rawling runt!' said Jake. 'We might not be able to lock you inside Blackthorn Lodge, but there are other ways of paying you back, now your brother isn't here to spoil our fun.'

Tim sighed and addressed Jake as though he were nothing more than an annoying insect. 'I don't need my brother to deal with the likes of you. This is your first and only warning: get out of my way, or I'll get you out of my way.'

Jake, Gary and Carl all laughed.

'I think the Rawling runt finally lost it,' said Jake. 'Well, crazy or not, this time you're gonna loose some teeth!'

Jake made a fist and pounded it into his hand.

Tim simply rolled his eyes, reached into his pocket, and took out a Hec vial. He drank its contents quickly then dismounted, striding towards them with such confidence that Jake took an involuntary step backwards.

'What was that you drank?'

Tim smiled. 'Magic potion.'

Jake snorted, and was about to throw a punch but Tim got there first. He struck Jake in the chest, sending him flying several feet across the path and into the bramble filled hedge.

Gary and Carl appeared confused for a moment then hurled themselves at Tim. But Tim struck them each in a one-two punch that had them sprawled on the ground. Wiping bloodied lips they looked up at him in amazement. Jake dragged himself out from the hedge, clutching his chest and groaning, but with a similar expression of disbelief.

Tim got onto his bike again and cycled past his former tormentors. He felt a surge of triumph at the way the tables had been turned on them.

It seemed that having a mad scientist as a close personal friend came in very handy for all kinds of things.

ALSO AVAILABLE: **George goes to Mars** by Simon Dillon

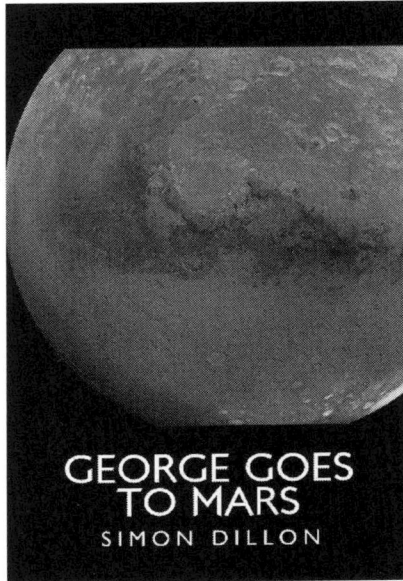

When George Hughes discovers he has inherited the planet Mars, he goes from poverty to becoming the richest boy on Earth overnight. Accompanied by his new guardian, a mysterious secret agent and a crew of astronauts, George voyages to Mars to sell land to celebrities wanting to build interplanetary holiday homes. But sabotage, assassination attempts and the possibility of an alien threat plunge him into a deadly adventure...

ALSO AVAILABLE: **Uncle Flynn** by Simon Dillon

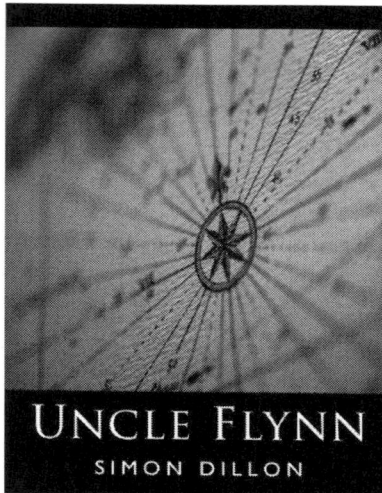

Max Bradley is a timid eleven year old boy with many fears. But when he embarks on a hunt for buried treasure on Dartmoor with his mysterious and dangerous Uncle Flynn, Max's life looks set to change forever. Together they decipher clues, find a hidden map and explore secret tunnels in their search. But with both police and rival treasure hunters on their tail, Max begins to wonder if his uncle is all he seems.

A gripping and thrilling adventure for all ages.

About the Author

I was born the year Steven Spielberg made moviegoers everywhere terrified of sharks, namely 1975. I lived the first twenty or so years of my life in Oxford, and am pleased to have spent so much time in the place where some of my favourite writers (including JRR Tolkien, CS Lewis and Phillip Pullman) wrote their greatest works. Things went gradually downhill from there as I attended University in Southampton and afterwards managed to muddle my way into television where I have worked ever since. I like to think I can write a diverting story, and as a result have penned a few novels. I might be sadly deluded, but that's for agents and publishers to decide. I currently live in Plymouth in the UK, and am married with two children. I am looking forward to brainwashing my children with the same books that I loved growing up.

Check out www.simondillonbooks.wordpress.com for further information about *George goes to Mars, Uncle Flynn, Dr Gribbles and the Beast of Blackthorn Lodge* and information on other works by Simon Dillon.

To contact Simon Dillon, email: uncleflynn@gmail.com

Manufactured by Amazon.ca
Bolton, ON

22569594R00136